DOVE EXILED

ALSO BY KAREN BAO

Dove Arising

DOVE
EXILED

*   *   *

by KAREN BAO

VIKING

TEEN
BAO

VIKING
An imprint of Penguin Random House LLC
375 Hudson Street
New York, New York 10014

First published in the United States of America by Viking,
· an imprint of Penguin Random House LLC, 2016

LIBRARY OF CONGRESS CATALOGING-IN-PUBLICATION DATA IS AVAILABLE
ISBN: 978-0-425-28773-6

Set in Apolline Std
Printed in U.S.A.

1   3   5   7   9   10   8   6   4   2

THIS ONE'S FOR MY BROTHER

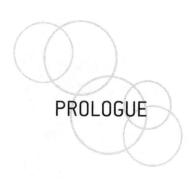

PROLOGUE

MY MIND IS UNRAVELING, LIKE A KNOT BEING picked by agile, persistent hands. Deep in its center, I find threads of memories I forgot I had. One tug, and they loop me into images of the past.

Mom and Dad are here, livelier than they'll ever be again. I wish I could see their faces better, but I'm only a meter tall.

"It's about time, Phaet," Dad says. He's my giant. His hands can lift big rocks, but they're always careful. He sets me on his lap. "Your little sister has a heartbeat now. Will you listen for me?"

I press my ear to Mom's rounded belly, which is growing day by day. *Ka-thump, ka-thump,* goes her heart.

Bop, bop, bop! goes Anka's.

"It's so fast," I tell Dad, and then bend down to listen more.

When I focus on the little heartbeat, I lose track of the big one. Mom's. I concentrate hard, listening for the *ka-thump,* but it's not there.

"Mommy? Is your heart okay?" I demand, crawling onto her lap to put my ear to her chest.

Her face is still. Peaceful, but still. I reach up to touch it. It's chilly, like the metal of an Atrium security mirror.

"Mommy?" *I'm not going to cry.* I don't want to make Dad worry. *"Mommy?"*

Screaming, I tumble off her lap. The tears start when I strike the floor—hard. *Why didn't Daddy catch me?* He likes to lie on his back, balance me on his shins, hold my hands, and make me fly like a bird. Never has he let me fall.

"Daddy, Daddy, we have to help Mommy!" I cry.

No answer.

Crumpled on the ground, he doesn't look like a giant anymore. Somehow, I know he's not playing a game—*ashes, ashes, we all fall down.* I crawl to him and put my ear to his chest, just as he taught me. *Can you hear the thump, Phaet? It keeps us all alive.*

His heart, too, is silent.

Violet light shoots across the room, bounces off the walls, the mirrors, the bodies of my parents. Hits everything but me.

* * *

I open my eyes to the real world's darkness.

". . . Wes, get more morphine from downstairs!" It's a woman's voice, clear like a raindrop landing on a glass pane. "Hurry, she's seeing things again!"

A pinch on the inside of my elbow, and I'm back in my childhood home. Sixty centimeters taller, eleven years older. The white walls are there; the smells of fruit rinds, green onion, and bleach; the little vacuum robot, Tinbie, shiny and new, both of his yellow eyes lit.

Maybe my family's sleeping. I walk into my brother Cygnus's bedroom, peer over the walls of his crib, and find nothing but a pile of white blankets. I run toward my parents' room, hoping they'll hold me close until this nightmare lifts.

But behind the door, there are no voices. Not a wrinkle in the bedsheets.

It's quiet, as quiet as I've grown since they died.

Except for a small sound that reveals itself shyly, warily. A sound that's scared to ask for my attention—a sound that I can't ignore.

Bop, bop, bop.

1

Four months later

THE WINTERTIME SUN MAKES A SPECIAL appearance to welcome Garnet River into the world. She's a squalling pink newborn itching to escape the arms of her mother, a freckled woman who looks weak from childbirth but delirious with joy. Garnet's father, a broad-shouldered fisherman with fluffy blond hair, tickles the baby under her chin. Her resulting sneeze is little more than a squeak. Cocooned in purple blankets, she's adorable—the roundest human being I've ever seen. Her cheeks are two half-moons, her chin a crescent.

There's something hopeful about new life, whether it's a seedling in the Lunar greenhouses or a yowling Earthbound baby. Garnet has every right to fuss—the movements keep her blood circulating, keep her warm. The stratus clouds that usually blanket Saint Oda may have lifted for today, but the cold hasn't.

All of the island community's citizens have gathered in the Overhang, their outdoor auditorium scooped out of the side of a mountain. There's a small platform at the far end, and beyond that lies the ocean. The stone floor slopes upward away from the stage, and a high ceiling shelters the auditorium from the elements. To the side, a disused off-white lighthouse casts its shadow across a thin sliver of the stage.

Eiders circle overhead, cawing. The birds' white wings are tipped with black; the color also appears on their foreheads and around their eyes. Their bills glint silver in the sun. Some birds dip down from the endless sky, fly low, and weave between glass orbs filled with seawater, which hang from the ceiling on hempen ropes around the room's perimeter. Though they're dull by day, the bioluminescent bacteria within them cast haunting blue light after sundown.

On the stage, First Priest Luciana Pinto lays a comforting hand on baby Garnet's forehead, calming her. Saint Oda's leader has a broad nose, wide-set eyes, and medium-brown skin that seems to glow. Even though Pinto's back is stooped from osteoporosis, the top of her head, covered in curly gray hair, hovers at least a meter and three-quarters off the ground.

"God is closest to our children," she says to the audience. She doesn't have a microphone, but her voice carries fifty meters to where I'm standing, slightly beyond the middle of the stone auditorium. The Odans constructed their gathering place to refract and amplify sound waves, so noises from the stage bend upward and outward. "He weaves a part of his spirit into every living thing before its birth. And so the youngest among us have most recently received his blessing."

"Amen," says the congregation. I move my lips but don't make a sound. Odan services make me uncomfortable, since I'm breaking rules from my old life just by listening. On the Lunar Bases, the Committee outlawed religion because it would supposedly counter scientific objectivity. I'd love to believe in the Odans' harmonious vision of the world, with its God who gives a bit of himself to every organism. I'd be happier. But it only takes one counterexample to disprove any theory, and I've come across several.

If God is good, and there's a part of him in all living things, why are the Committee members evil? If God is powerful, why couldn't he stop them from killing my mother? And why won't he drain away my grief? Sometimes, so much sorrow clogs my body that my tears can't flow. I want the Committee—all six faceless murderers—to suffer as I have, as the Lunar people have. To experience hunger so complete that the pangs no longer register; to weather the pain of electric shocks and laser fire. To lose a loved one, if they're still capable of loving anybody. What would *their* screams sound like?

My desires shock me, and they'd appall the Odans, for whom needlessly harming another of God's creations is the greatest sin.

The only person who knows I'm not a believer is Wes, who's standing on the other side of the Overhang with the rest of the men. His face is solemn and his eyes focus on Priest Pinto, but three fingers of his right hand toy with a loose string on his brown wool sweater, coiling it around and around. He saw the same things I did on the Moon—maybe even worse things—and now he seems out of touch with his countrymen's beliefs too.

We keep our doubts to ourselves.

Priest Pinto raises her left hand. Three minuscule red dots—ladybugs—scurry across her palm. She rolls back the baby's right sleeve. "Today, we accept this child as a citizen and a member of our congregation. With these three ladybirds"—the Odans' name for the insects—"I join the divine in me and the city of Saint Oda to the divine in her. Let us welcome Garnet River into our midst."

"Amen!" we chorus.

The three ladybugs scuttle from Priest Pinto's hand to Garnet River's. The baby squeals, delighted or simply tickled.

I smile, remembering the scratching of the insects' feet on the crisp November day when the Odans accepted me as one of their own. It's the happiest event in my recent memory. Wes's grandmother, Nanna Zeffie, spoke on my behalf: "Our garden has become more fruitful than I've ever seen it. The lass does wonders for God's greenest creations—he blesses the work of her hands." Her speech, along with Wes's goodwill, convinced the crowd to vote in my favor. Immigrants like me must receive majority approval from the congregation's adults to become citizens. If they had rejected me, Saint Oda would've sent me away. All the other places I could have gone—floating cities, nomadic pirate ships, the wilderness—would have been hellish compared to this haven.

"Now let us pray," says Priest Pinto.

I bow my head with the women around me.

"Lord, thank you for trusting us with this child. May she grow tall as a fir and sturdy as an oak. May she swim with the dolphin, fly with the eider, and run with the wolf. With your love, may she never find herself alone. Amen."

"Amen," the congregation says.

*   *   *

The ceremony complete, the Odans mill about, congratulate Garnet's parents, drop off gifts for the baby girl, discuss the good omen of a birth on a sunny day. Men and women from the opposite halves of the hall mingle. By separating the sexes during religious proceedings, the Odans claim, they minimize distraction from God. It's one of many bizarre practices that make me wish I had a digital encyclopedia on Earthbound cultures. Now, whenever I want information, I have to ask someone instead of looking it up on my handscreen, creating much undue social awkwardness.

I trail Wes's older sister, Murray, as she moves through the crowd toward the River family. She and I made our own gift for Garnet; per Odan tradition, we'll present it together.

Dozens of eyes follow Murray, though she's unaware of it. She's tall—if she so chose, she could stand directly behind me without surrendering her line of sight. Sunlight illuminates her tangled hair, the color of parched soil, and the scar, pink against her pale skin, that runs from the left side of her forehead through her drooping right eyelid. I never asked what maimed her. When I first regained consciousness and saw Murray bent over me, I yelped, but I figured that the fear would go away if we didn't talk about it. Besides, asking would've been insensitive. Murray healed my laser burn–riddled arm, stuffing it full of herbs and salves, and stayed by my side for weeks. The least I can do is respect her privacy.

Lewis, her domesticated nightingale, perches on her left shoulder. He's a brown bird the size of a fist, with a white breast and reddish tail feathers. Every few seconds, he ruffles his wings, tickling Murray's cheek; she scratches his belly with one finger, and he chirps in delight. Pets are commonplace at Odan gatherings; today, several attendees carry falcons, frogs, or cats. At the back of the Overhang is an assortment of larger animals: dogs, cows, even horses. I can smell their damp stink from here, but no one else seems to notice or mind.

When we reach the young family, I try my best to smile.

"Fay and I made this for Garnet," Murray says in her high, ringing voice. She holds out the hair clip she's assembled. "Lewis helped too by shedding some feathers he didn't need anymore." The clip has two brown wing feathers on the sides and a longer, reddish tail feather in the center. A chain of pink seashells from clams, scallops, and snails dangles from the feathers' quills.

"As for the shells," Murray continues, "Fay and I picked up whatever caught our eyes during our walks on the shore."

"Oh, this is lovely." Willet turns the clip in her hands, admiring it from all angles. "Garnet's going to wear it the moment she sprouts actual hair." She strokes the white-blonde fuzz on her daughter's head. "Aren't you, my little duck?"

Garnet snuggles against Willet's chest and lets out a snore.

"We'll ask her again when she wakes up," Garnet's father, Larimer River, says with a chuckle. He and four of his brothers, all of whom have sunburnt skin and blond curls, supply and run Wes's mother's favorite fish stall in the marketplace. There's a fifth brother, too, but he's gone to the Moon as a spy, like Wes did. It's odd, and sad, too, that several men from this beautiful city have had to leave it for the bases' barren hallways.

"I remember when *you* stood here," Larimer says to me, "for your own induction. How are the snowdrops?"

Earlier that day, Larimer approached me with his brothers and dropped four bulbs into my hand. "For you," he said. "Snowdrops. They'll flower in the winter when nothing else does. White against the white snow."

I've buried the bulbs like secret treasure, and I'm waiting for the shoots to appear. To answer Larimer's question, I shake my head and shrug.

"Lassie's still got a frostbitten tongue," Larimer teases me.

I shrug off his comment, because he's only trying to make me open up. Since I'm new—and *different*—most Odans don't yet know what to make of me.

But Murray doesn't let Larimer off so easily. She puts a hand on my upper back and steps forward as if to shield me. "Keep mocking her and she'll never thaw out."

Her smile is just wide enough to mask any aggression she might be feeling. Did people poke fun at her appearance when she was younger? She's hyperaware of anything that might be taken for a taunt directed at me, catching things even Umbriel, my best friend on the Moon, might've missed.

Facing me, Larimer's wife shrugs. "Better not to say anything than sound like a nitwit."

"You know you love nitwits, Willet." Larimer plants a kiss on her cheek.

I give them a half grin, the most communication I can afford. Speaking more than a few words at a time would be dangerous. Wes tried to teach me how to talk like an Odan, playing with the pitch of every vowel before moving on to the next, but my efforts sounded like the clucking of the hens behind his house. My normal, consonant-heavy accent would trumpet my Lunar origins; the islanders here never forgot the invading Militia's idiosyncratic speech, not in the nine years since the Lunars attacked, stealing grain, water, metals, and lives. We might be the only living things Odans detest, and we deserve it.

Months ago, Phaet the fugitive, a Lunar rebel's daughter, was reborn Fay, a former engine room slave from Pacifia. Since I'm Asian, like more than half of Pacifia's population, it made the most sense. Wes told the Odans that he made an emergency pit stop in Pacifia, got caught trespassing in classified locations, and was slated for execution; that I—Fay—helped him escape his jail cell, and he brought me to Saint Oda out of gratitude. While this city welcomes immigrants from all over the world—Priest

Pinto's family came here only fifty years ago, from South America—most Odans are Caucasian and can trace their families back generations on this soil.

Murray tugs on one of my silver-streaked pigtails, bringing me back to the present. "Snowdrops are your soul flower, Fay." It's strange to be associated with snow, something I've never seen. "You'll see when they bloom. . . ."

The crowd stirs, drowning out Murray's voice. At first, I worry that we've lingered too long with Garnet's parents, but the Odans are looking past us, at the ocean, where spots of light twinkle in the distance. They squint at the horizon, some pointing, others shaking their heads. Stern-faced parents hurry their children away to higher ground.

"A *mobile city*?"

"It must have already breached the Sanctuary boundary!"

I follow their gaze, dread making it harder and harder to breathe. The lights on the horizon have grown brighter. I can make out various colors—scarlet, deep violet, glassy green—even though their glow is shrouded in smoke.

The wind picks up, carries the rotting odor of sulfur to my nose.

"Everybody move inland!"

"Where is Coordinator Carlyle? Somebody call for him!"

"Are he and his boys mobilizing yet?"

They're talking about Saint Oda's law enforcement cohort, made up of twenty or so young men—called Sanctuarists—and led by Wes's father. Unlike the Lunar Militia, the Sanctuarists are so unobtrusive that I sometimes forget they exist. They dress like civilians and rarely take people into custody. What's more, the Odans love them. When Wes walks the city's narrow footpaths, adults greet him by his first name, boys look at him in awe, and girls giggle into each other's shoulders. But I usually stave off jealousy by convincing myself that these young women don't really care for him. If they did, they'd know that he'd rather exchange blows with Lunar soldiers than banter with them.

But there's no laughter now. Several boys and men within the crowd are running about, shouting, or fumbling in their pockets. The Sanctuarists are assembling, but will it do any good? The disorder reminds me of the breakout from Shelter, the Militia chasing the residents and shooting them as if for target practice.

The blood has stopped flowing to my toes. Disturbed, I shake off the memory.

"Outsiders." Willet holds her baby closer and shields Garnet's eyes with her hand. "Fay, we haven't had unannounced visitors since those *demons* came." *Demons*: the Odan word for Lunars. "God forbid someone's here to take the rest of us."

2

"NO," MURRAY MUTTERS. "THIS ISN'T REAL—
it's fake, fake, *fake.*" Her thundercloud eyes widen—the right
only slightly, the left until I can see every white striation in the
gray iris. *Like lightning.* Her hand clutches the oval amber locket
at her throat, an ornament I've never seen her without.

"The last time this happened . . ." she says to no one in particular. Without warning, she runs uphill, stumbling over the
stray rocks—and small children—in her path. The injury that
disfigured her face also compromised the vision in her right eye,
giving her poor depth perception. Above Murray's head, Lewis
flies in circles, screaming her alarm to the island.

"Murray!" I call out, stunned and terrified that she's leaving
without me. Never in the five months I've known her has she
failed to see me home. I'm torn between fleeing uphill with
her and staying to learn something, anything, about what's
going on.

Beside me, Willet argues with Larimer. "They certainly
didn't come to congratulate us," she says. "I'm taking Garnet
out of here."

He glances worriedly at the mass exodus from the Overhang.
Bodies block every exit. "She'll get jostled. Or worse, trampled."

"There's a Pacifian ally only minutes from us," Willet says
through her teeth. "I will *not* let them ruin this day. . . ."

Upon hearing the word *Pacifian,* I, too, take off running. My mind's splitting along fault lines I thought had stabilized during my recovery, and it's terrifying, this loss of control over my own consciousness. *Get away and keep it together,* I order myself. Living on Base IV, I learned to slip through crowds with ease, and the familiar rhythm of dodging bodies gets my synapses firing.

This unknown city is an ally of Pacifia, the city-state Wes and I discovered is working with the Lunar Standing Committee toward some mysterious and terrifying goal. A floating metropolis with millions of inhabitants, Pacifia is the capital of the eastern hemisphere's hegemon here on Earth. With half the planet under its control, its military could kick aside a city of Saint Oda's size like a pebble in its path.

That wouldn't happen if Saint Oda allied itself with Pacifia's archenemy, the city-state of Battery Bay. But Saint Oda would never cooperate with the biggest single polluter on Earth.

An announcement from the approaching city—read by a grating female voice—thunders through the still air. "Odans, remain where you are. We are the municipality of Tourmaline, and we come in peace, bearing a message for all of you. We repeat: remain where you are."

Many Odans freeze, staring at the floating city as if down the barrel of a massive cannon. That might well be the case. Who's to say that at this moment, Tourmaline doesn't have metric tons of ammunition ready to fire at us?

I run faster, the back of my neck prickling. The announcement's amplification and commanding tone sound too much like a Committee address. My past has followed me *here*, even though I've run 400,000 kilometers away from the Moon, where everything happened.

Passersby will think I'm retreating uphill, to the shelter of Wes's family's home; it's what any young girl should do, for safety. But what if Tourmaline's visit has something to do with me, a Lunar rebel's runaway daughter? Given this island city's connections to Pacifia and therefore to the Moon, that's not outside the realm of possibility.

Responsibility and morbid curiosity win out over self-preservation. Instead of disappearing into the tunnels weaving through the mountain, I run behind a boulder and toward the lighthouse. Hand over hand, I climb the tower's creaky metal ladder. Overgrown layers of rust cover the rungs, and each feels jagged against my palms.

I won't be seen up here, fifty meters off the ground. And it's doubtful I'll receive an unexpected visitor. Odans avoid the observatory because they believe that the "restless souls" of those killed during the twenty-second century's storms and the recent Lunar invasion reside there, scanning the seas for future threats to their kin. The Odans even keep away from the lighthouse's base, as some have seen the "ghosts" of people they lost darting about there.

Earthbound myths don't faze me—or Wes. He told me that years ago, he snuck up here with another spy-in-training, Alex, to howl and moan, to scare people and laugh at their reactions. Nostalgia amassing in my heart, I imagined the two of them were like Umbriel and me.

Umbriel was also a trickster. He'd drop worms down people's shirts instead of tending the greenhouse plants.

I'm glad Wes had company during his training. Alex, from an immigrant family, was two years older—the only Lunar agent close to Wes in age. Wes left for Base IV three and a half years ago, when he was fifteen, and Alex set off for Base VI ten months later.

I reach the lighthouse's tip and sneak into the back door. The observatory is octagonal and painted light yellow; old piping bulges from the walls like veins on an angry man's forehead.

The older Sanctuarists departed for the Moon years before Wes and Alex. Camden, the former Sanctuarist on Base I, hijacked the first Hemispherical Registered Processor, or HeRP, for the Odans' Earth-to-Moon communications system. But he struggled to connect it with a midpoint receptor in the Alps. By the time he succeeded, the Militia had detected abnormal signals from his HeRP, and they captured him. Through the weeks of torture preceding his execution, Camden held on to the secret of his home city. Ironically, his death allowed twenty-something Micah River to pursue his lifelong dream of spying for Saint Oda. Though he wasn't ready, he begged Wesley Sr. to let him take Camden's place. Wes thinks Micah became a Sanctuarist to distinguish himself from Larimer and his four fisherman brothers. "He wanted to be different," Wes told me. "To be a hero, whatever the cost."

A hero. . . . Not like me. I've been useless, and a liability.

Shaking off the thought, I walk past a panel of defunct buttons and levers—the beacon hasn't shone in a hundred and fifty years—and peer through a dusty window at the Overhang and the Odan harbor. I'm exhaling heavily from exertion; my breath fogs the glass, and I wipe away the condensation with my sleeve, which has a texture similar to that of human skin. My shirt's made from yeast film. I still haven't gotten used to the Odans' bizarre natural products—moss carpeting, fungal medicine.

But like so many traditions here, their manufactures are rooted in their faith. Odans work toward unity with all their fellow creatures. Why employ alloys and synthesized materials for any purpose, they reason, when materials from a divinely infused life form could serve just as well?

On the other hand, Tourmaline, the uninvited city, gleams with artificiality. Scarlet, green, and violet lights block out the indigo sky. The reflections in the black water oscillate and swirl as the massive raft parts the ocean waves. For balance, the circular city has been constructed in the shape of an upside-down mushroom; the base slopes upward into interconnected buildings, and a cluster of golden skyscrapers rises in the center. Pounding, hysterical music plays, somewhere on the near side. It sounds as if all the computers in the Lunar InfoTech Department are shorting out at once. Most Pacifian allies are destitute, I've learned, but this one, with its colorful lights, seems decadently wealthy. Pacifia must have designated Tourmaline as an ambassador city to intimidate other states.

A pair of silver-plated binoculars hangs above my head; I put the string around my neck, raise the lenses to my eyes, and focus them, the way Wes showed me last month. Now I can see people dancing—or rather, thrashing—to the beat, their clothing lighting up and powering down with their movements.

Tourmaline scintillates like the gemstone that shares its name, but it also proves that brilliance is best presented in small quantities. Visually, aurally, the city is too much. So is the small group that now struts across the Overhang's stage, their footfalls accompanied by jangling metal.

The Tourmalinian soldiers are decorated in every sense: their pants are amethyst purple, their jackets emerald green, and their narrow-brimmed caps cinnabar red. Golden badges and frills cover their uniforms from their collars to their pant hems. A middle-aged brunette woman with an arrogantly arched back heads a unit of guards wearing red jackets with purple lapels. They carry meter-long muskets.

At the sight, I suck in my breath; though the guns are primitive, they're still an unwelcome presence on an archipelago that's pacifistic to the core.

If First Priest Luciana Pinto is affronted by Tourmaline's militant display, she keeps the sentiment off her face. Sanctuary Coordinator Carlyle, a tall man with graying red hair and asymmetrical, skeptical eyebrows, stands four meters behind the priest, wearing his usual smart brown jacket with golden buttons.

"A lovely day," the Tourmalinian lady says. I hear every sharp note in her voice—the sound travels all the way to the lighthouse, demonstrating the incredible acoustic properties of the Odan amphitheater. Her tone implies that the evening isn't inherently lovely, but lovely because she says so. The vertical lines around her mouth look like cracks in dried mud.

In the sparse Odan crowd below, mostly made up of men, a copper-haired head shakes. Wes. I imagine him smiling dimly at the spectacle before us, even though I know he'd rather run straight at the newcomers to flush out the adrenaline. His fingers loop through the loose thread of his sweater and tighten it around his wrist like a handcuff. I wish I could untangle him before he cuts off his circulation. I wish he were next to me.

"Saint Oda extends to Tourmaline the hospitality of the Lord and all the creatures in his keeping." Pinto folds her hands, resting them on the belt of her scratchy-looking wool dress. "I don't believe we have met. My name is Luciana Pinto."

"And I am Ambassador Everett." The Tourmalinian wears what looks like a lime-green silk blanket wrapped around her waist and draped over her shoulder. When she moves forward to shake hands with Pinto, she takes tiny steps so that she won't trip on the skirt.

"What brings you here?" Pinto asks. "Trade? Do you require a place to rest?"

"No. As you can see, our city provides more than adequate accommodation." Mouth twisted in a condescending sneer, Everett sweeps her hand around, as if to contrast her glamorous city with Saint Oda's primitivism. "We have not traveled far; we have been conducting diplomacy in Europe. Today, Tourmaline's duty is to come here, on direct orders from the President of Pacifia."

A shudder rattles through the Odan crowd.

"No need to fear!" Again, self-importance pervades Everett's words. "Our visit is cause for celebration. The Pacifian alliance is welcoming Saint Oda, and allowing you to join us."

3

THE ODAN MEN'S ANGER MATERIALIZES AT once. They puff out their chests like frigate birds and inch closer to the stage.

"How profane!"

"A military alliance? We renounced weaponry centuries ago."

"I pray for the souls within them!"

They're shaking their heads and glaring at Ambassador Everett. I've lived here only five months, yet I find that I'm offended, too. Although Saint Oda's people have seen and felt war, they've never instigated it. They've only suffered and done their best to recover, to forgive. Joining the Pacifian alliance and taking part in the standoff with Battery Bay would run counter to the Odans' instincts, like forcing blood to flow backward through their veins.

On the stage, Wesley Carlyle Sr. moves swiftly to Pinto's side. In the audience, his son raises a narrow tube to his lips, hiding it from view with his other hand. It's a blowgun, used to fire hardened pine needles dipped in toxic wolfsbane—one of the only hunting tools permitted in Saint Oda. Blowguns are excellent weapons for Sanctuarists: small, all-natural, nonlethal. Should a Tourmalinian show aggression toward Pinto or his father, Wes can knock the stranger unconscious with a puff.

Several other young men cover their mouths with their hands, among them Finley, Wes's fifteen-year-old cousin, and Maurice, a nineteen-year-old Sanctuarist who'll leave soon for the Moon.

"Matters of state are outside my concern, Ambassador." Pinto's speech remains dignified, as does her posture. But through the binoculars, I see the skin beneath her left eye twitch. "I can help in the realm of spirituality, even hospitality—but never hostility. Please redirect your inquiry to Sanctuary Coordinator Carlyle."

With that, Pinto turns her back on Ambassador Everett and shuffles off the stage. The Odans look bewildered. I've seen Pinto act graciously to fussing toddlers, but today she insulted a lady dressed like an ancient Earthbound queen. It takes a lot to infuriate Pinto, and the Tourmalinians have done it in a matter of minutes.

Wes's father takes Pinto's place at center stage and brushes something invisible off his shoulder before speaking. "You seem to have forgotten, Tourmalinian, that we have not communicated with another state in nearly a century. It will pain me to give you a lesson in Odan international affairs in front of my people, but it seems to be necessary. Do you remember the incident ninety years ago with New Joudo, your fellow Pacifian ally? And the oil wells at the border of Odan's waters?"

My stomach lurches. Saint Oda wasn't always isolationist? No one mentioned that to me.

"Of course I know the story." Everett glares sideways at Priest Pinto. "What do you take me for, an uneducated Luddite?"

Hissing from the Odans.

"New Joudo tried to negotiate with your . . . tribe," Everett continues. "When you didn't cooperate, they *utilized* the oil wells—"

"*Seized*," says Wesley Sr.

"Battery Bay swooped in, assaulted New Joudo, offered you an alliance—"

"Which we rejected."

"—and took over the oil wells—"

"Which we had never used!" Wesley Sr.'s face is the color of a blood orange.

"And you let them, because in return, Battery Bay declared that . . ."

The two finish together: *"No state shall violate the sovereignty of the International Sanctuary of Saint Oda."*

So Saint Oda benefited from Battery Bay's help, even though its residents claim that they ignore the outside world, and always have? Do Odans play the international affairs game like everyone else? I rub my eyes, feeling cold disappointment in my gut. *They have no other choice,* I tell myself.

"No matter. Pacifia knew that the cost of a war with the Batterers was not worth some xenophobic tribe's oil." Everett sniffs, staring down her wide-eyed Odan audience. "Now that your history has been so tiresomely elucidated, let me warn you: your 'sanctuary' is about to become an inferno. The cold war between Battery Bay and Pacifia is getting hot. And it will move here. Has Battery Bay helped you prepare? Has it warned you about what is to come? No. The Batterers are not your friends, as you might think. We in the Pacifian alliance will place you under our protection. We will modernize Saint Oda and give its people a fighting chance. Trust us—you will *need* to fight."

In the audience, several people nod, but the majority shake their heads. Wes practices aiming his blowgun, his eyes narrowed at Everett.

"You are purely self-interested," Wesley Sr. says. "The Odan archipelago is strategically located in the center of the North Channel. If we joined you, you would control the Irish Sea and the British Isles, where you have factories, reserve corps—"

"Your city would never again be defenseless!" Everett cries, cutting him off. "Not even from Lunars. Pacifian intelligence has learned that the 'demons,' as you call them, mean to increase the frequency of their Earth invasions, which will endanger every city on this planet—even Pacifia, our great benefactor. Of course, this has escaped your notice."

She's acting as if she knows nothing about the recent Lunar-Pacifian alliance. Maybe she doesn't; the Committee's kept it from the Lunar public, and Pacifia's leadership may not have informed its allies yet either. Most Earthbound probably think that the Lunars wouldn't touch their planet with a 400,000-kilometer-long pole.

After Battery Bay led Pacifia in a failed attempt to democratize the warmongering Moon thirty years ago, the Lunars supposedly retreated into isolation. Without a common enemy, the Batterers and Pacifians have turned on each other. Each expanded its individual alliances in case war broke out. Pacifia pursued the less developed nations most degraded by centuries of free-market global trade, appealing to their ingrained bitterness. The capitalist and democratic Battery Bay labeled Pacifia a bully and set out to protect economic and political openness worldwide. Or so they claimed.

Most people don't know that without telling the Lunar populace, the Committee began using the Moon's Militia to attack nonaligned Earth cities and seize their resources—cities like Saint Oda. Now Everett is using fear of Lunar brutality to persuade them.

"The Lunars have grown even more barbaric of late." Everett turns to one of the soldiers behind her, who holds a small black cube. "Play the video. They should know what happens to those who are captured."

The cube spins and clicks in the soldier's hand and then projects a high-resolution image on the stone wall at the rear of the Overhang. At the activation of an electronic device, several Odans *tsk* their tongues in disapproval. But they all turn to watch the video.

The boy is alone.

I recognize my little brother one feature at a time. The blank eyes are the same shape. The mouth, if those cuts were erased, might resemble his. But the sunken cheeks, covered in bruises that bloom like violets . . .

Cygnus is exhausted, bald, and horribly thin.

Then the electric chair comes to life, and he's in that white cylinder of a cell with a monster.

My brother's eyes scrunch shut. Beneath the electricity streaking across his bruised face, he's screaming.

"T two A one G—"

The binoculars slip from my hands; the observatory floor rises to meet my knees.

"Stop, please," I murmur to myself.

But Cygnus keeps hollering nonsense. *"T two A one G three omicron C-E-T alpha C-O-L alpha P-H-E dodeca-chordata T two A one G three."* He gasps for breath; my heart lurches. *"T two A one G three omicron C-E-T—"*

"That is more than enough." Wesley Sr. plucks the cube out of the soldier's hand, hurls it to the ground, and crushes it beneath his moccasin-clad foot. His face reddens as he points toward the ocean. "Out. *Get out!*"

I look through my binoculars again. Many of the remaining audience members are fleeing the scene, their faces contorted and disturbed. The people that have stayed cluster near the stage, hurling words of condemnation at the Tourmalinian entourage. Never have I heard the Odans' musical speech turn to wrathful howling.

Ambassador Everett's jaw quivers. "We only meant to—"

Wesley Sr. looks at the audience and taps his lips with one finger. The scattered plainclothes Sanctuarists raise their blowguns to their mouths.

The Tourmalinian entourage turn on their heels and retreat toward their floating city, Ambassador Everett glaring at the Overhang as she goes. At the last moment, her eyes seem to find the lighthouse, the look in them venomous enough to kill.

I battle the overwhelming urge to shout, to run, to kick something and relish the pain. Instead of taking entire seasons to recover, instead of enjoying the company of Wes and the other Earthbound people I've met, I should have been clawing my way back to the Moon. I sit with my back to the lighthouse window, catching my breath.

The Militia troops sent footage of Cygnus's brutal capture to me and Wes as we escaped Base IV, and yet I didn't turn back to save him. Guilt has caught up with me, but it's months too late.

The Tourmalinians showed the torture video to intimidate the Odans, but in doing so, they've stirred up a fierce energy inside me. I'm an arrow pulled tight against a string, and if I don't fly toward the Moon before time runs out, I might splinter bit by bit.

4

I STAY IN THE LIGHTHOUSE, CURLED IN A ball, until night comes. When the temperature drops, tears freeze on my face. The Carlyles will worry about why I haven't come home, but whatever Wes has to say, whatever Murray's reactions or the Odans' declamations against Lunars may be—I don't want to hear it or be expected to respond.

The waves advance and retreat, the sound like crackling electricity. To my ears, the keening of Saint Oda's nocturnal animals resembles a young boy's screams.

When it feels like the next howl will light a fuse in my head, I slide down the lighthouse's ladder, ignoring the potential for blisters, and begin to climb the mountain. Moments later, I reach a gaping hole in the rock face and duck inside.

Saint Oda is a burrowing city. The interior of Koré Island, the central landmass in the archipelago, is shaped like a cone, with a spiral staircase leading upward. Murray says that both the stairs and the dwellings are modeled after the curves of a snail shell. The frigid air smells of brine; Odans find bleach and ammonia nastier than the gunk those compounds dissolve. During high tides, or when storms blow through, ocean water floods the lower levels. It happened just last month, leading homeowners and shop proprietors to complain at the city council meeting. People lived on a floor below the current lowest level as recently as fifty years ago, when the Earth was cooler and the sea farther down. Only crabs and eels pass through those rooms now.

I emerge into the night air near the peak of the highest mountain. The bioluminescent bacteria in the glass bulbs cast their blue glow, brighter than yesterday. Murray must have fed them flour while I was gone. Despite her family's stature, she's expected to maintain the lighting near Koré's peak and contribute labor to the community like any other adult.

Far below, footbridges float atop the ocean, also glowing blue, bobbing gently with the waves. They connect the four auxiliary islands to each other and to this one. Usually, the vista strikes me dumb with its beauty; today, it impresses my eyes but not my mind. I've been stricken enough already. I wipe sweat from my forehead, looking up at the Moon while I catch my breath.

Even if I climbed the highest mountain on Earth, I'd still be too far away to help Cygnus. Somewhere on Saint Oda, a wolf cries, and all I hear is my brother's pain. Earth is taunting me, and it feels like yet another sign that I belong back on the Moon. But although I'm absent, several Odan agents, Wes's colleagues and friends, watch over their respective bases. *If I could just talk to them . . .*

My feet pick up the trail again, energized by a new idea. I keep my eyes turned upward. Unaware that a lost girl is watching them, the stars—and my cratered homeland—continue to shine against the dark.

*　　*　　*

Unlike most Odan dwellings, the Carlyle family's home isn't underground. It's not aboveground either: a hollow rock formation makes up three walls and half the ceiling, while lumpy glass shields the rest of the interior from rain and wind. In the absence of mechanized industry, Wes explained, people made these materials by hand. Primitive, a Lunar would say, but I find it charming.

The house is only quasi-subterranean—with one glass wall—because the Sanctuary coordinator needs high ground and an excellent vantage point. Not that Saint Oda is often attacked, but Odans want at least one person to remember that it's a possibility.

The front door is a wooden block dyed green with foxglove leaf extract. I pound my fist against it until Murray swings it open. Her expression is standoffish and stale, and her gaze dodges mine when I try to make eye contact.

"*Cheep! Cheep! Chirrreeeep!*"

Having announced my arrival, Lewis rises off of Murray's shoulder and coasts into the kitchen. As he swoops across the dinner table, a gigantic hollowed-out tree stump, his wing knocks a clay dessert bowl to the floor. *Crash!*

I stumble into the entryway. Wes's parents take in my disheveled appearance, and their jaws settle, firm, like they're cast in iron. In the corner, Nanna Zeffie, an old woman with spectacles and white hair that coils like sheep's wool, looks up from slicing an elderberry pie and frowns.

"I *told* you she would come home, Murray!" Emberley, Wes's eight-year-old sister, says, taking Murray's hand and skipping around her in a circle. "Knew it the whole time." The young girl's hair is the upbeat orange of tiger lilies, even in the blue light. Beside her, Murray turns her face toward the shadows.

The youngest Carlyle, six-year-old Jubilee, blinks at me. She's the most like her parents, the hardest to impress.

Wes rushes forward as if he'll embrace me. Remembering our audience, I raise my hands to prevent a high-momentum collision, and he touches my elbow instead. My heartbeats grow too frequent, and not only because I've been running.

"Don't scare me like that again," he whispers. "That video smelled like bait."

I look down at the muddy hem of my skirt.

"I'm sorry. That was inconsiderate. There was no way you could have prepared for those . . . those *images*."

"Did you say something, Wes?" Murray's voice is higher than normal, as if her vocal cords have been stretched too tight.

"Don't worry about it." Wes has used that phrase at least twice a day since we arrived. He picked it up from me—without fail, it shuts down unnecessary or unwanted conversation. But as I've learned through hard experience, it also keeps people at a distance, and I'm not sure if Wes will want that in the long run.

"Calm down, Marina." The house's matriarch rarely uses Murray's full name. Square-jawed and stout, Wes's mother, Holly Carlyle, rises slowly to her feet. The gray color of her dress highlights the silver at the roots of her brown hair. "Emmy, Julie, sit down and finish your supper."

Mrs. Carlyle uses the same cajoling tone to address her little girls as she does with her grown daughter.

I've missed dinner. Every day, at exactly eight "p.m."— or 20:00, as a Lunar would say—the Carlyles gather around their circular wooden table, clasp hands, and recite a prayer to thank God for the plants, animals, and fungi that lost their lives or tissues so the family could eat. Tourmaline's visit hasn't disrupted this routine—until now. Wesley Sr. looks anxiously at his two younger daughters and clears his throat. "In fact, it's Emmy and Julie's bedtime."

Nanna Zeffie stops cutting the pie midslice, parks the knife in the golden crust. "I'll tuck them in."

Next to me, Wes gulps. Mrs. Carlyle, Murray, and Wesley Sr. must want to discuss the day's events. I brace myself for the scolding I'll get when the little girls and their grandmother are out of earshot.

"It's getting cold, Nanna," Wes stammers, trying to spare me. "Fay and I could help you stoke the fires in their rooms."

"You'll stay right here, Wesley." Mrs. Carlyle's voice grows shriller. "And so will Fay."

"Mother!" says Emberley. "It's not nine o'clock yet. And I'm not tired!" She pouts and points at the huge analog clock by the wall. It's so old that its wooden bits are rotting at the edges. The name "grandfather clock" suits it perfectly; Wes told me it dates back to the twentieth century. At that time, I suppose, it was acceptable to use a tree's worth of wood to construct a mere timepiece.

"You're never tired, Emmy." Nanna Zeffie shuffles toward her, tugging a pouting Jubilee by the hand. "Time for bed."

Jubilee fixes me with a tight-lipped glare that seems unnatural on her plump face, as if she knows I've caused her early imprisonment. Then she disappears down the hallway with her sister and grandmother. I hear their slippered feet climbing the spiral staircase to the second floor.

I can't bear to look at the Carlyles, so instead, I direct my gaze to the wall above Murray's place at the table. Hanging there is what looks like a photograph of a teenage girl, except her features look smudged and the shadows don't fall quite where you'd expect; it must be a painting, an Earthbound image that I know takes longer to create. The girl in the picture has dark skin with a luminous pallor and thick black hair that hangs in a braid over one shoulder. Her big eyes seem to see everything—sometimes they follow me around the room—and her unyielding lips are pressed shut.

I've looked at her countless times: when Wes's mother needles him about his interactions with Odan citizens, when his father asks about the minutiae of his exercise routine, when Murray tries to mediate their conversations and the whole scene melts into heated argument. But no one has ever explained who the girl is or why her picture hangs here.

When I can no longer hear Nanna's or the girls' footsteps, Wesley Sr. begins to speak. "Fay. Explain yourself, and the quicker you are about it, the sooner you can resume your customary silence."

I nod, hoping I look calmer than I am.

"Why didn't you return to the house with Murray when Tourmaline dropped anchor? And why did you stay out so long past sunset? I thought you had heeded our warnings about our island's nocturnal wildlife."

Brown bears, wolves, and wild boars roam Saint Oda at night; the Odans consider themselves blessed, as these species nearly went extinct elsewhere. But the predators occasionally attack the city's people, whose faith forbids fighting back. Wesley Sr. knows I'm terrified of these unfamiliar creatures. Flat-ended bees were the most dangerous creature I ever encountered on the Moon.

As if seeking help, I lock eyes with the painted mystery girl. I can't risk exposing my Lunar identity by admitting that the boy in the torture video was my brother. Although the Odans treat every living thing peacefully, we are the singular, unnatural "demons" they cannot tolerate. If Wesley Sr. finds out I'm a Lunar, he'll throw me off Saint Oda into the open ocean, where I'll drown or be captured. Wes would face exile too, for harboring an enemy.

"Tried to leave," I enunciate. "Crowd trapped me near the lighthouse."

Mrs. Carlyle and Murray shudder, as I hoped they would. Wesley Sr. rolls his eyes, unimpressed.

Wes walks toward them. "Want to know what Fay told me, just a minute ago?" His voice grows hushed as he launches into a lie. He developed his technique in preparation for his spy stint and perfected it during those years on the Moon, away from his family. They don't realize what he's doing. "She saw the wandering souls of her family—her mother, her brother, everyone who died breathing engine exhaust in the Pacifian motor room."

Murray throws an arm around her brother's shoulders and squeezes. "Oh, Wes, I've been so insensitive. I didn't know." She approaches, hands outstretched to hug me. "And Fay . . ." In her embrace, I can feel her body quivering with emotion.

"My deepest sympathies." Mrs. Carlyle gives me an awkward pat on the shoulder.

There's a twinge of guilt in my midsection. Wes and I have upset them—but these are necessary lies. Wes told me once that he forgives himself for deceiving, stealing, hurting, even killing, because he commits those crimes with the noblest intentions. It's how he stays sane.

"I got stuck. Near the lighthouse." I will my lower lip to tremble, as if I'm about to cry. Then I remember Cygnus's screams, and I'm no longer faking sorrow. "Had to walk and clear my head."

"That explains why you looked rattled when you arrived home." Wesley Sr. crosses his arms. "Odd, though. I didn't expect you to be superstitious, given your *background*."

My mouth twitches involuntarily. Does Wes's father suspect I'm a Lunar? I retrace each of my steps, my every word, wondering what could have blown my cover. Tears of panic sting my eyes, but in this case, they're opportune.

"Look what you've done to the poor girl—she's ready to cry!" Mrs. Carlyle steps forward as if to protect me. "How can you say such things? Pacifians have legends of their own; only those Lunar *demons* are godless." She turns to me, using the same tone she employs when Jubilee stubs her toe and cries, or when Murray looks glum for no reason. "Dear Fay, I'm sorry for your ordeal. Really, truly sorry."

I've never heard her speak this softly to Wes, not even when he took over some of his grandmother's duties, cooking and cleaning and tucking in his sisters, during the week in November when Nanna Zeffie fell ill.

"But I beg you," Mrs. Carlyle continues, "don't stay out late again. Haven't you noticed how Emmy and Julie adore you? That's why it's so good to have you here, aside from all the help you've given us. You must set a good example for my girls."

I nod, relieved. I'm safe for today. But Mrs. Carlyle's speech reminds me of my own mother's lectures, which I'll never hear again. Except in my memories.

The cracks in my mind open further, and a surge of grief escapes its deep confinement. *Stop right there.* Too many tears will give everything away.

"Thank you, dear." Mrs. Carlyle smiles at me, then stands and circles the table to her husband. She hugs him; his face loses all its suspicion and fills with love. He pats her on her back, brushing his hands over her wavy hair. They share a brief look, and in only a second convey the affection and trust they've built up over long years of living together in safety.

I clench my eyes shut—hard, hard, *harder*, even though the pressure hurts. Mom must have held Dad like that, must have felt what Mrs. Carlyle's feeling now. Maybe more. But I can't ask her, so I'll never know.

She looked at me, through me, in the seconds before she died. Did she know how much I'd miss her?

"Fay . . ."

I open my eyes.

Wes moves toward me, one hand extended. I don't think he's even aware of the gesture.

"I believe I can take care of this." Murray swoops in, loops her arm through mine, and forces a smile. She seems unusually intent on preventing me and Wes from spending time alone together. What's she worried about? Social norms? Pleasing her parents? "There's no such thing as too much fresh air."

With that, she leads me back out into the cold.

5

AS MURRAY AND I WALK THROUGH THE garden behind the chicken coop, our arms remain entwined. It feels more like a restraint than an embrace.

She's thought hard all day; I feel it in her faraway gaze. My left hand automatically worms under my right arm, as if to cover my handscreen's now-defunct audio receptors. The old habit persists, even on Earth.

While I was in recovery, Wes disconnected my blood vessels from the handscreen's wiring, and removed the Lunar Positioning System chip. Then he used stolen Medical Department supplies to induce my skin to heal over the wound, scarlessly. Without the handscreen, I'll be dead to the Committee if I return to the Moon—no, *when* I return. At first I felt a gnawing sense of loss. My blood had pumped through the handscreen's battery since I was five, allowing me to receive communications, play games, and introduce myself to others. But the device held me prisoner: Medical watched my vital signs, the Militia tracked my location, and government eavesdroppers listened to my most private conversations. Now I have freedom, and I've embraced it, though sometimes I still doubt it's real.

"Here." Murray's holding out a currant roll, which she must have nicked from the table, and I think with a strange detachment that I haven't eaten since noon. The bread's not as soft as it was this morning, when Nanna Zeffie and I pulled the batch from the mud-brick oven, but it's warm from Murray's body heat.

I nibble. Lewis hops along the ground behind me, snapping up the crumbs I leave behind. Whenever I find a currant in the bread, I suck on it until the skin bursts. There's sweet juice inside each one. Nanna Zeffie knows how to keep the currants from dehydrating.

Around Murray, Lewis, and me, bare branches reach toward the yellow Moon as if begging for light or love. They receive neither.

The forest must have been beautiful during the autumn, when, Murray tells me, leaves filled every twig. For each color you've seen in a fire, she said, there was a leaf to match. I wasn't sure what she meant, because I'd only seen tiny blue flames in the Primary Chemistry labs, and leaves don't turn blue. Because I slept until November came, I missed the fire in the treetops.

And all that time, Murray watched me sleep.

We pass a clump of green shoots; each has two or three long, straight leaves that extend toward the sky. They come up to our ankles now. *My snowdrops*, I think. *They'll flower soon.*

Lewis lands in the middle of the patch, swallows a pebble as roughage for his gizzard, and takes off, calling loudly.

"I know I'm a bad role model," Murray says, "but you shouldn't let strong feelings lead you to make stupid decisions."

She turns to me, a spark of concern in her intact eye. Her words, her every gesture, seem to warn against my plans for later tonight. But she wouldn't know about those; she's speaking about her own experiences. I remember her stunned face and her shaking hands as Tourmaline's lights appeared in the distance.

"Why did you leave the Overhang so quickly?" I say.

Murray's throat tightens. With the hand not holding mine, she absently rubs her locket between her fingers. "Tourmaline made me feel thirteen again. The world was splintering, and everything in it was dark and new."

Silence falls. This time, it feels awkward. I swallow the last of the roll and dust off the bits of flour clinging to my fingertips. "Are you talking about the Lunars?"

"The demons? The one night they spent here, they killed us. Just to steal our things. They might have *asked*. We would have given them whatever we could spare." Murray drops my arm and runs a finger down the scar across her eye. In the blue bacterial light, her old injury looks like a rocky lunar canyon. "They gave me this."

Grief—for Wes's sister, for this city—rises in my chest.

Murray fiddles with the locket's clasp and wrenches it open. In the left half, shielded by a thin glass cover, is a black-and-white drawing of the girl whose painting hangs in the Carlyles' dining room. On the right half, the glass has been smashed, the paper ripped, but I can make out the strong shoulders of a man in a black jacket. His face is a mystery.

"I grew up with her." Murray gestures at the girl. "She didn't say much, but she seemed to see and hear everything. The way she looked at me, I knew she understood me. You're like that too. It made me like you the day we met."

My heart hitches. She's wrong—I hardly understand her at all.

Murray nods—half to herself and half to me. "Yes, you're like Cassia—Cassia Murray."

"What?" I blurt. Murray's first name is this girl's last name? That can't be an accident.

"My birth name is Marina. I only started calling myself Murray after the raid." Murray utters her next words in one breath. "Cassia was set free." The Odan euphemism for death.

"Her parents and brother left Saint Oda because they couldn't bear to see reminders of her everywhere. Sometimes I wish I'd left with them."

Murray hugs herself as if to keep out the cold, but it's coming from inside her. Moving closer and rubbing the middle of her back, I calculate that Cassia couldn't have been more than thirteen when she died.

"We were sitting on her back porch, talking and looking out at the blackberry patch, when the demons landed. Her family lived right outside the cave entrances, which was where the soldiers wanted to go. So they swept across the farm. We didn't know what the stomping noises behind us were. . . ." A tear dribbles down Murray's face, but she doesn't wipe it away. "I didn't do anything but watch."

Stop remembering, if it makes you sad! But maybe talking about her trauma is cathartic, like letting air gush out of something that's about to explode. Not everyone tries to hold it in like me.

"Cassia g-got shot. . . . She had blackberry juice on her lips. I screamed and screamed until a different soldier cut me with a shard from a clay pot."

I wince, imagining the pain, and put my arms around her. Murray looks up at me, composure regained, voice eerily calm. "Before she did it, though, the soldier flipped up her visor so I could see her eyes. They were almost like yours, Fay. But she was dreadfully thin." Murray shakes her head, smiling coldly. Her features seem to change shape as she cycles through emotions. "I still wonder how she had the strength in that arm to cut me and knock me unconscious. I must have looked dead to the world. No demons hurt me afterward."

The soldier must have been new when the raid occurred;

only a fresh Beetle would knock a girl out to prevent the team from killing her. It's harder than leaving people to die, which doesn't require looking into their eyes and acknowledging their humanity. Only someone soft, unhardened by months of dealing out cruelty, would make the effort. During my time in Militia, I found that the longer soldiers served, the less they valued others' lives.

Murray squeezes the locket. "Sometimes, I wonder if she meant to kill me. But she didn't. She made it so hard for me to see and be seen—for life. Is that any better?"

I wouldn't know. I stare at Murray's hands, feeling sadness and shame in equal measure. Her voice is pretty; so is her big heart. But because of her angry scar and permanently mismatched gaze, that beauty took me a long time to see.

Maybe the Lunar soldier didn't know that Odan medicine, unlike ours, doesn't include facial reconstruction and can't erase a scar. Or maybe I'm making excuses.

The locket rotates beneath Murray's fingers. The broken glass on the side opposite Cassia Murray's picture reflects the pasty moonlight.

"Things returned to normal after we cleaned up the demons' mess—well, as normal as they could get, with Wes and the other five preparing to go to that . . . lair in the sky. I felt blessed to live in this city, where people were so *different* from the Lunar demons. I believed our faith would keep us kind. But I was naive." Murray snaps the locket shut. "There are selfish Odans too."

"Who?" I ask.

Murray clasps both hands around the locket, squeezing until they shake. "I don't like remembering. Every time I mention his name, the memory of him gets stronger."

"Sorry, I didn't mean to—"

"Not a problem." She taps her foot. "Why do you lean on my brother so much? How can you be certain he won't go somewhere far away and leave you alone and so awfully *cold*?"

I gape at her, bewildered. She and her parents have separated Wes and me at every opportunity; I don't need her warnings about spending time with him when she doesn't know any of our secrets.

Murray turns away from the blue light, and her face is just shadows on shadows. "I'm sorry. I've talked too much, haven't I?"

"Don't be sorry," I say. "Better to say too much than nothing at all. After my dad died, I . . . I went mute for a year and a half." I only spoke in my dreams after I lost Mom. But Murray heard all that.

"You talk now, though," Murray points out. "Not much. But you talk."

"When I was mute, people thought I was crazy." *Why am I telling Murray this?* I've hardly discussed it with Umbriel, and he knew the most about me as a child. The answer comes to me in an instant: *Because Murray's experienced something similar.*

"People thought I was crazy for a time too." Murray's laugh is more like a bark. "My parents and my brother were afraid I'd poison my sisters with my darkness. Wes spent every free moment with Emmy until he left. By then, she was five years old, and she could block me out. Jubilee was just three. She had a favorite lullaby—this one."

And she begins to sing, to herself more than to me.

> "*Snowy trees and snowy seas,*
> *Frozen you and frozen me.*

One foot, two, two feet, three—
Snow and ice will set us free."

The words, rendered in her clear, cold voice, induce in me a creeping sadness—the last line in particular. Chills run through me.

"How could you teach a toddler about death?" I ask. She threw her little sister into the shadows before she'd seen the sun; I couldn't do that to my siblings—not intentionally.

"Those were some strange years for me, Fay," Murray says. "My thoughts were completely outside my control. First, I denied what had happened; then I wanted to stop . . . existing. Then I wanted revenge."

"But you're not like that now," I blurt, watching the composed young woman beside me.

"Back then, a different girl inhabited this body—not me. When she got angry, she attacked the people closest to her. With words on good days, with blows on bad days. Because she couldn't strike the ones who'd actually hurt her—they were too far away. And this fiend-girl stayed with me until years later, when I told myself I'd outgrown the terrible memories, and put them out of mind's reach—like you'd stash out-of-season clothes in a chest of drawers somewhere. But since Tourmaline docked, they've been spilling out again, all moth-eaten and foul."

I think of all the experiences I've tried and failed to erase over the past few months. They bring me nightmares and tears, not rage—but is that any better? "Do you think the memories will ever disappear completely?" I say.

"I don't know, and I don't care to know." She blinks at me—only one eye fully shuts. "I only want to make it through each day. Why should I wonder about a time that might never come?"

6

THREE HOURS LATER, I BREAK AND ENTER.
I'll get help for Cygnus tonight, and I don't give two grits if Wes
finds out. It won't be enough, but it's all I can manage.

The door leading to the basement, where Wes's father and
the Sanctuarists hold their meetings, is a piece of wood cut and
painted to blend in with the stone floor. But it's lighter. The
hinge is located a third of the way down, forming a lever. I stomp
on one end, and as the other pops up, I lift it and slide inside.

The spiral staircase is made of old wood, which sags and
moans with every step I take. Every night, a Sanctuarist or two
is on watch duty here. In the past, I've secretly accompanied
Wes on a few of his shifts. But in the wake of today's events, all
two dozen young men are out patrolling and collecting material
evidence of Tourmaline's visit, leaving the room empty.

With the exception of the Sanctuarists' meeting place, Saint
Oda is devoid of digitization and electronics. Not a soul, except
for the men in service and me, knows about the equipment in
the Carlyles' basement. There are exercise machines with beeping monitors, links to cameras that film the ocean from the hill-
top, and a primitive but powerful computer. The Sanctuarists
hide even the industrial-sized chemical battery that powers the
equipment, driving the only electrical circuit in the city, and
they maintain the levels of zinc and mercury ions themselves.

I park myself in front of the computer monitor mounted

on the stone wall. On the upper left corner of the screen are six circular icons, each labeled with a Roman numeral; these must represent the Odan agents on their respective bases. To my disappointment, only *IV* and *VI* glow green; the rest are red. This means just two of the agents can send messages to the Odan machine at the moment, and neither of them is on Base I, where Cygnus is being held.

Last month, I pestered Wes about how he and the other Sanctuarists communicate with the spies on the Moon, and he showed me the basics. First, he records a voice message, which is coded into a radio wave, encrypted, and sent to a midpoint in the Alps. The ultraviolet beam travels to another midpoint on the Moon's far side, then to any Sanctuarist on the Moon with a switched-on receiver. The receiver, usually a jailbroken HeRP, decrypts the message and plays the sound clip. The entire process takes only milliseconds, but it's secure. Because the bases' handscreen network uses longer-wavelength transmission, Info-Tech's surveillance equipment doesn't detect the Sanctuarists' messages. The two midpoints also ensure that even if detection occurs, the bases can only trace the lasers' origin to useless terrain. As an added precaution, the Sanctuarists have landed prestigious jobs on their respective bases, affording them private offices in which to talk.

I'd leave a message for Micah on Base I, but what if he replied and one of the Sanctuarists on Saint Oda intercepted it? I'm hoping to keep tonight's conversation—with whomever I manage to speak—as quiet as possible. To avoid accidental interception, I must talk to a Sanctuarist whose icon is green.

But Cygnus is not the only one in danger. My mental image of my brother's tormented face melts into that of a helpless young girl's. Anka, my little sister, could be facing any amount of abuse from the Militia—all alone. While I have the chance, I must ask the Base IV agent to watch over her. All I've heard from Wes is that the agent is new, a recent transfer from Base II who's posing as a Psychology assistant and experimenting on "patients" in Shelter.

I'm wagering that this man—Lazarus Penny—is as kind as his countrymen and that, like them, he'll want to protect people who can't protect themselves. Hopefully, he's spent enough time around Lunars to realize not all of us are evil; hopefully, too, he won't hate me as soon as he learns of my nationality.

Will his humanity prevent him from turning me in to Wesley Sr.? If not, I could face deportation—or worse. But that would still be nothing compared to Anka's vulnerability or Cygnus's pain.

I tap the Base IV icon.

"Hello? Anyone there?"

After several long seconds, the computer beeps. The words Voice message received appear on the screen. I key in the six-digit code I watched Wes use to unlock messages.

"Wesley Junior? This is rather unanticipated. Your speech sounds . . . shriller than usual."

Every soft sound that escapes this unseen man's lips brims over with grace and fluidity. It's lovely but elusive; listening to his voice is like trying to hold warm water in the palms of my hands.

"It became apparent after our last one-on-one communication that you preferred not to speak with me directly," the Base IV agent continues shyly, as if unsure of himself. "I did not wish to disrespect that position if you still held it."

End of message, reads the screen.

Does he have a problem with Wes? If the two of them have had a disagreement, it would be unwise to associate myself with the boy who brought me here—but Wes is so agreeable, and this man seems the same way. After all, they're still teammates.

Pushing back my momentary hesitation, I square my shoulders and put my lips to the small perforations on the side of the screen.

"Have they hurt Anka Theta? Umbriel Phi?"

Lazarus's reply does nothing to ease my worries. "Pardon me, young miss, but your identity seems to elude me. Without that information, I'm afraid, I cannot aid you in your endeavors." He pauses, waiting for me to say something. When I don't, he fills the silence: "I *am*, however, familiar with those personages of whom you speak. From your evident distress, may I conclude that you are personally bonded to them? Those unfortunate youths . . ."

"Yes," I blurt. "Please, tell me anything you know."

"Ah, I understand the situation now. Permit me to ask— might you be the alleged female engine room slave from Pacifia? Your appearance on Saint Oda coincided curiously with the flight of one Phaet Theta, criminal-ess extraordinaire, from the Moon."

So, he knows who I am. The only good outcome of his quick reasoning is that he's saved me some explaining. But at least he seems sympathetic. I must continue tugging at his heartstrings, and must humble myself. He seems like the kind of person who'd want to help a young woman begging for aid. Unfortunately, with my limited speaking skills, I'm not much of a beggar.

"Tourmaline played a video of Cygnus Theta's torture at the Overhang today," I say. "Please, Mr. Lazarus, sir, can you tell me what's happening to him? Or to Anka? My sister? If you help them, I don't know how I'll ever repay you."

"Your sister is alive, Miss Phaet, albeit destitute in Base IV Shelter, and your brother is alive, albeit suffering on Base I." Lazarus speaks haltingly, as if unwilling to believe that his words are true. "Umbriel Phi has not left Anka's side since your withdrawal to Earth, and I commend his dedication to her. I regret that I cannot elaborate, because we do not have unlimited time to speak."

I gulp, and then ask, "Has something else gone wrong?"

Lazarus's sigh blows air across the receiver, making a muffled static noise. "I connected to the network in the middle of the night to disseminate my recently acquired knowledge about the present emergency circumstances. Circumstances, I am afraid, that involve you."

One word sticks in my brain, refusing to budge: *emergency.* Memories of my loved ones play out in my mind: Cygnus's fingers scurrying across the HeRP in our old apartment, the image so real that I can smell the spotted banana in his other hand; Anka, grinning, arranging two prunes and a handful of dried cranberries in a smiley face atop a bowl of porridge before handing it to me; Umbriel and the Phis; Nash; even Yinha, my former training instructor, neighbor, and friend, who turned out to be a covert member of Dovetail, the rebel movement. I didn't know until the day of Mom's trial. At the time, I was furious that Yinha had never told me where her loyalties lay. Now I'm worried that my anger will be the last memory she'll have of me.

"Twenty-seven hours ago, the Base IV General ordered an immense dispatch of his soldiers to Pacifia," Lazarus continues. Although he doesn't raise his voice, I can hear genuine worry in each word, and I can almost see him solemnly bowing his head on the other end of the line. "They touch down in two days. Every base has been made aware of the Lunar-Pacifian alliance, and the General is lobbying to assemble a conglomerate force of soldiers from all six."

I swallow hard. The Base IV Militia is coming to Earth? And a massive attack force might follow?

Lazarus pauses, allowing the silence to dilute the terrible news.

"I lament that I must inform you, but you are very much in danger. Because you are one root cause of the impending invasion—by no fault of your own, I assure you—you have the right to know first, before I inform Coordinator Carlyle and the other Sanctuarists." The content of his speech is awful, but now I can't shake the feeling of . . . enjoyment. Every word he says is a silken masterpiece. It's hard to imagine the owner of that voice sitting on his handscreen, watching out for base security, even though I know that's what Lazarus must be doing.

Now Lazarus inhales, preparing to deliver still worse news.

"Pacifia and the Base IV Militia will attack Saint Oda in less than a fortnight—eleven days, to be more precise. Pacifia wants its strategically located archipelago, and the Lunar Bases their runaways. The Militia has found you, Phaet Theta."

7

"THEY KNOW I'M HERE?" I'M NEARLY
shouting. "How? Does this relate to Cygnus? Does anyone
else know?"

Somehow, the Tourmalinians must have detected Wes's or
my presence the day they docked. But our handscreen trackers
couldn't have given us away, because they're out of commission. Did they see us? Impossible; Wes was amidst the crowd,
and I never emerged from the shadows. They might have used
infrared scanners, but those only detect body heat. They can't
distinguish one human being from another.

However they did it, our presence has placed an entire city
in danger. And we came here thinking only of me, trying to save
my life.

Why do I cause catastrophe everywhere I go? I shudder where I
sit, my throat constricting so that I can't force words out.

"Shh, Miss Phaet, please moderate your anxiety! I can hear
you shuddering from here," Lazarus says. "I will address your
inquiries one at a time. First, your discovery. For some time,
the Lunar authorities were in a state of uncertainty about
whether you and Wesley had lived or died, so they sent soldiers
to their Earth allies to achieve verification. Unfortunately, the
business of locating you was so straightforward that, using the
facial-recognition software installed in their telescopes, even
those Tourmalinian peacocks could manage it. They seem to

have detected your face in the lighthouse window."

I bury my head in my hands, feeling like an imbecile. I wish someone would slap me. Lonely, ugly, weak—I'd rather be any of those things than *stupid*.

"But how did they know where to look?" I say.

I wait anxiously while Lazarus records his response.

"After your departure from Base IV, your spacecraft tumbled into the North Atlantic, which provided a general geographic range. And Wesley's vigilance in disguising his accent must have lapsed whilst he lived on the Moon."

I nod, even though he can't see me. Wes's speech always sounded funny to my ears.

"The Information Technology Department acquired hand-screen and security pod recordings of his voice," Lazarus says, "and, through fastidious analysis, placed his origins in the British Isles. The authorities dispatched low-level Militia to scour all stationary and floating cities in the vicinity. Staying on Tourmaline was convenient for them, because, as you know, the Militia lacks vehicles suitable for extended travel on the Earth's surface. Without delay, the Committee informed the Lunar population about Wesley's and your location, and put seven-figure price tags on your heads, using their wealth to exact revenge like the despicable despots they are."

"But if they know Wes is from Earth . . ." *Then they know about the rest of you.*

At this, Lazarus lets out a long sigh. "Yes. The unveiling of Wesley's identity has alerted the Committee to the presence of spies from Earth, and they have commanded all citizens to be vigilant for others like him."

"I'm so sorry," I whisper into the microphone.

"I understand that you had only the best intentions, Miss Phaet," he says. "However, you must know that four hours ago, voice analysis tests were implemented to root out Earthbound agents. Poor Alex on Base VI will have to scramble to hide both his Kings Port accent—which trumpets his Caribbean origin—*and* his Odan one. Thank God he is the Astrophysics editor and needn't speak much on the job."

Lazarus's message isn't over. "Any other questions or concerns, Phaet? I am all yours."

"N-no," I stutter. "But I want to thank you for your time." This call was unpleasant but informative—and I seem to have gained a new ally in Lazarus. "I'm going back to the Moon as soon as I can. For Wes's sake, can you keep my Lunar identity secret? Just don't tell any Odans until I get home. Please?"

"I certainly could keep it confidential," Lazarus says, "but would it be the right thing? With all my heart, I want to help you, but I swore to guarantee my country's security."

"Please, sir, I'm begging you. Wes only brought me to Saint Oda to keep me alive."

"Whether I disperse intelligence crucial to Odan security is not for you or me to decide; it is written into the very core of Sanctuarist principles." Impatience and anger have, at long last, crept into his smooth voice.

Unquestionably, I deserve the rebuke. But if he follows his code of honor and reveals information about me, I will be flushed into the open ocean.

"But Lazarus, sir—"

"Beaters approaching," Lazarus breathes. I hear bags zipping shut, lights switching off, and Militia boots clicking on tile. "I must go. I recall that you apologized to me earlier, but I am the one who is sorry now. Truly, I wish everything were different, Miss Phaet."

The Base IV icon turns red.

"No!" I shout, pounding my fist on the machine. Thankfully, nothing breaks; it's solid and unshakable, just like Lazarus's integrity—integrity that overruled his sympathy for me. It makes me direct all my anger not at him but at myself.

There's no noise but the whirring of the room's circuitry. Memories of Lazarus's voice trickle through my head like a lukewarm stream that roars louder and louder, until I can no longer hear my own thoughts.

8

I TAKE THE SHUFFLING FOOTSTEPS AS A SIGN
that I should give up trying to sleep.

Wes has come home. His father heel-toed his way in through the green front door perhaps two hours ago, having sent Wes on another round of patrolling. But now he can finally rest.

I slip out of bed, thick wool blanket wrapped tight around me. The cold seeps in through the openings in my cocoon, near my neck and ankles. Keeping my leg joints supple, I pad down the first-floor hallway, my shadow a dark pillar against the faint blue light illuminating the slate walls. Insomnia has created a buzzing sensation between my ears.

I turn the corner and see him. He's unlacing his boots while standing up, one ankle crossed over the other knee. Those usually dexterous fingers are fumbling, numb with cold. Although shadows obscure his face, I can imagine him wearing a lopsided, frustrated grimace.

I tiptoe closer, and he looks up. His arms extend, beckoning me to him. I step into them, selfishly. Inside I find warmth, safety, a home of sorts. He doesn't yet know that because of me, the Odans might lose theirs. But he will by tomorrow, after Lazarus reports to his father. Worse, he'll find out that I revealed my Lunar identity—our secret—only when he gets punished.

I should tell him now, but selfish affection seals my lips. This hug might be our last, and I want to settle in these arms for as long as possible.

"My boots are wet," he murmurs. "They probably smell swampy."

An uneasy laugh is my only reply.

Seemingly of its own accord, the wool blanket leaves my shoulders and covers his.

"Phaet, you don't need to . . ." he protests.

"Shh." As I bend down to pick at the knots in his wet shoe-laces, I feel a warm weight settle on my upper back. He's leaning on me, and it makes me feel useful, if not less guilty. I'd do any-thing to take some pressure off his feet.

"No trace of the Tourmalinians"—he yawns—"except for a rogue submarine near the northern island. I ran an extra round to make sure of it."

"Wish I could have helped," I say. Patrolling would've giv-en me something productive to do, to counteract the harm I've caused. It would've been more useful than tossing and turning under the covers with the incessant buzzing in my head.

Wes slips off his boots, straightens, and wraps me in the blanket with him. Together, we shuffle away from the front door. My face growing hot, I pull him toward the spiral stair-case, intending to walk him to his bedroom, because he looks as if he's about to collapse. We begin climbing—slowly.

"Your taking on blanket duty is help enough for me," he quips. "But I know what you mean. It would've been just like training to have you there. Since I've come back, it's been strange operating without you. Did you know that you always calm me down? It's not just the fact that I trust you; you've got this peaceful aura about you, even though there's so much going on in your head and heart. Even now, when . . ." His face falls, and I imagine he's remembering the video of Cygnus. "Were you having nightmares again? Is that why you're awake?"

I shake my head; I stayed up partly to keep from dreaming.

We walk past Murray's door—ajar, by just a few centimeters—before reaching his. The day's first red rays of sun, passing through his window's white sheet of a curtain, highlight his room's minimal furnishings. The bed is a rectangular mattress on the floor, off-white sheets impeccably smoothed out and tucked in. The desk is a flat shelf of stone protruding from the wall, and it's barren, devoid of writing implements, paper, or anything else a normal Earthbound person would have left there. Nothing hints at the fact that someone grew up in this room and sleeps here still. It's as if he's afraid to settle back into his living space, because he doesn't know when he'll have to leave again.

He follows my gaze, and suddenly everything—the placement of our bodies, our shivering—feels uncomfortable. He takes a step away from me but stays under the blanket. *Does he want me to come into the room with him? Does he think I want that?* I wander past a mental barrier and imagine sleeping next to him, as I did with Anka years ago to keep her safe from the Militia soldiers she thought were living in our closet. Embarrassment and regret strike immediately after happiness does. Wes might keep the ghosts away, but we'd add another complicated layer to our relationship. We can't afford that, not in the middle of a crisis.

Although I dread letting his warmth slip away, I take the blanket back, leaving him in the cold.

"Good night, or good morning," I say quickly. "Take your pick."

"The latter," he says, teeth chattering. "*Good night* sounds too much like good-bye."

It's too much. Does he know how many good-byes we're

about to say? Perhaps even a good-bye to each other.

I nod and head back down the stairs, feeling like the biggest coward on the islands.

Lying in bed, I imagine my heartbeat decelerating, my cellular machinery slowing to a crawl. Finally, when I feel as if I'm the same temperature as the frigid air, I fall into cold-blooded sleep.

*　　*　　*

In the morning, the sky is ashen and dripping.

I follow Wes, matching him step for sluggish step, as if our feet are chained together. In a straight line, we walk behind his father to the very edge of the Carlyles' backyard, where the garden ends and the pine forest begins.

Wesley Sr. stands not a meter away, staring me down. I look up—not at his slate-colored eyes, but at the deep creases that separate his jowls from the rest of his face.

"Phaet Theta," he spits, every syllable a staccato bullet.

The sound of my own name, made hideous by his disdain, makes me flinch.

I steal a glance at Wes. His eyes match the sky: gray and filled with moisture. He trusted me and my judgment. Both failed him. My heartbreak over Cygnus overrode my common sense.

His father's tirade is a welcome distraction from my guilt. "You've had quite an intimate and prolonged association with the Sanctuarists, haven't you, Lunar girl? Impressive. I hadn't any idea until Lazarus informed me."

"Father, you're mistaken. She's *Pacifian*." The words waver on Wes's tongue. He glances at me just long enough to smite me with fear and shame. *What have you done?* his eyes demand. I bow my head, cursing myself for failing to tell him last night.

Even if he hasn't guessed that I used the Sanctuarist network without permission, it's only a matter of time before he gives up on our shared lie.

But for now, Wes continues to reason against his father's suspicions, futile as that effort may be, and my heart sinks more with every second. "How can you take Lazarus Penny's word over mine? Not only am I your son, but he's the least upstanding man I've ever met. And I encountered some rotten characters on the Moon, so that's saying something. Ask your daughter sometime."

That can't be. If Lazarus were any more upstanding, he'd have a meter stick for a spine.

"It's not your place to question Mr. Penny's honor." Wesley Sr. doesn't so much as glance at his son. "We will speak of your punishment later." Keeping his eyes on me, he says, "Hiding your nationality, using our communications network—"

"What?" Wes's eyes bulge. "Fay, you never told me—"

I shake my head, an apology drying up in my throat.

Wes's father silences him with a glare. "You have quite a few things in common with the men under my command, Phaet. It is clear that you'd like to live and work as we do, in spite of being female and Lunar. What do you say to eradicating this cognitive dissonance?"

His tone is as emotionless as my old vacuum robot Tinbie's beeping utterances, but more menacing. Nothing I say will make a difference, so I remain silent, listening to the patter of the rain.

"We need your help undoing everything you have set in motion. Last night, we captured a Tourmalinian submarine as it attempted to circle Koré Island to spy on us. This vehicle perfectly suits my *assignment* for you."

I'm taken aback by the Sanctuarists' capabilities. Their

equipment is primitive, but they move silently, in unison. Maybe they ensnared the submarine in a fishnet or forced it into a nasty current.

"Go to the harbor beneath the caves," Wesley Sr. continues. "Board the submarine. It's been programmed to take you to Pacifia. Once you dock, stop that city from reaching these islands. My agents' intelligence indicates that Pacifia is floating past the Gold Coast of Australia, and is heading this way. Therefore, you have about ten days to complete your mission before it arrives to demolish our home."

Raindrops splatter against the rocks, the sound filling the stunned silence.

"But . . . that's impossible," Wes protests, giving voice to my thoughts before I can. He's still fighting for me, despite the fact that I've betrayed him. I'd have felt less shame if he'd turned against me.

"Surely not for Phaet," his father says. "Isn't her homeland allied with the Pacifians?"

The government of my "homeland" wants me dead, and he knows it.

My stomach twists as I piece together the meaning of Wesley Sr.'s assignment. It's a suicide mission. He's skirting Saint Oda's lack of a death penalty by sending me to a hostile floating city with a population of twenty million. I must traverse kilometers of treacherous water, and he knows I can't swim. That fact came to light on a Carlyle family trip to the beach in the fall, and must have contributed to his suspicions. What native floating city dweller not only can't swim, but also shrinks from seawater as if it were poison?

Now I cringe away, and picture all the things I'll face on

my journey: storms at sea; pirates and outlaws; hostile troops, Earthbound and Lunar alike . . . and Lunar spacecraft, which they've probably stationed on Pacifia.

Could I turn my death sentence into a homecoming?

"You're sending her to Pacifia? Alone?" Wes demands. "Father, you don't understand. She's got traumatizing memories of the place."

"So she should be keen to succeed in her assignment."

No, but I'm keen to begin my journey. To get away from this foreign planet and back to the thirteen-year-old boy who needs me.

"Imagine how strange it'll look if she disappears," Wes says. "How will you explain it to everyone?"

"She volunteered." Wesley Sr. locks his fingers around my right wrist; his grip is the closest thing to handcuffs on Saint Oda. "I will send you off now, Phaet."

He pulls me across the barren garden. I don't resist. Behind us, Wes jogs to keep up, talking animatedly. "Think about what you're doing! Sentencing a girl to die based on one man's word. I've kept silent about this for almost five years, but I'll be quiet no longer. Father, Lazarus Penny lied to my sister. Your daughter."

My mind won't wrap around the thought. What could that man possibly have lied about?

"Why wouldn't he take the next step and lie to *you*?" Wes demands.

Wesley Sr. walks faster, as if driven forward by his son's words. We're approaching the front of the Carlyle house, where the trail dips down the mountain.

"You have spoken out of turn long enough—"

"He broke a secret engagement to her!" Wes shouts.

The mountainside seems to tilt around me. Did Lazarus's

kind words blind me to his faults? Or . . . could Wes be lying? His accusation seems too outlandish to be true. I push numbers through my mind: Lazarus left for the Moon four and a half years ago. Murray was seventeen then, too young by Odan standards to seek a relationship.

Wesley Sr. has stopped in his tracks. We're right outside the front door.

"Don't be ridiculous."

"He cut her off just before she turned eighteen, before she became an adult and could officially declare the partnership. And because he was on the Moon, he designated me as his messenger!"

"Lazarus is a full decade older than your sister, and he is a good man. He would never harm a fellow Odan."

"That's what he wants you to think!"

That's what he duped me into thinking, apparently. But should I trust my instincts or Wes's accusations?

We hear footsteps along the path up the hill, the sound of someone running. Murray limps into view, a sack of flour in her hand, sweat on her brow. Although it isn't noon yet, she's already finished feeding the bacterial lights. The illumination helps prevent foot-traffic accidents on foggy days like this.

A few meters away from us, she halts. The glass orbs hanging from a nearby fir tree glow an intense blue, throwing her scar into sharp relief. A twitching, agitated Lewis sits on her shoulder; his feathers are puffed out to make him look larger—a self-defense mechanism.

Murray takes in her father's hold on me and the angry words being exchanged. "Will someone tell me what this is about?" Her voice is a whimper.

"Your brother claims that you were secretly engaged to

Lazarus Penny," Wesley Sr. says. "Do you confirm or deny this?"

Lewis abandons Murray then. He flies in an upward spiral until his dun feathers blend in with the trees.

A puff of white escapes the opening of Murray's flour sack as it hits the ground. Another cloud filling the air between us.

And Wes's sister flees down the mountain, toward the green-gray sea.

*   *   *

She makes it only five meters before her toe catches on a gnarled root. Wes, who's followed her, grabs her elbow before she falls.

"You *told* him?" Murray yanks her arm away, snarling. Now I can see her at thirteen, grieving and raging against her friend's death, against her own misfortune. "Those months of happiness were *mine*, to hide or reveal as I chose. My past belongs to *me*! Don't you know it's all I have left? None of you Sanctuarists can be trusted, not with anything!"

Lazarus couldn't have left her without a good reason. I feel embarrassed, stumbling upon these feelings, these secrets that would have been better hidden in the lunar dust or sunk deep in the Odan harbor.

The hand gripping my arm slackens.

"Which of you has disappointed me more? I cannot decide." Wesley Sr. looks from one child to the other, his expression of fury softening into sadness—this man of stone being sanded down one grain at a time. "We have much to discuss. But first, we will remove this Lunar fugitive from Saint Oda."

With the pressure back on me, my pulse starts rattling away in my throat.

Wes tries to argue one last time. "She's not a—"

"I am," I say, thinking of Cygnus. "I've endangered this place just by being here. Let me get what I deserve, Wes."

Murray lets out a bark of laughter. Her smile doesn't reach her eyes, in which an electrical storm brews. "So! My little brother smuggled a Lunar lady back home! Wes, you're no better than *him*, with all his plaything females and fancy words. What is it about you Sanctuarists and demon girls?"

"What? No!" Wes shakes his head as if clearing fog from his vision.

"This racket is unbearable!" Mrs. Carlyle marches out of the house, holding something Odans call a broomstick. She points the handle at us, and her voice slices the air, making way for her body. "I'll wager that the lichen mats in the lower levels can hear you too!"

"We're discussing Odan security," says Wesley Sr.

"From what *I* heard, it's more a matter of vice." Mrs. Carlyle turns her glare on Wes and Murray, and continues in a harsh whisper. "You have both substituted hedonistic comforts for faith. How did I fail to teach you better? Weren't God and nature enough for you?"

"Did God let me forget my past for hours at a time?" Murray says. "Did he ever say he loved me?"

Mrs. Carlyle scoffs. "Lazarus Penny's *love* was evidently fleeting."

"But it was enough! When we drank the wine we made together, when we watched lunar eclipses from the mountaintops, I felt whole. Like I'd never hurt my eye, like the raid had never happened!"

"Shame on you." Mrs. Carlyle shakes a finger at her daughter, her lips a straight, colorless line. "Shame on you!"

"I know, I *know*! I've carried enough shame for the two of us, me and him both." Murray twists away from her mother, facing Wesley Sr. Her knees strike the muddy ground; her open hands reach for his. Lightning flashes in the distance. "I hate myself for it. I should have run to the other side of the Earth. Oh, Father, forgive me!"

The jagged edges in her voice cut me deeply. It's a cry for Wesley Sr.—and, perhaps, a cry for God.

Wesley Sr. slaps Murray's hands away at the same moment God sends a clap of thunder to shake the island's bedrock. Turning to his son, he says, "What's *your* excuse?"

"You mean my rationale?" Wes tears his eyes from his sister's broken form. Does he regret sharing her secret now, even though he did it to protect me? "Bringing Phaet here was a practical choice, not a personal one. She's a prominent Lunar rebel's daughter. If she died, the resistance would lose all hope of overthrowing the Committee's rule. If she lives and they succeed, it'll benefit all of humanity. Imagine a benevolent Moon, Mother. Think what that would mean for everyone on Earth."

"It seems to me," says Wesley Sr., "that you've attempted to make peace by inciting a war. Pacifia is en route to Saint Oda, with Lunars on board. Lazarus says the attacking force is substantial."

Mrs. Carlyle's jaw clenches and unclenches, as if she's biting back screams. "God help us."

"He won't," Wes growls.

His mother advances on him. "Shame on you, too. You've betrayed your family. And your city. For one girl—one *demon* girl—"

"*Don't*," Wes hisses, "call her that."

Mrs. Carlyle is silenced.

"How can you value everything that lives," Wes continues,

"except for people who happen to be born up there?" He points at the sky. "It's inconsistent. Illogical."

"You," his mother says, "haven't the right to judge *anyone*—"

"Stop!" Murray claps her hands over her ears. "Stop fighting, won't you?"

I move to put an arm around her, but she twists away. "Don't touch me!" she hisses. There's a corresponding twist somewhere in my heart.

"The demons treated us like scum," Mrs. Carlyle says. With her eyes on Wes, she's oblivious to Murray's rejection of me. "Their behavior is *unnatural*, and so are they."

"You're wrong—look at her." Wes's hand touches my back. "Look her in the eye and tell her she's anything less than human. Can you do it? Can you tell her that her life is forfeit because of where she came from?"

Mrs. Carlyle shakes off his words and looks past me, as if I'm not even here. "How dare you speak to me that way," she tells Wes. "I'm your mother."

"You're a hypocrite," Wes shoots back.

I count my heartbeats as the seconds go by.

Mrs. Carlyle recovers quickly. "You had a choice: protect us, or her. We *raised* you—*she* only entertained you." She singes me with a glare and turns back to her son. "Evidently, you hold this demon child in higher esteem than all of us."

"I . . . I—" Wes begins.

"Very well," Mrs. Carlyle says, cutting him off. Her face spasms, but after a moment, it settles back into an expression of cold neutrality. "Then you are no child of mine."

"Holly!" Wesley Sr. booms. "Consider what you're saying. What that means."

"It means that I'm no more welcome here than Phaet. Understand that I'm not picking sides, but merely putting myself between a dear friend and her certain death." Wes points toward the Odan harbor, the way obscured by shifting mists, and then looks me in the eye. "Let's go, Phaet. Pacifia's waiting."

9

WES AND GRAVITY PULL ME DOWN THE
mountain. He leads me by the hand into the damp tunnel system,
but we take an unfamiliar path—probably heading to some secret
dock known only to the Sanctuarists. His family's shouts blend
into echoes behind us, but they can't hope to match our pace.

"How can you leave them like that?" I demand, my voice
lost in the smack of cloth soles on rock. I wish now that I'd had
time to fetch my Militia boots before leaving; Wes hid them in a
cranny in the Sanctuary Room while I was recuperating. "What
if something happens to them, or to us, and you never get to
apologize? Will you ever forgive yourself?"

My hand slips in his, and his grip tightens. I've imagined
holding his hand more often than I'd like to admit, never an-
ticipating that the contact would be this clammy or harried. Or
full of anger.

"What do you want me to do—leave you to die alone out
there?" As usual, running doesn't fragment Wes's speech in the
slightest. During Militia training last year, we'd dash through Defense together, having clumsy conversations that grew more coordinated as the weeks passed. Now we're like antagonistic new
trainees again. I'm hurting, like I did then, but not physically.

"I hope you're not coming with me just to spite your *family*."
I regret my words as soon as they hit the air, because I need
him. If I set out alone, Earth's ocean might swallow me before
the Pacifian alliance gets a chance.

"I'm taking a break from them. With you." He lets go of my hand, and the air feels especially cold where his skin was touching mine. "Even though you sent messages to the Moon— and to Lazarus, of all people. Why didn't you tell me you were planning to do that?"

"You'd have stopped me."

"Yes! I said we could only trust each other on Earth. Now do you see why?" Wes pulls ahead, as if trying to put me out of sight. "Why can't you believe in me, after all we've been through?"

"You lied to me on the Moon," I say. "For months."

It's true; he let me believe he was Lunar until we were en route to his home planet—Earth. He quits arguing.

The hallways grow dimmer, their bacterial lights out of commission. Our feet begin to slip on the stone floor; we slide on algal growths and splash through puddles of salt water into an open cavern, where water laps against the rock on which we stand.

At the far end, a semicircle of gray sky is visible. The Sanctuarists have partially beached the submarine, which resembles an oversized ripe eggplant. Though small—only six meters long from nose to propeller—it's striking. Like most Tourmalinian artifacts, it lends itself more to show than stealth. Perfect for a suicide mission.

Wes and I push the vessel into the water, wade in up to our calves, and climb into the hatch. Buttons, gauges, screens, and switches cover the rounded walls from the floor to the low ceiling. I bang my head as I stumble to one of the two rear seats.

Wes sits at the helm and touches the controls with easy familiarity. He probably had to steer a similar vehicle on his initial journey to the Moon. He taps the monitor on the wall, entering passwords and overriding commands to take us from SET DESTINATION: PACIFIA to MANUAL.

His comfort with the vehicle worries me. *No going back now.*

We sink into the water, and the propeller switches on with a roar. Just before we dip beneath the surface, I notice movement in the rearview screen. Two figures—one male, one female—rush into the cavern, holding hands. Wes's parents. His father's eyes cling to us as a man dangling from a cliff clings to a ledge. His mother's face is buried in the shadow of her husband's shoulder. She can't watch us go.

For a fleeting moment, my mind's eye replaces her features with Mom's. Then the black water blinds us to everything but itself.

*　　*　　*

Days and nights merge together. The dimly lit interior of the submarine never seems to change, nor does the murky water outside. From a face-sized window, I look down at the so-called mid-Atlantic kelp "forests"—*patches* better describes them now. Clusters of the green-brown algae reach only a meter or so high, grasping at stray beams of sunlight. According to Nanna Zeffie, the kelp used to extend from bedrock to surface, undulating in the gentle waters and growing as much as half a meter in a day—until pollutants like industrial fertilizers caused phytoplankton to bloom in the photic zone, preventing light from reaching the kelp below. Above us, at the surface, patches of accreted plastic waste dim the water even more.

Sometimes, a bale of sea turtles or a pod of dolphins swims straight past our headlights, frightening me despite Wes's insistence that they're harmless. Grayish tumors cover some of the bigger turtles' faces and flippers, and many dolphins have skin that is crusted with the yellowish parasites that grew abundantly after the oceans warmed last century. Although skinny and few in number, the animals seem amused by our awkwardness, the way we struggle to move through the fluid realm that belongs to them. It's a realm that humans almost decimated centuries ago. Life came back, as it has after every one of Earth's major ecological disturbances—as it always does. But in a form our ancestors wouldn't recognize.

Wes and I have tacitly partitioned the vehicle. He holds the helm, while I occupy one of the backward-facing seats in the rear of the cabin. When he needs to eat a can of oats and beans or use the tiny bin of a water closet, I hold the controls steady.

At night, we tether the submarine to rock formations. When breathing the recycled air gets unbearable, we surface and pop open the hatch. If other vessels come too close, we dive deep and flee, whether they're freight barges or scouting submarines carrying bombs; everything out here is a potential threat.

And always, we utter the bare minimum of words necessary to coordinate these activities.

Five days into our journey, I track our progress on the satellite-generated map of Earth and realize with a start that we're moving away from Pacifia.

"But Pacifia's in the Arabian Sea," I say, not looking at Wes. It has made startlingly fast progress from Australia to its current location.

"We're going to Battery Bay," he says, pointing to the map and similarly avoiding my eyes. Examining the map, I see that Pacifia's rival is sunning itself off the southwestern coast of Africa. Although most of the continents are still technically habitable, their climate is so volatile that life is more manageable floating on migratory cities than staying in one place.

"We'll beg them for help," I say. "Or guns."

Years ago, the Batterers promised the Odans protection when they declared the city an International Sanctuary. Wes's plan makes sense.

"If they say no," he says, "I'll turn back and help my father set up Odan civil defenses. But you're free to go home, if Battery Bay gives you a ship. And that's a big if." Battery Bay's border security is notoriously harsh; they're known to imprison undocumented visitors or throw them overboard to die. "Honestly, I think you *should* go home. Away from me and Saint Oda."

His words sting, and my arms automatically wrap around my torso to nurse the wound. If I managed to board a spacecraft on Battery Bay . . . I could fly home, gather all the information I can, and then somehow hide Anka and Umbriel somewhere safer, and end my brother's suffering. Memories of Cygnus's toothy grin, which I may finally see again, flash through my mind without bringing me happiness. Would it be fair to rescue one boy and leave a city to burn? Not when the threat of Saint Oda's destruction exists partially because of me. And especially not when it's the refuge that saved my life.

"Now I wonder if that . . . peaceful silence that's always about you . . . just meant whatever I wanted it to mean," Wes mutters. "It turns out you're not so silent. After that stunt talking to Lazarus, how can any reasonable person trust you?"

The hurt in his voice makes me want to take back everything that happened that night.

He sighs. "Phaet, say something. Please. Don't make me do all the talking when you know I'm not so good at it."

I wish I could do as he's asked. There's so much to say, but none of it seems adequate to repair the trust I've broken. The friendship that I feel drifting away, like debris into the deep sea.

10

ABOUT FIFTEEN DEGREES NORTH OF OUR destination, the ocean seems to tremble. According to our radar screen, the floating city of Recoleta—Battery Bay's ally—is five kilometers north of us and quickly approaching.

Panic hangs heavy in the air.

"Could they have detected us?" I ask. "We may have gotten too close."

"Hopefully not." Wes looks straight ahead, his jaw set; he hasn't met my eyes for days. "In the grand scheme of things, this little submarine isn't that important." He points to the satellite-generated map above our heads. "See New Joudo— the Pacifian sidekick—swooping in from the south?"

The water trembles again, shaking our vessel. What looks like a radially symmetrical tuna fish zips by, just missing us. Alarms screech in my head. *What was that?* Back in Militia weapons training, we learned about Earthbound weapons; the underwater ones were called . . . *torpedoes*, I think.

Wes exhales, relieved that we weren't hit. "My question is, what are they fighting over?"

Well, what do the Earthbound usually fight over? "Metals? Minerals? Combustible detritus?"

"There *are* significant oil deposits near the mouth of the Cuanza River." Wes takes us away on full throttle. "Not sure how much is left, though."

These cities are fighting over congealed rot from the Carboniferous. On some level, it's amusing that these powerful Earthbound nations live off dead matter, but in the moment, the humor feels hollow.

Wes curses. A swarm of needlelike objects is following the torpedo. Pipefish bombs—tiny, hydrodynamic explosives. Their susceptibility to currents and eddies means they have poor accuracy, but enough of them at once can do serious damage. Wes dodges the projectiles to the best of his ability, taking the submarine on a swinging, unpredictable path. I wish I could help, maybe even steer, instead of sitting uselessly—

Wait. The submarine's controls might be different from those of the spaceships I know so well, but that doesn't mean the principles of battle have changed. Location still means everything.

Squinting, I make out the Recoletan submarine that fired the pipefish bombs. Its outline is blurry in the orange-tinted water, but it grows clearer with every second. It's squat and compact, with a cone-shaped nose and an arm dangling in front of it like an anglerfish's lure. I imagine the crew uses the arm to grasp their prey after disabling it.

My eyes dart to the speedometer. "Wes. Get us out of here."

"If we try to flee, they might think we're the enemy!"

I reach over him and pull a lever that I've learned will take us farther down. "Then we have to move to deeper water."

Tap-tap-tap. The submarine shudders. I wonder if it was all in my head—but then I hear a series of pings and the horrible hissing sound of water spraying into the cabin. We've been hit.

"The pressure gauge is going berserk!" Wes calls out. "All this water above us—the cabin could cave in."

Pathetic Earthbound contraption! I want to pound the dashboard of this fossil of a submarine, but instead I pull the lever in the other direction, taking us upward. *Can't even take a few pipefish bombs to the hull.* Not like the Militia ships' self-repairing carbon fiber, which knits back together even after being clobbered by a hailstorm of small asteroids.

The hissing quiets as we ascend and stops when we break the surface. The sky is orange with early morning light and opaque with smoke. Triangular black planes glide overhead, sowing explosives across the water. Flames bloom from the boats and one-man scooters that they hit.

Wes takes us farther out to sea at top speed, aiming toward an area where there's no chance of being cornered by the two cities and caught in the crossfire.

As we move, Recoleta and New Joudo approach from either side. Matched in military strength, they are comparable in beauty too. The former is an oblong city, larger than Tourmaline. Its rectangular buildings have façades painted peach, rose, and yellow. Great granite columns and semicircular arches support heavy roofs. I can just make out narrow canals between the structures; today, though, the waterways are empty.

Twisting, I look toward New Joudo, a roughly squarish city. Every building seems to be topped with blue, green, and silver structures shaped like tulip bulbs, each of which supports a thin golden cross. From this distance, the bulbs sparkle like reptile scales.

The cities' foundations were laid on land millennia ago, long before the rising tide forced them to float out to sea. They weren't predesigned for efficiency, like the bases. They rose and expanded organically, changed as their people did. It seems unjust for the earthwide scuffle to endanger their beauty and their history, but any one individual—especially one in a damaged submarine—lacks the ability to protect them. From here, I can only watch their devastation.

I look longingly at the two cities even as we speed out of the crossfire and into the open ocean.

*   *   *

"You were right about the fact that something could happen to us, or to them."

A salty night breeze blows Wes's sweaty hair back. Because of the damage from the pipefish bombs, we have no choice but to float at the ocean's surface, and the submarine's hull received the full brunt of the sun's radiance during the day. The result was a greenhouse effect in miniature, as the interior warmed to unbearable temperatures. We'd activate the cooling system if it wouldn't waste precious fuel. Sitting atop our vessel, on a ridge near the hatch, is the next best option.

I raise an eyebrow at him, needing context for his words.

"This war is real. One of those cities could've blown us up back there. I'd have died, and my parents' last memories of me would have been . . . less than pleasant. My sister's, too. And yours, if you'd survived."

I nod in sympathy. Wes focuses his eyes on some invisible path through the ocean, refusing to look my way.

"If I could tell all of you I was sorry, I would."

In the blank quiet after his words, I hear an invitation. To end our stalemate. "Then let's make up while *we're* both here," I blurt, full of hope. "I'm sorry. About that night, and Lazarus, and the secrets."

Wes sits up straighter, seeming to embrace the peace offering. "You only called him to ask after Cygnus, yes?"

I nod.

"It's impossible to imagine a better sister than you." Wes looks at me with an admiration that I perhaps don't deserve. "Explains why I never really stopped trusting you—you're so good to people you care about."

If only you knew that you're one of them, I think, my flushed cheeks hidden in the dark.

"Now I regret even more the way things ended with my family," he concludes, changing the subject, to both my relief and my disappointment.

The ocean's swells bump us up, float us down, make splashing noises against the hull. A breeze rolls in, carrying the sharp, salty smell of life and its inevitable decay.

"Why didn't you think that through before you spoke, back on Saint Oda?" I say.

"Not everyone's got a checkpoint between their brain and their mouth like you," he says, shrugging. "I thought I did, but it broke down that day. Maybe after three years of living away from my parents, I got used to making choices without their judgment."

I imagine Wes as a little boy, then an adolescent, unable to escape from his mother's razor-edged words, his father's suspicious eyes, his sister's secrets.

"Why can't we choose our family the way we choose our friends?" Wes asks without warning. "We can't get away from blood relatives until we've 'grown up'—and not even then. I didn't choose to be born to parents who wanted their son to save the world."

The corners of my mouth pull down in a frown.

"What did your parents do to you?" I ask.

"Took me out of school when I was ten so I could prepare for my mission. Mother gave me endless lessons on God and God's preferences and God's plans. Father drilled me for two hours a day—in addition to the three I spent with the other spies-to-be. I never doubted them. I thought my mission would save Saint Oda, and the Lunars too. Save you all from your 'hateful ways.'"

"Sounds like very underage Militia training."

"If I'd had a choice, I would've picked different parents, ones who let me be. A sister who knew how to forget, if not forgive." At last, he turns. "But you—you were the first to know me, outside of my family and the other Sanctuarists. My first real friend. I picked you, Phaet."

His words fill me with slow, flickering happiness. "It was more than that," I say. "We were like the vines I worked with in the greenhouses. Quietly looking until we found someone to grow with."

"That . . . that's beautiful," he says.

I no longer feel stranded on the tiny submarine. Sitting with him like this, I could soar across the entire shimmering sea.

"But if not for your parents," I say, "we wouldn't know each other. You wouldn't be able to beat back anyone who tries to harm you. You wouldn't have seen the world—seen beyond this world. Think about it, Wes. Your family gave you everything you have."

"And they tried to take away all you had left," Wes points out. "Your citizenship, your safety, your *life*. How can you forgive them so willingly?"

Because you fought with them on my behalf, I think, *and it hurt to watch.*

"I missed them like mad on the Moon," he says. "This'll make me sound like a mummy's boy, but almost every night, I wished someone would take care of me, or just hold me. Feeding myself, coming home to an empty apartment—it made me lonely. But when I lived with my parents again, the tiniest things about them drove me mad."

"They are . . ." I pause, searching for an appropriate word. "Intense."

"That's an understatement. They make our Militia instructors look like lackadaisical dolts. Still, they mean so much to me. I'm afraid to show them how much—I'm almost worried they'll reject me."

I remember Mom, whom I avoided for the last month of her life, and think, not for the first time, how quickly the people close to us can be lost. "Love them while you can," I say.

Wes raises his eyebrows as he makes the connection. "That makes me want to turn back, kiss the ground by my front door, and apologize."

"You won't, though," I say. Not when we're so close to Battery Bay and the chance, however slim, of preventing Saint Oda's demolition. Of sending me home to rescue Cygnus.

"Exactly." Wes's eyes find a distant spot on the horizon; his face settles into a purposeful expression. "I have to show them that I care. Which means I can't go back empty-handed."

11

A FREAK SUMMER STORM TOSSES US INTO Battery Bay's path. Although it's midafternoon, the sky is dark and tinged with green. We ride the graphite-gray waves up and down, changing orientation every few seconds, like we're balls being juggled. I sit in the front passenger seat in a vain effort to avoid motion sickness. Through the sideways sheets of rain, Battery Bay appears to be a conglomeration of colored lights so densely packed that they look solid. The city is far enough from us that we aren't in danger of colliding with it, but it's close enough to intimidate. Its enormous size makes estimating distance a challenge, even with what I know of parallax.

The submarine tilts forward, and only my seat belt keeps my body from falling onto the control panel in front of me. I retch my half-digested lunch into a seasickness bag.

Oblivious to my distress—or pretending to be—Wes submerges the submarine ten meters, trying to evade the surface turbulence. Again, we hear the hissing sound that started when the pipefish bombs punctured our hull.

"What I wouldn't give for a self-repairing carbon fiber shell now," Wes grumbles.

I peek at the controls. The pressure gauge has swung into the red zone, indicating that we should stop descending, lest the water column crush the craft.

"There's no hiding." Wes reluctantly brings us back toward

the surface. "Not from the Batterers, and not from Neptune."

"The planet?" I say, confused. Cold water touches my toes. Holding in a yelp, I pull my feet away.

"The ancient Earthbound god of the sea!" Wes replies in a mock-scary voice, his eyes widening. He hasn't noticed the water yet. "He's sent powerful waves to kidnap many beautiful maidens. You could be next, Phaet."

I hope the submarine is dim enough to hide my blush. *Is he teasing me as he would Emmy and Julie?* I wonder. *Or does he really think I'm beautiful?*

The moment our vessel breaks the surface, rainwater begins to leak through the ceiling. A perfectly round drop falls on Wes's nose, and he swears under his breath. "Neptune's impatient today."

I frantically check the radar. We're several kilometers from land. In this weather, we'll never make it.

Before I can think of a way to safety, a blinding light sweeps the tiny chamber—a search beam from Battery Bay, pulsing through the pilot's window.

I'm relieved at the prospect of shelter from the storm. But that relief fades when I remember we're in a Tourmalinian submarine.

"Neptune will have to wait," I say, dread pooling in my belly. "The Batterers found us first."

*   *   *

"Hands behind your heads! Up, up, up!" shouts one officer as her colleagues pull us out of the submarine, now docked at an outdoor pier along the north edge of Battery Bay. She has brown skin and pale green eyes, a striking combination.

The air carries the smells of pollen, cooking oil, spent fuel, and a thousand other things I can't identify. It must be almost

310 Kelvin out here—a few degrees warmer than Earth's summer temperatures three centuries ago, before the anthropogenic greenhouse effect kicked in. Now, the atmosphere itself has a fever. The combination of sweat and humidity glues my Odan winter clothes to my skin.

But the steel tip of another soldier's handgun is cool against my left temple. I try to keep my fearful shuddering to a minimum. The square-faced young man looks all too eager to use his weapon.

We're on one of what seem to be countless balconies, having traveled upward through the system of pumps and water-lock chambers that comprise Battery Bay's primary port. Discarded fuel canisters and outdated gadgets floated past us as we climbed, shimmering outlines appearing and fading again in the cloudy water. The refuse might've gotten there hundreds of years ago or yesterday—the Batterers wouldn't know or care. The ones on board with us didn't spare a glance at the debris.

As I stand up, I take a better look at the officer in charge. She wears a close-fitting, knobbed metal helmet that looks like solid gold. No—upon closer inspection, it's not a helmet. It's her hair. Annoyed, she brushes raindrops from the top of her head.

"Tourmalinian nationals captured on Dock 427," the officer says into a tooth-sized microphone by her mouth. "We *shouldn't* detain them?" Pause. "Yes, sir. Be there soon. Yes, of *course*, taking the greatest security measures."

Trailed by a horde of curious onlookers, we march into a narrow glass tube. It's at least a kilometer long and climate-controlled to about the same temperature as Base IV's interior—or is my memory fooling me? I've been away from home for too long.

So has Cygnus.

Don't think about that. I have to survive Battery Bay before I can help him.

I glance at our followers' reflections in the hallway's glass walls. One man's shoes enable him to hover several centimeters in the air; he wears a floor-length violet gown with a high neck and minimalist design. He looks vaguely South Asian and wears his straight maroon hair in a high ponytail. Another woman, who might be of Pacific Islander descent, has black hair that flows seamlessly into her short, lacy dress; the garment appears to be made of her hair wrapped around her body.

I also hear snippets of conversation in several languages I don't recognize. Like the Moon, Battery Bay seems like a melting pot of ethnic backgrounds, but it obviously hasn't stamped out the cultures or traditions its citizens arrived with.

Small hovering vehicles speed by, above and below and around us, weaving through the rain and nearby buildings. Battery Bay's architecture reminds me of the colorful geometry block sets I used in first-year Primary; I see elongated pyramids pointing to the sky, sturdy octagonal prisms, cylinders of various diameters stacked atop one another to form towers. Video advertisements play on every flat surface. One nearby building consists of a loop-the-loop through which dozens of vehicles zoom. Painted every fluorescent color imaginable, the transports have both wings that extend on either side of their cabins and wheels for land travel. I can't see the ground—a sign near the ceiling says that we're on the 117th floor. I unfocus my eyes to avoid looking at the petrifying drop. A button falling from this height could strike and probably kill someone at ground level.

The Batterers' imposing architecture and widespread technology surprise me; on the Moon, I learned that the Earthbound had degraded the environment to the point of warring over resources like oil and metals. I whisper to Wes, "I thought the Batterers didn't have the materials to make all this fancy stuff."

"Who told you that, the Committee?" Wes whispers back. He's trying to sound nonchalant and collected, perhaps to impress me, but excitement bubbles in his voice. "Even in Saint Oda, we know the Batterers have got half the globe—their alliance, I mean—feeding them raw materials. Wouldn't be the richest city on the planet without some draw-on clothes and thousand-foot-high buildings."

"So the Batterers aren't desperate, but a lot of their allies still are," I say. The Committee made all of Earth sound primitive, polluted, or both, but it seems a handful of places might defy that propaganda—at the expense of their allies.

"I hear you two chattering," the officer says. "Before we go on, you need to give me your documentation."

I close my gaping mouth, remembering the danger we're in. Odans don't keep official papers or electronic records, so how will we prove we're not from Tourmaline? Fail to convince the Batterers, and they'll throw us in jail or deport us.

The young soldier next to me pushes the muzzle of his gun harder against my temple. "*Documentation*, alien. I could buy that the boy's Odan, but you? Not likely."

It's because I don't *look* typically Odan, thanks to my Asian features. Eyes wide, I shake my head and curse myself for failing to prepare. Should we say I'm a Pacifian emigrant to Saint Oda? Or would that complicate the narrative too much?

"We're from Saint Oda, and we carry no records," Wes rattles off, unfazed, in an exaggerated Odan accent. "People of every nation are equal in God's eyes."

I suppress an eye roll at his theatrics. But behind us, the crowd presses closer, watching with interest. Although the Batterer soldiers' faces remain unyielding, Wes's antics have appealed to the civilians.

"Odans? In a Tourmalinian submarine? This should keep Battery Bay entertained for the next few hours." The woman in the black hair-dress reaches into a pocket and pulls out a curled sheet of plastic. She unrolls it—it's rectangular, about the length and width of her face—and it lights up. Wes and I see our haggard faces reflected back at us, with the word INTERVIEWEE(S) flashing at the bottom of the screen. Behind her, other people press forward, trying to film us, shouting for the woman to make room.

She ignores their pleas. "Turn this way. I'm shooting you for my vlog." She changes the angle of the camera screen. "It's called *The Seaway.* I show my followers the most interesting people who pass through BB Customs, live."

I look away and keep walking. Why would this woman seek attention rather than shrink from it? My Lunar background taught me that standing out is dangerous, and I saw that firsthand in Militia training, when Jupiter and Callisto attacked me for threatening their positions at the top of our class. On the Moon, a Journalist wouldn't dare interrupt an official procedure—and I should know, as my mother was one. But I remember from Earth Studies classes that Battery Bay prides itself on "chaotic broadcasting" and maintains strong independent media outlets. I just didn't think they'd take the word *independent* so far.

"Amalie, wait for an interview until they've seen the Diplomacy Minister, or I'll throw you overboard too." The officer walks faster. "Don't Odans think anything with an electrical current is diseased? You're inviting voodoo from these two."

"If they're Odan like they claim to be," says the soldier who's guarding me.

The officer and Amalie know each other? The latter must be a regular fixture here. Law enforcement officers and vloggers seem to stand on equal footing; these so-called journalists chronicle what they want. If Mom were here, she'd be delighted and envious. I feel only trepidation. This city is so bizarre, its customs so foreign. I could make a lethal mistake without knowing it.

The long glass tunnel leads us to a circular building edged with spikes. It resembles an immense sea urchin (Wes showed me the spiny creatures in the tide pools of Saint Oda). Although the spikes themselves are solid metal, the center portion is transparent. Anyone can see into the hall from outside. Oblong pods with wings—Batterer vehicles, I assume—swarm around the building like a school of fish. Where the walkway connects to the urchin building, the narrow space opens into a wide hallway that slopes downward at an angle of about thirty degrees.

The horde of vloggers seizes the chance to move closer to Wes and me. I avoid looking at their cameras, instead examining the cerulean walls, the golden seats implanted in the floor. At the end of the hallway sit a gold desk and a short, pale man whose transparent hair reflects light like water. *Is it an optical illusion? Or is there water enclosed in some kind of membrane around his head?*

As he stands up, his hair ripples but does not splash away from his skull. His dark blue eyes are as cold as the ocean's abyss.

"Minister Costa, here are the passengers we found aboard the Tourmalinian submarine," the officer says to him.

"Please, Minister," Wes begins, "we're Odan. Pacifia is heading toward our city as we speak, and we had to travel here quickly, using the first vehicle we could find—"

To cut off Wes, Minister Costa raises his right hand and pinches his forefinger and thumb together. His quiet voice thrums with strength. "You'll need a better reason to stop me from deporting you, one that's not a lie."

The vloggers begin hurling questions at us. One shouts, "You, the girl—Odan, Tourmalinian, whatever you are—are the minister's suspicions justified?"

I numbly shake my head.

"Do you feel you were treated fairly by the Coastwatch?"

I continue shaking my head, eyes wide. The combination of fear and claustrophobia is giving me a splitting headache.

"What are your names?" "What are your plans after deportation?" "Why have the Odans finally broken their silence?"

In the middle of answering one journalist's question, Wes catches my eye. Even as words issue from his mouth, he looks worn, frightened—the same way I'm feeling. He can fight for hours on end, but he can only bear this level of scrutiny for a few minutes.

Sighing, Costa sits behind his desk and presses a button; a transparent, flexible screen like Amalie's unrolls in front of his face. The sight sucks the noise out of the room—perhaps he's dictating our fate based on what he's heard. "The situation has spiraled out of control," he says to the screen. "Can't deport them without exacerbating the hullabaloo. . . . Fine, come if you must."

The crowd begins buzzing again, and my heart takes off, beating fast as a lab rat's.

Several unbearable seconds later, the mahogany doors behind Minister Costa swing open. A tall, bearded, relatively unadorned man walks in; he looks to be Central American. He wears a simple white shirt that buttons up to his chin, and a gold silk scarf is tied around his neck. His hair is parted on the right; the top is long, but the sides are buzzed short. The outline of a falcon's head has been shaved onto his scalp.

Whispers of "Prime Minister Sear!" fill the air, and the reporters press ever closer. Amalie whips out a small tube from her pocket and begins drawing on her legs. Wherever her pen goes, new fabric appears, elongating her short skirt. Soon, she's dressed modestly enough to appease even an Odan.

The newcomer leans against the wall behind Costa's desk. His yawn, though silent, looks like a bear's roar. He moves with the ease of someone aware of his power, who doesn't need to prove himself to others. Like a Committee member—but not quite: we can all see his face.

"Half the city is streaming this event," Sear says. "The other, younger half, while stuck in class, are aware that they are missing something monumental. Odan natives! We teach our children about the Sanctuary Act, but we've never acquired decent footage of these mysterious people. And now two of them have voluntarily come to us. Fascinating."

Costa's water-hair sloshes as he shakes his head. "They *claim* to be Odan—"

"I cannot speak for the girl—" Sear says.

"Exactly," Costa says, turning to me. "Explain yourself."

Freezing up, I force out words through locked jaws and hope my Lunar accent doesn't rear its jagged head. "I came to Saint Oda. From Pacifia. Very recently."

"See?" Sear says. "She's telling the truth. English doesn't seem to be her first language."

Ugh. I pinch my lips together to keep from grimacing in distaste. Since the Pacifian alliance absorbed much of former China and all of North Korea, it makes sense that he'd assume I learned a different language first. But I speak English as well as Sear does, even if I do so sporadically.

Costa's expression softens. "What about the boy?"

I slowly breathe out, letting relief fill me up. Wes will pass their test far more easily. Suddenly, I'm thankful that Sear made assumptions about me. Now, I can be my quiet self without arousing suspicion.

"Minister Costa, I have a memory for faces." Sear looks hard at Wes. "I remember the boy's."

Wes sits up straighter in his chair. "What? How?"

I'm equally stunned. If this isn't a cruel joke, we can take immediate deportation off our list of worries.

"I visited Saint Oda—what was it, two weeks after the Lunar attack? At the time I occupied Diplomacy Minister Costa's current position. I spoke privately with another Wesley Carlyle— your father, yes?—about Battery Bay's offer of aid. You refused to leave the basement. Your father said you believed bombs would fall on you if you went upstairs. Although you were too young to understand what was happening, we still needed to remove you before proceeding with our discussion."

Another episode in Odan history I wasn't aware of; another hidden part of Wes's life that's come to light. Next to me, he twists his hands in his lap, clearly embarrassed. He told me that he survived the Lunar attack by hiding in the Sanctuary Room, but not that he feared leaving it for weeks afterward.

"Your father rejected my offer, to no one's surprise," Minister Sear continues. "Which leads me to ask: why should we send Saint Oda military aid now, when you said no to the food and supplies we offered you nine years ago?"

Wes gathers himself, arranges his features into that practiced, purposeful expression. "Back then, we wanted to rebuild the city as a community, without foreign intervention. We could accomplish that alone, but we can't make it through a Pacifian attack without you. Think of all the innocents who could die, Prime Minister. Please, send just one regiment—even drones . . ."

Minister Sear holds up his hands. "It's not me you need to convince. You must win over the people of Battery Bay. Our citizens have elected a five-hundred-member Parliament, which meets in the spheroid of this building. Parliament alone can approve military action, and they must do so by a majority vote. And if we are to travel to meet Pacifia, city to city . . . well, that will require a public referendum."

With an unreadable smile, he opens the mahogany door through which he entered. "Our surveillance readings tell me time is short. Let's not waste any more of it. Parliament's waiting."

Wes and I stand. My legs feel weightless as they carry me toward the exit.

The Prime Minister of Battery Bay waves us through first. "After you," he says. "Don't forget to smile."

12

THE BATTERER PARLIAMENT'S MEETING space is a vast sphere with small balconies embedded in the wall, one for each legislator's district. The room is painted a mosaic of different blue-green shades; a silver chandelier in the shape of Earth's continents dangles from the ceiling. We could almost be underwater, peering upward at speckled sunlight. Legislators, aides, and pages occupy each balcony; their clothes are mostly white or some other neutral shade, but they've accessorized with scarves, pins, or hair doodads of gold, teal, and a smattering of other colors.

On the floor, Batterer citizens mill about, their flexible screen-cameras pointed upward. All around us, the lights of hovercraft shine in through the transparent walls, brighter than stars.

"The spherical shape represents the global reach of our alliance," Minister Costa explains. As he speaks, the balcony we're on moves toward the center of the sphere. I look behind us and see that it's attached to the wall by a long metal arm.

"About half of Earth belongs to the Pacifians," Minister Sear says. "Most of the remaining patches are allied with us. But a patchy sphere wasn't a sound architectural concept."

"Half the balconies are empty," Wes points out.

"Those legislators can vote remotely. This week, many are paying visits to their districts, located around the globe. Don't worry, they'll be watching."

Before our balcony reaches the sphere's center, the politicians begin to argue among themselves. Those wearing gold accessories voice their support for Sear; those wearing teal seem frustrated by his mere appearance. Separate political parties, perhaps? I suck in my breath, intimidated. My Primary teachers said multiple factions often ripped Earthbound countries apart, making Lunar-style one-party rule the best form of government.

"Border control, Sear?" shouts a woman wearing a beige dress and teal hairnet. "With you in charge, our border's like a sponge—absorbing any slicks that wash up."

"They're foreign nationals with useful information," Sear says. "Let them talk before you condemn them."

"They're after our guns! We saw the memo," says a man in a silk teal poncho. "Don't expect *our* party to vote for your coffer-draining lunacy."

Sear steps back and gestures for Wes and me to address Parliament. "They're all yours."

He won't help us? *Obviously not.* He wants to wrap up our moment of infamy as quickly as he can.

I wonder how the Batterers will respond when I request a vehicle to take me up to the Moon. They'll thoroughly investigate me, maybe expose my identity. Will I have to steal a ship to avoid the danger? Impossible. I don't even know where the airfield is.

Parliament's faces and the reporters' cameras swim before my eyes, becoming a brownish-beige soup. Wes has to talk, at least until I work up my courage.

And he does. "Saint Oda needs very little, in proportion to the size of your forces. A dozen aircraft would be enough. Consider that a small price to pay for disrupting Pacifian supply lines in northwest Europe, for a new ally, and"—he swallows painfully—"access to our natural resources. There's more oil under Koré Island. And coal, shale, zinc, iron . . ."

I inhale sharply, along with everyone who's listening. If Saint Oda survives the invasion, it will become a mining metropolis as well as a Batterer ally. The clear Eloisa River will run yellow with silt; the tunnels will fill with dust from dynamite explosions. Oil refineries' towers will obstruct the eiders' flight paths. Wes's people might never forgive him for compromising their core values, but he's doing it anyway—to save their lives.

His tone gets more aggressive. "Battery Bay designated Saint Oda a protectorate nearly a century ago. If we are attacked—not once, but twice—imagine how that will look. Does this nation keep its word or not?"

Hisses of annoyance from Parliament. Dozens of representatives wave their hands as if brushing him aside. The noise escalates, and I hear shouts along the lines of "Dump 'em back in the Atlantic!" Reporters' remote-controlled video screens flit about the auditorium, recording the ruckus.

I rub my temples, despairing. If the Batterers won't send drones to Saint Oda, they definitely won't help me get home.

"Look at this mumbo-jumbo mess." Two meters from me, one of Sear's aides—an elderly man with triangular spectacles— catches my attention.

Another aide, a young woman with green eyelashes like blades of grass, lets out a sigh. "The constituents will love it," she says sarcastically.

"Morbid amusement and love are different beasts."

Did Mom really want to introduce disorder, inefficiency, and bad manners into the bases' government? Then again, how could she have known that in practice "democracy" looks like *this*? Still, it must beat having only six people in charge, with nothing to check their power.

Wes sits down by my side, legs shaking. "That didn't quite work. Sorry to throw you to the wolves, but I need you to win them back."

We both know I can't. If he's bad at public speaking, I'm utterly incapable. My chest constricts, my head pounds, and the soup of people bubbles and lurches before my eyes.

"Phaet, please," he says. "If you love Saint Oda, even a little . . ."

I think back to the islands: how the Carlyles took me in even though I was a stranger, how Murray healed my arm. The tickle of ladybug feet on my hand as I became an Odan. I owe them something. I stand and walk to the microphone.

"I'm a new Odan citizen," I say. My voice is weak, but it's high-pitched and audible over Parliament's ruckus. Legislators and reporters alike focus on me; the attention makes me want to duck under the balcony's railing. "When I arrived, it was the first time in my life I felt truly safe. The first time I experienced the kindness of strangers. I'd never imagined a people could be so generous, so close to nature, so good to one another." I try an ideological approach, name-dropping the values Batterers hold dear and choosing words that feel almost truthful. "With its direct democracy, Saint Oda is the last beacon of freedom in an increasingly Pacifian part of the world. If Pacifia captures the archipelago, northwest Europe will be *theirs*. Please, do not let this happen. I beg you, defend Saint Oda from the encroachment of my . . . my horrid home country."

Representatives sit up straighter in their seats. Though I'm too nervous to look into their eyes, I can feel their opinions shifting.

"The Odans saved my life. But who can save *them*?" The question hangs in the air while I scramble for words with which to end this awful ordeal. "Only Battery Bay. Only you."

I walk backward to my seat, footsteps loud in the suddenly silent hall.

Did I really do that? I feared the words wouldn't come, but they did—entire sentences.

Conversations begin around the hall, but the voices sound different. Quiet. Respectful.

Wes squeezes my shoulder. "You didn't just say all those words for their benefit, did you? Did you mean them?"

I'll miss making bread with Nanna Zeffie, playing hide-and-seek with Emmy and Julie, walking along the cliff side with Murray as she sprinkles flour into the bacterial lights. I might have chafed at their religion and their rules, but I can't allow Pacifia to destroy the Odans' way of life the way the Committee destroyed my family's.

Family. Wes shouldn't have to see his suffer the way I did mine. I remember his face, lit by the sunset on our submarine; his voice, when he told me how much he loves them.

"I'll go back to Saint Oda with you," I say quietly. I doubt I can do much to fight Pacifia, but it's almost entirely my fault that the hegemon is attacking the island in the first place. Could I bear the guilt if I left Wes's city to burn?

"*Really?* But Cygnus—"

At the sound of my little brother's name, I cringe. Visions of his torture tug at the invisible ropes pulling me upward, back toward the Moon.

"Are you *sure* you want to do this?" Wes whispers. He sounds happy that I'm accompanying him. Or am I imagining it? My heart sinks in my chest like an anchor, heavy and sharp.

"Cygnus . . ." I say, "will have to wait a few days longer." I'll use the time to brainstorm a real plan to save him, to compose a mental list of allies and safe hiding places on Base IV.

Wes gives me a quick one-armed hug, and my decision is cemented. He's saved my life twice over. I can't return to my home until I'm sure he still has one.

Parliament's discussion has concluded, and legislators are voting on whether to send a dozen fighter jets to Saint Oda. It's the starting point for military aid. On one side of the sphere, a scoreboard of sorts keeps track of the numbers. On the forward-facing side of each balcony, a glass bulb lights up as the representative sends in his or her vote: green for yes, red for no, yellow for abstain. My pulse thrums; I can't bear to watch. But when I close my eyes, the backs of my eyelids make everything look red.

"It's all okay now." Someone taps me on the shoulder—Costa's aide, the woman with the grassy eyelashes. Shuddering, I risk a look—and see green has triumphed by a slim margin: 235–226.

Relief floods through me. Wes is hugging himself, thanking God under his breath.

Battery Bay will send help, even if it's only a dozen planes. It's something. But perhaps not enough. The thought puts an end to my relief. The entire *city* of Pacifia will invade Saint Oda, and soon. Our submarine's satellite-generated map indicated that it would take only two and a half days' travel for Pacifia to reach the archipelago. And that was this morning.

Minister Sear gives Wes and me a satisfied smile and sits down between us. "Excellent. We'll wait twenty-four hours, then, for the referendum to move the city."

Twenty-four hours? Battery Bay will need at least thirty-six to travel northward—and that's if the referendum passes. Should their dozen jets prove insufficient, Pacifia will have burned Saint Oda alive by the time the city itself travels to join the battle.

Wes and I exchange nervous glances. Sear reads the anxiety on our faces. "The twelve aircraft will take off in approximately two hours and land before morning. You're more than welcome to travel with them."

Wes and I nod vigorously.

"Try to get some sleep en route," Sear continues. "I find that dreams have a preventative effect on airsickness, whether they're sweet or bitter."

And while we're aloft, Battery Bay will cruise onward, brightly, chaotically. Forgetting we were there until, perhaps, Pacifia gives them a reason to remember.

13

AN OFFICIAL HOVERCRAFT CARRIES US FROM
Parliament to the airfield. The roadways, which consist of lanes demarcated by beams of light, soon become an aerial parking lot. Civilian vehicles pass us; many have no ceilings, and people shout furiously, waving their flexible screens like flags. ODANS: BB WANTS YOUR OIL, they've written in blood-red type. MAKE WISHES, NOT WARS. And, SEAR LIES, TROOPS DIE.

They'll never pass the referendum, I think, despair nibbling at my heart.

Below us, through the thicket of antiwar protesters, I see a rectangular park several kilometers wide, walled in by skyscrapers of every shape and size. Although it's nighttime, light is everywhere—so much that I can't make out a single star above us. Beams of it pour out of windows, illuminating the park's fields, forests, small ponds, and one big, amoeba-shaped lake—all that photosynthetic life, I imagine, thriving on the CO_2 output from other parts of the city. If only we had time for a pit stop there. These plants were obviously cultivated, as in the Lunar greenhouses, but they're not prodded, snipped, and forced into single file. How would ours look if *they* could decide where and how to grow?

At almost every "intersection," we pass stationary hovercrafts that project pictures of food onto nearby windows. Their proprietors hawk pungent meats, which customers eat off colorful plastic sticks; deep-fried whole sardine sandwiches; and

DESSERT PIZZA!!—white chocolate melted on flatbread, topped with raspberries. The oily smells seep into our vehicle and tickle my salivary glands.

Quieter neighborhoods occupy the area north of the park— but that doesn't mean they're *quiet*. Atop centuries-old row houses far below us, people wearing strange geometrical and sparkling clothing dance to stuttering beats. The houses' walls have been painted over with children's faces, women in sunny dresses, bearded men in wide-brimmed hats. I notice a few granite churches sandwiched between other buildings, their walls uniquely bare.

As we approach the city's northern edge, fewer protesters bar our way. Heaps of garbage several stories high are piled near the docks. Freight ships bob near shore, waiting to carry the litter away and deposit it where no Batterer will have to think about it. Just like the Committee, dumping Lunar waste into Earth's oceans, letting it sink out of sight.

The Batterer airfield, twelve long runways bordered by patchy brown grass, is unimpressive compared with the rest of the city. When we walk onto the tarmac, I squint to see the outlines of the stealth aircraft. I hear the pilot say that, using fisheye cameras positioned on the body of the planes, the hulls can change color to match their surroundings. They're mostly hazy gray now, with smatterings of white pinpricks—the reflection of glaring city lights.

"If Battery Bay can invent undetectable aircraft," I ask the pilot, "why are the streets and airways so . . ." I wrinkle my nose.

"Smelly and hot?" she says. "Most of us want to change that, but no one wants to pay for it. Proposals keep getting voted down."

"Doesn't matter to me," another female pilot says with a

snort. "I don't spend enough time sniffing this place to care."

As we near the aircraft, I see that they're shaped like boomerangs, with no real fuselage or tail. Their wingspans are about twenty-five meters, but they're only two and a half meters tall. The bellies are a brighter silver than the dorsal side, so that they're countershaded like fish, and their names are textured—not painted—onto the wings: *Flounder, Tuatara, Tree Frog*. The planes and their animal namesakes can disappear into any background. A dozen aircraft will fly to Saint Oda—one carrying Wes and me, the other eleven bearing an assortment of explosives with which to fortify the islands when we arrive.

Our pilot, dressed in drab brown, helps us climb into the cockpit through the roof of the craft that will take us home. Like the aircraft we passed before, it bears the name of a camouflaging species: *Cuttlefish*. Inside are seats for three crew members, with no room for passengers. The Batterers push a crate against the wall and buckle us down. One of them holds out two green pills, one for me and one for Wes.

"Sleeping meds," she says. "You're both new to acceleration to high subsonic speeds while meeting wind resistance from all angles. Trust me, you don't want to be awake for this."

We swallow the pills without water, and the crew members fit each of us with noise-canceling headgear. Still, I feel the thrum of the engine reverberate through my chest.

As we head into the air and accelerate upward, some part of me imagines—for a moment—that we're aiming for the Moon.

*   *   *

Someone shakes me awake. I lift my eyelids, feeling like I'm drawing back curtains made of lead.

It's Wes who has disturbed my sleep. He absently rattles my shoulder with his hand while staring out the tiny window behind us.

We've landed. I follow Wes's gaze and see the familiar outline of Koré Island—but something about it looks foreign. Though the sun is high overhead, it shines down on an empty beach and bare cliff face. Sandbags made of flour sacks and scraps of old clothing seal off the entrances to the island's tunnels, and there's a gaping pit below the Overhang from which the Odans presumably took the sand. Apart from the occasional scavenging seagull, the very life Saint Oda holds so dear seems to have gone missing.

Wes and I step out of the plane into the freezing air.

Beside us, the Batterer airmen scope out the beach. I stand with Wes, watching them, digging my boots into the tan sand. How odd the visitors look with their guns and gadgets, their flight masks still in place. It's as if they think the air of Saint Oda could poison them.

"They don't belong here," Wes says.

"Do we?" I ask.

Wes glances at the back of his left hand, at the round plastic handscreen that blends seamlessly into his skin. He says nothing.

Several Odans have appeared, hiking down the slope. They're Sanctuarists; they hold blowguns to their lips as they scrutinize the strange newcomers and their aircraft.

One Sanctuarist—Finley, Wes's cousin—ventures farther out than the others. When he notices the two of us, a smile breaks out on his face, and he jumps up and down, waving. He looks like a more animated version of his cousin. Still smiling, he turns to run back up the slope toward Wes's house.

It takes several long minutes for Wes's parents to arrive on the beach. Wesley Sr. acknowledges our presence with a nod, but instead of approaching, he stops to talk to one of the Batterer pilots. *Coward.* He must not want to admit he was wrong to distrust me just yet.

Mrs. Carlyle, however, careens down the slope. She runs to us, kicking up flurries of sand, and I scoot sideways to avoid getting flattened. Taking Wes by the shoulders, she kisses his cheeks over and over. When his face turns scarlet, I smile and think of my own mother tucking my silver hair behind my ears. Seeing his happiness makes the ache of missing her bearable.

Wesley Sr. finally approaches, flanked by Batterer airmen. He claps Wes on the shoulder and ignores his son's instinctive flinch. "Good Sanctuarists obey orders word for word. The worst of them associate with our enemies and flee to distant cities when Saint Oda needs them most. Yet you, my son, are among the best—because you came back, bringing us more than a sliver of hope."

Wes blinks in surprise, staring at the ground. He looks too abashed for words.

"And Phaet," adds Wesley Sr., "I treated you with excess caution, relying on the intelligence I had at the time. I do not regret my actions. But know that you are . . . appreciated here."

It's a bad apology—and clearly a grudging one—but still I receive it with a curt nod. At least he sounds glad that I didn't die.

Touching Wes's shoulder to get his attention, Wesley Sr. changes the subject. "This officer here says that a referendum is currently taking place that will decide whether Battery Bay itself comes to meet Pacifia head-to-head in Saint Oda's defense."

"They'll quit voting five hours from now." The Batterer pilot has a buzz cut with swirling pinwheel designs shaved onto the sides of his head. He must be in his late thirties, but he hasn't outgrown the sarcastic smirk of a teenager. "Turnout's high and getting higher. But the last time I checked, the citizens were voting to stay the hell away from this place. I'd bet my badges they don't want to leave southern Africa. They like the sun, and traveling costs tax money."

"So would fighting, yes?" Wesley Sr. says.

The pilot nods. "Not to mention they'd put their lives up for grabs by entering a war zone. Until they've decided, all we can do is provide modern weapons to incorporate into your defense plans—so you're not stuck chucking rocks at Pacifia."

Wesley Sr.'s fingers curl into a fist at the jibe, but his demeanor remains unruffled. "We have strung large nets between the Odan islands. With any luck, they'll jam Pacifia's propellers. Wes, Phaet, and the other Sanctuarists can tie the smaller explosives you brought onto the nets, set them to explode on contact. But first, we need to finish setting up sandbags and Punji sticks."

"We've also brought new toys for your troops: assault rifles, machine guns—"

"No, thank you," Wesley Sr. says. Although the firearms aren't exactly the Sanctuarists' style, I'm surprised he's rejecting them. "I will not let my men bet their lives on contraptions they've never seen before. We will use the methods we've relied on for centuries."

I'm skeptical that booby traps and poison darts will be enough, but I'm not about to offend the Sanctuary Coordinator again by speaking up in the pilot's defense.

A pained expression flickers across Mrs. Carlyle's face. "I need to check on Murray and the girls, back at the shelter. They must have heard about the Batterer . . . *apparatuses* by now." She turns to go.

"Mother?" Wes calls after her. "Is Murray . . . is she all right?"

"She's stable," Mrs. Carlyle says. "But you shouldn't see her. She hasn't acted like this in years. Last night, she was railing about you and Lazarus Penny—every wrong you two have done her. Seeing your face could set her off, and she needs to remain calm if she's to survive the attack."

Wes inclines his head, touches his eyelids with his fingertips. "But Mother—"

"Good-bye, my boy." Mrs. Carlyle hurries toward the north entrance, located halfway up the mountain. It's the only cave opening not sealed shut with sandbags.

"Listen to me, son. Your mother will care for your sister. She's done it for twenty-two years," Wesley Sr. says. "And you've got work to do. Phaet too—we need help from everyone who's willing to use potentially lethal objects. In the meantime, if possible, I will persuade the civilians that there's no need to fear the Batterer contraptions occupying their entire beach."

Wes and I scramble away with the Sanctuarists to work on last-minute fortifications. Continuing the work they've done already, our task is to set up Punji sticks, contaminated wooden spikes concealed by holes in the ground. Their sharp ends will puncture the enemies' boots, infect their flesh.

Next, we prepare scores of wolfsbane darts for blowguns and select skull-sized rocks for makeshift catapults. The young men give me a wide berth, preferring to talk among themselves about me and, if they must, talk to me through Wes.

I read the assumptions in their eyes—all the racy things Wes and I must've done on our voyage, the reasons *why* I'm allowed to work alongside them despite being female. Soon, Wes and I grow so uncomfortable that without a word, we split off from the group and head toward the remotest part of the islands.

I respect the Sanctuarists' efforts to prepare, I think as we trudge, but they seem like child's play. Wes and I are the only ones here who have seen firsthand the full capabilities of the Militia, who know what's coming when Pacifia arrives.

We don't mention this to his comrades. They need their courage.

14

AS THE SUN SETS, WES AND I REACH THE southeast harbor. Using the Batterers' gifts, we'll rig the nets here to explode.

Our nonstop travel has returned us to the fuzzy, sleep-deprived state so familiar from our Militia days. Working with Wes reminds me of happy memories from late-night training back on the Moon—the thrilling clicks of knife on knife as we swiped at each other, reveling in our skill and our recklessness.

We appropriate a smelly rowboat belonging to some fisherman—he's no doubt taken refuge in the caves with his family—and paddle toward the north island's southwest cliff. I gulp, reminded anew of my inability to swim. What if the boat springs a leak and wells up with water, like the submarine?

"Don't worry." Wes takes a seat at the stern. It's easier to steer from there. "You're not getting wet. In fact, you needn't leave the boat."

I shake my head in mock exasperation, but shelve my doubts and step onto the prow. The boat's rocking throws me off balance, and I hastily plant my rear on the wooden plank that serves as a seat.

"I see Base IV," Wes says from behind me.

I continue paddling, trying to keep the rowboat on course, but I do steal a look at the Moon. He's right. I can make out my home city, a cluster of white lumps like fungus, cowering against the wall of a large equatorial crater. I almost feel sorry for it.

"It's so small, I could squash it between my fingers," I say. "But everything I ever did happened there."

Everything until I came here.

"You glad to be going home after this?" Wes asks.

"Glad I can try." I stand, shifting my weight to counteract the boat's rocking motion. With the rope attached to the bow, I tether our vessel to the chain of nets in the water.

Behind me, Wes nods. *Try.* The battle and the journey ahead will test everything we have.

No, everything *I* have. Wes isn't coming. Will memories of him be enough to keep the little light in my heart alive? Or will I forget him and the warmth that fills me when he's around? Separated from him, I might go frigid from the inside out.

We reach the site where we'll plant the explosives. Only a few blue dots illuminate the north island; I see its ragged rock formations in silhouette. Wes turns away from me, shrugging off his wool jacket.

"When Pacifia gets close, they'll start sending submarines to the islands. If we can hijack one, we can get you aboard the city and hide you in Moon-bound cargo before they make landfall on Oda."

I hear him shiver on the last word. It's probably less a reaction to the cold than an anticipation of it. He has to jump into the wintertime Atlantic to complete our task.

"But I want to help fight," I say, my throat constricting with frustration. Running away while the Odans struggle against Pacifia seems unfair to Wes. "It's my fault that your city needs defending at all."

"Phaet, you've done more than enough for us." Wes stands, causing the boat to buck and nearly throw me overboard. I shrink back, and he lowers his voice. "Don't make yourself crazy. I'm as accountable as you are."

He kicks off his tough leather shoes and stands at the stern in his socks.

"But . . ."

"I wish I'd made different decisions, Phaet. Every waking hour, I wonder at least once if I could've kept you alive without bringing you to Earth and blowing my cover."

He leaps from the boat. His body forms a magnificent arc and makes a neat splash when he enters the cold water, fingertips first. A long moment later, he surfaces, shaking wet hair out of his eyes.

"But that's months in the past. What matters is the near future. Several hours from now, Pacifia will invade. You'll head to the Moon and keep as many innocents alive as you can. I'll do the same here. I'm sure we'll find a way to communicate after things settle."

Something within me goes brittle. Over the past three seasons, some of the steel in Wes's eyes has passed into my spirit. I can only hope it will linger when he's not around.

"Let's start the future today. With this." Hands heavy with sorrow, I pass him the end of a string of explosives, and we begin our work in earnest. After I hand Wes the short cords, he submerges himself and ties sections of the explosives chain to the fishing nets. He gasps for air every time he comes up, his lips going purple from the cold.

As he progresses, I tether the boat to the net conglomerate near him and feed him more of the chain, ensuring it doesn't tangle. *Why can't I swim?* I'd join him in an instant to speed up his progress. Helpless and swallowing frustration, I watch his movements grow stiffer.

"It's okay," he calls, teeth chattering. "Before I left for the Moon, Father made all of us swim in cold water. Once a week, every winter!"

That's why he and the other Sanctuarist spies are so tough. Someone who can spend twenty minutes in the wintry ocean knows how to endure. I'd be hypothermic in five.

Days seem to pass before we're done. Finally, I take Wes's icy hand and help him back onto the rowboat, patting the water off his torso with the empty cloth satchel we used to carry our supplies. As Wes shifts into a sitting position, his movements are slow, his limbs rigid. Panicking, I pick up the wool jacket and slide his arms into the sleeves, one by one. My own hands shake as I fasten the three buttons up the front, and not entirely because of the cold.

"You're so warm," he says.

I wrap my arms around him in an off-kilter half hug. He reciprocates. As he shudders from the cold, I feel the energy go up and down his spine. A moment passes, and neither of us releases the other.

"Phaet . . ."

"Hmm?"

"What are you thinking?"

If you don't let go of me, I'll never make it home. But my heart's too full to say it.

"You tell me," I mumble instead.

"I'm not so good at this," he says, releasing me. "Serious talking, I mean."

I raise an eyebrow. *Really?*

"Fine, you win." Wes smiles queasily, and swallows. "I'm thinking that . . . that I'm going to miss you terribly. I can see it now, my life after you leave. It'll be like going around barefaced after you've gotten used to wearing spectacles. Even if you try to forget it, the knowledge is there, the sense that things aren't as good as they were. Everything will be blurrier without you, Phaet. Lonelier too."

I take in his words, swirl them about in my mind, and then I wrap my arms around him again. Honored and joyful beyond expression, I hold his heartbeat in my hands. A steady but rapid *ka-thump, ka-thump.*

But then thoughts break through the euphoria. My arms slacken and a cold wind rakes across my skin. I don't want to return home and agonize over an Earthbound boy, not while I'm trying to save my two siblings, help my lifelong friends. The more joy I feel now, the more it'll hurt to lose Wes when I go.

"Miss me in a few hours," I mumble, pulling away. In the distance, I see the demonic red light of a floating city—a star that's fallen onto the ocean, damp but still glowing. "First, we have to make it through them."

15

KORÉ ISLAND RISES BEHIND US, ONE SHADE
blacker than the starless sky. There's not a single bacterial light
aglow. Blown by intense winds, sparse white grains careen
through the air in every direction except straight down, a snow-
fall that's more like a dust storm.

From a small watchtower built into a rock outcropping, we
see Pacifia looming larger and larger on the horizon. I can discern
its oblong outline and block-shaped towers rising out of a woolly
blanket of smog. Only a few sections of the city are lit, at the prow
and the stern. Pacifian citizens probably don't go out much at
night; I learned in my studies that law enforcement in the massive
floating city is underfunded and corrupt. I don't want to imagine
what dangers await unwary Pacifians in the darkness.

Wes and Finley have been assigned watch at the big island's
north shore, where the mountain meets the pastures. The boys
hunch over a paper printout of Pacifia's floor plan; one of the
Lunar spies accessed it in the Militia databases and sent it over
digitally. Wes, Finley, and I will oversee the booby traps that
activate automatically, set off those that need triggering, and
take down what foot soldiers we can. Then Wes and Finley will
board Pacifia with a group of other Sanctuarists and try to shut
down the command center—if there is one; the Batterers aren't
sure—and I'll look for a spaceship to carry me home.

Mrs. Carlyle couldn't fathom a girl working alongside young

men in a war zone, but Wesley Sr. convinced her that my departure was for the best. Most Odans, including almost all of the Sanctuarists, still don't know that I'm a Lunar, and Wesley Sr. didn't want to suffer the consequences if they were to find out.

The Carlyle women have taken shelter with the other civilians in the upper levels of Koré Island. Though several dozen Odans have fled to distant islands or to other cities, most resolved to stay until the end.

In the darkness, I shudder at every sound: the tumble of a pebble, the keening of a hawk. In my jacket pocket is a rubbery sleeve that fits over a forefinger, embossed with some Lunar Sanitation worker's fingerprint. Wes used it to sneak around Base IV all those months ago. He passed it on to me—a gift for my trip home. I squeeze it to stay close to calm.

It's not easy. I dread our first encounter with the enemy—especially the Militia contingent. Among the attackers, there'll be Committee loyalists who hate me with every cell in their bodies. But there may also be my friends, who made Militia bearable for me. Will I have to fight Nash, Eri, or Io? What about Orion? I couldn't extinguish his lazy smile and dry wit. Unless he . . . Would any of them attack me? As for the soldiers who are only following orders—can I bring myself to kill them, if the only other option is being killed?

Shaking, I call out in my thoughts to anyone who might listen—the Odan god, perhaps. *Please, please, don't let it come to that.*

Finley's holding up better than I am. Something in his expression reminds me of my reedy, off-kilter brother. It's his curiosity, I suppose: the curiosity to see things he's been shielded from until now.

"Remember, lock the Lazy after you've snitched it," Wes instructs him. "If you stow it unlocked, you'll put a hole through your pants—if you're lucky. If you're not, it'll go through your leg."

We've gone over this before; Wes is repeating himself to calm us down. As one of our first moves, we'll knock out some soldiers—preferably Lunar Militia, because they have the best, most familiar equipment—and steal their uniforms, armor, helmets, and weapons.

Finley nods, staring out the window. Hulking and angular, Pacifia plows through the water, wind, and snow. The churning waves in its wake reflect light from the crescent moon. If Tourmaline was big, Pacifia is a monstrosity, like Battery Bay. It must be as tall as Koré Island and twice as long from stern to prow. The smokestacks pumping waste gases into the air are rectangular prisms. Crooked monorail tracks snake between the buildings; some end in midair, the cutoff a lethal drop hundreds of feet down.

At the prow is a tower that spreads out into an expansive tabletop. It looks like a giant hand balancing toy planes in its open palm. *The aerospace complex.* If I'm to go home tonight, I'll need to make it there.

Another, smaller tower points up from the hand's center like a toothpick. That must be the command center, where people watch the runways and give orders so that ships don't collide with each other.

As Pacifia enters the passage between the north and west islands, I catch my breath. The Sanctuarists watching the area, two old hands named Jean and Grenby, had better vacate before the chains of explosives go off.

Ba-ba-ba-BAM! Bright explosions distort the ocean's surface, but Pacifia doesn't shift from its course. The massive craft doesn't even rock. What must we do to defeat them—sink the city? Blow a hole in the side? Both seem impossible. The Batterer stealth jets won't join the battle until later. Based on Pacifia's seeming impermeability, we'll need the element of surprise.

"Don't worry," Wes whispers to Finley. "The Pacifians probably weren't expecting that. I'll wager they didn't even know we'd prepared for an attack."

I gulp, suddenly wishing I were in the Odan shelter with Wes's mother and sisters. Pacifia will stop moving soon. When they reach shallower water, they'll likely send out submarines.

"Amphibious warfare has proved difficult throughout history. We should be fine." Wes used this tone when he told me his fake identity, back in training. He doesn't think we'll be fine at all.

"When's Battery Bay coming?" Finley asks.

Wes sighs, apparently tired of ungrounded optimism. "I don't think they will." As he speaks, I imagine the Batterers' antiwar protests spiraling out of control. "Whatever happens, Fin, keep your head up."

Beside me, Finley swallows. He looks terrified.

"You ready?" Wes asks his cousin.

"Sure," Finley says, but he doesn't sound sure.

Wes's eyes shift to mine. I pull up my pant leg, reach my hand into my battered Militia boot, and take out one of my three remaining daggers.

16

"WHY HAVEN'T THEY PULLED OUT THEIR BIG guns?" Finley loads another homemade grenade into our makeshift catapult.

The sun has set, but we wear simple infrared glasses—an outdated model Wes gave me long ago on Base IV, to ward off sneak attacks from jealous Militia trainees—and aim at large areas with a mean temperature of ninety-eight degrees Fahrenheit, the outdated temperature metric used by the Sanctuarists. Our attempts so far have all been misses; the grenades explode off target, causing the squads of soldiers to shift to one side. Invaders keep coming in an endless wave. It's as if Pacifia is spilling its every able-bodied citizen onto Saint Oda's shores.

Wes and I exchange a look. We can't say what we're thinking: the attackers haven't used bomber aircraft or self-destructing drones because they hope to capture me alive.

"I'm not sure. But that's first-rate aim, Finley," Wes says, smoothly distracting his cousin. Finley beams. "Go ahead, chuck the thing."

I light the fuse, Finley pulls the lever, and we watch the grenade sail through the air. I know it'll hit its target, and the calculating, aggressive part of me gets a cold sort of satisfaction. It's the part I've kept in check since I was a captain in Militia and I attacked a thief in the Atrium with an Electrostun. I've wanted to forget that it's still in me.

Through my infrared glasses, the explosion below us appears

in blinding white. It scatters the red dots in my modified vision like a spray of blood. We've hit the invaders dead-on, which means we didn't waste ammunition like we did with our last few shots. A shivering thrill zips up the back of my neck. The Beater in me is rejoicing, and the rest of me hates it. Would I feel like this if I hadn't undergone Militia training? Or did it not matter? Do all people, regardless of their experiences, enjoy watching their enemies burn?

Human beings are getting tossed into the air, and they're dying—or sustaining horrific injuries—before they hit the ground. The carnage makes me feel as if someone's frozen my insides. We've taken people's lives, and we can never return them.

On the island and in the water, more explosions bring down the Pacifian attackers. Three of the Batterer jets have finally joined the fight; they twist, turn, and fire air-to-water missiles at the enemy. Broken submarines sink, sending up bubbles and smoke. But for every vessel that goes down, five more make it to shore. One Batterer jet flies too close to Pacifia, and some sort of electric cannon—probably connected to one of the power plants—sends it tumbling into the sea. The truth hits me like a slap: *Saint Oda and eleven aircraft aren't enough to fight this city.* Unless Battery Bay decided that confronting Pacifia in these frigid waters is worth sacrificing their time and safety—which doesn't seem to have happened—we're doomed.

I need to move. If I keep watching grenades explode and souls leave the world, the Beater I was on the Moon might come back.

"A lot of soldiers have already landed," I say. "Should we check the Punji holes?"

Wes loads another grenade into the catapult and fires. "Sure. Finley, go with her."

I descend the spiral stone staircase, Finley behind me, and

crawl out the half-meter-high door. We swerve to the right; in the path's center is the first trap, which we've covered with a thin layer of sticks and leaves. About a meter and a half deep, so that a soldier will fall in past his shin armor, are sharpened sticks dipped in diseased manure, their tips pointing downward. If we trap an attacker, and he tries to pull his leg upward, the sticks will puncture his thigh, making escape from the hole impossible.

Finley and I duck into a copse of firs, counting as we go. The Sanctuarists have dug Punji holes on the far side of the third and sixth trees on our left, and installed trip wires between several pairs of trees in between. Dark shapes shift in the middle distance; frantic voices murmur. Our prey is closing in.

"Should we get Downers out?" a male voice whispers. In Militia lingo, "Downers" are tranquilizing guns that fire darts filled with sedatives.

"Obviously, fuzzbrain!" a woman replies. Foolish Lunar soldiers, talking with their visors up. "Didn't you hear Alpha's order back on Pacifia? We're supposed to take any really good fighters prisoner. For questioning."

In case a prisoner turns out to be me—or Wes. Do they suspect he's here too?

Then the rest of the soldier's words sink in, and for a second, I forget to breathe. *Alpha's order, back on Pacifia*. That can only mean one thing: the General's here—the head of Base IV Militia; father to Jupiter, my rival from Militia training; and the primary executor of the Committee's orders. A hulking man with sharp eyes and a powerful, cruel body, he seems to have been selectively bred for devastation. I'd track him down and make him suffer—if I weren't petrified by the very notion of him.

"Hmph. The General's clueless about how many natives are running around here." The first soldier stands and adjusts his utility belt, which holds a spare Lazy, an Electrostun, a dagger, and what looks like sensor equipment. "I'll take backup. Elara, Puck, Mayuri—go knock out whoever was screaming. Sounded like a little girl."

Finley and I nod to each other. Three of these soldiers will head for Wes if we don't take them out now. As one, we raise blowguns to our lips. Before the Militia soldiers can lower their visors, Finley puffs a dart at Elara. It burrows into her forehead, and she falls atop one of the males. His stumbling gives me an excellent shot at his unarmored thighs—a much larger surface area than the forehead. I puff once and manage to hit the side of the soldier's leg.

"What the fuse!" one of the men cries. "We're under attack!"

The two remaining soldiers flip down their visors, turn on their helmets' headlamps, and fire their Electrostuns in our direction. Feeling the pounding of my heart down to my toe bones, I duck behind the nearest tree, angling my body sideways to make myself a smaller target. Nearby, a yellow beam illuminates Finley's face, and I see his openmouthed expression of fear. Wesley Sr. and the other Sanctuarists must have lectured him about these weapons for years, but this is the first time he's seen them in person.

We've lost the advantage of surprise; the soldiers know our locations, and their weapons make ours look like toys.

The other traps. Nearby stand two trees connected by a trip wire. When pulled, it will cause a looped rope on the ground to snag around the victim's ankle and pull him or her four meters into the air. I face Finley, put a finger to my lips, and gesture toward the trip wire's location. He only blinks at me. *Fine. I'll do this alone.*

With careful strides, I sprint toward the trip wire. Relaxing all my leg muscles, I leap over it and take shelter behind a tree, then stamp my feet as if I'm still running, creating a racket in the carpet of dry leaves covering the ground.

Both soldiers' helmets swivel in my direction.

Get over here.

One sprints toward me; the other continues firing toward Finley. *Blast.* I reach into my boot, pull out a knife, and estimate the revolutions it'll take to reach my target. Holding the dull end of the blade, I throw the knife at the second soldier's helmeted head. It clunks against his helmet, knocking him off balance. He continues staggering forward, but Finley, shaking off his fear, takes him down with a blow dart to the neck.

Without warning, someone's helmet lamp blinds me. The other soldier is sprinting in my direction, an incredulous expression on his face.

"Hey! Your hair!" he yells, stumbling.

Finley runs after him, but it's too late: the Lunar soldier's recognized me. The unmistakable silver strands on my head have been growing in aggressively of late. If he continues talking, whoever's listening to his headset feed will find out exactly where Phaet Theta's hiding. If they do, it's all over.

I hear strangely heavy footsteps behind him. Reinforcements? How could the Militia have found us already?

"Bear!" Finley shouts. "Watch out, Fay!"

I dive behind a nearby spruce without a second thought and then look back, unable to believe Finley's words. The stomping grows louder, a rumble in my ears, and in the next instant a huge, furry mass barrels into view. The animal is two and a half meters long, and must weigh as much as seven or eight adult humans. Dark blood drips onto the snow from a wound on one of its hind legs; it probably sustained an injury from a trap set by the Sanctuarists for the Militia. The Lunar soldier twists around and, with a shout of surprise, shoots the bear in the jaw.

Looks like we won't need the trip wire after all.

Roaring in anger, the wounded animal rears up on its hind legs, standing twice as tall as its attacker. I'm rooted to the spot, stunned by the spectacle. *This is why Odans stay inside at night.*

The soldier fires Electrostun pellets into the bear's belly—he's probably too frightened to think of switching to his Lazy. There's nothing like this creature on the Moon. Still roaring, the bear charges. Paws the size of Sanitation manhole covers, topped with pointed claws, swipe at the lone soldier, and powerful jaws close around the back of his head.

"C'mon!" Finley dashes toward me from the side of the tree opposite the bear. He pulls me up and leads me away from the scene, but I can't tear my eyes away from the beast, which is stomping across its enemy's body, snapping ribs and flattening organs. Only when the soldier lies limp does the bear flee back uphill, whimpering in pain.

The quiet that falls means we're safe. I exhale slowly, relishing the sound of my breath, the thump of my still-beating heart. Then, after triple-checking the area, Finley and I move back in and collect three soldiers' worth of clothing, gear, and weapons. We don't touch the dead body of the soldier mangled by the bear.

Our treasures are damp with blood—blood we drew. I can't stomach the idea of putting on the uniform or handling the blasters as if they were my own. But within the next hour, I'll have to.

Arms laden, Finley and I tread back toward our hideout.

17

IN THE OBSERVATORY, THE BOYS AND I TURN our backs to one another to put on the stolen Militia uniforms. It feels good to wear the getup again, if only because I know I can fight in it. Elara had a larger frame than mine, so extra fabric bunches around my shoulders and hips. But the uniform isn't riddled with holes or soaked in blood, since Finley got her with one dart to the forehead.

We wear the Lazies on the left side of our utility belts, rather than the customary right. The Sanctuarists agreed beforehand that this would distinguish enemy from undercover friend.

I'm helping Finley buckle down the last piece of his stolen chest armor when we hear the explosion—from behind us. Wes pokes his head out the window and immediately retracts it, cursing. "A red flare at the top of the mountain."

Finley gasps. "You mean, the emergency signal—"

"Exactly." Wes jams a helmet over his head and flips the visor down. "The civilian shelter's about to be attacked."

Blast. Pacifian and Lunar forces have already neared the mountain's peak?

The next sounds we hear confirm our worst suspicions.

"We are about to breach your caverns," a deep male voice booms from Pacifia—and from Koré Island. All the foot soldiers have cranked their audio devices to the maximum, the better to broadcast their commanders' threats. *"We will show you mercy*

if two conditions, and only these two, are met. One, surrender your is-
land. Two, give us all your information and evidence concerning Lunar
fugitives Wezn Kappa and Phaet Theta. Both were 1.67 meters tall,
plus or minus half a centimeter. The male had red-brown hair. The
female's was black and gray. Generous compensation will be given for
any revelations. . . ."

They can't ask the Odans to turn Wes and me in without
revealing to the Militia that we're still alive. But they can ask
for clues.

"Gray hair. Phaet." Finley scrunches his face. ". . . *Fay?*" His
body lurches backward. "She's . . . she . . . Wes, you knew she
wasn't Pacifian, didn't you?"

Wes and I look at each other helplessly. We must tell yet
another person my secret—and risk the consequences if Finley
is captured.

"They committed treason and espionage, among other crimes. In-
vestigation is continuing," the announcement blares.

"Fay, you're a *demon*?" Finley's face shifts from horror to awe
and back again. "A demon *criminal*. What did you *do*?"

Wes looks at me expectantly; this explanation is mine to
give. "The demon government killed my mother." The words
feel like another language in my mouth, and yet the Committee
are demons, more than any other Lunars I've met—save only
the General.

Finley's face settles into a confused expression. "But—"

Wes interrupts him. "Fin, listen to me. When I was feeling
most hopeless on the Moon, I met Phaet, a girl who'd do anything for her family, who'd never hurt anyone or anything in her
entire life. I've defended her to the death, and I'll continue as
long as I'm able. If my thoughts and feelings mean anything to

you, Fin, treat her like she's come from heaven. Not hell."

I don't understand the last bit, about those supernatural realms, but it doesn't matter. *This is how he feels about me?* I make eye contact with Wes and smile, unveiling my happiness— happiness that has no place in this battle.

"I believe you, Wes." Finley turns back to me, tilts his head sideways. "Why would they go through all this trouble to find you?"

"They can't wait to tell the Lunars that we're dead," I say.

The announcement resumes: *"Hand over the fugitives, or their remains, and you will be shown mercy."*

Then a thought strikes me: *If the soldiers capture me and Wes, then maybe the Lunar forces will retreat. Odans shouldn't have to die for us.*

"We should turn ourselves in," I blurt.

Wes freezes in the midst of buckling his new utility belt and looks at me as if I'm a total stranger. He, Finley, and I have formed a triangle with our bodies. A three-way standoff.

"Surrendering won't do any good," he says. "The Pacifians are here for our territory, and the Lunars have to fight for them until Saint Oda's in their possession. Even if they got us, the invasion would go on."

He's right. Guilt has made me stupid.

"Let's head out," Finley says. His determined expression ages him. "Wes, your father told us to go straight for the enemy's command center if things got bad. That's where their spacecraft are, right?"

"Yes." In Wes's voice, I hear the itch for action. "Look, Lunars— maybe Pacifians too—can't function without directions from their headsets. I've seen it. They stampede around like a herd of bulls surrounded by red flags."

He's right. I've seen Militia organization implode only once, but it was memorable. After the hundreds of impoverished Base IV residents living in Shelter witnessed my mother's death, they stormed the Atrium. In the ensuing chaos, a little girl from Shelter, Belinda, was killed. The violence escalated, and Beetles moved in to put the Shelter residents down. But through a hacking masterstroke, Cygnus disconnected their headsets. The soldiers went from mitigating mayhem to causing it: officers struggled to keep their units together, and dozens of soldiers dropped their weapons and fled the scene.

Can we achieve something like that now?

"All right, then," Finley says, as if sifting through my thoughts. "Let's cut some transmissions."

I slide the visor of my helmet down over my eyes. It's time to board Pacifia.

18

PACIFIANS TRAVEL IN HORDES. ALTHOUGH the gray-clad soldiers move more slowly than the small squads of Lunar Militia, they raze the land as they go. The battalion advancing toward us covers an entire wheat field. Rather than wade through the crop, they spray fire, systematically burning it down. The orange flames oscillate with the wind, and smoke clouds hover over the land like a specter of death.

I've looked at wheat stalks under a microscope and harvested kernels in the Base IV greenhouses—it's a beautifully complex organism. Witnessing its annihilation hurts me, makes it difficult to keep walking downhill.

In the corner of my vision, I see a wild boar and her offspring fleeing the flames; their path takes them along the edge of the enemy line, and my stomach clenches as I watch a Pacifian soldier shoot the mother boar down. Some of the piglets scatter; some hover by their parent's body. Tormented by the sight, I turn away, and we press onward, slipping through the snow, ducking behind foliage every few seconds to blow poison darts at nearby troops. To keep Lunars from hearing our sporadic conversation, we keep the microphones inside our helmets turned off, but we leave reception on so we can hear their orders.

A hundred meters across the field, violet light zips across my field of vision. Though far away, the sight is enough to toss me back into the past.

I'm at my mother's trial, unable to shut my eyes before they fire the fatal shot. The snow falling around me seems to materialize into a white cylindrical wall, and it's coming closer, closer—

"No!" I cry, falling backward. "Stop! Mom—"

My voice is muffled. Someone's got an arm around my mouth, someone strong, now dragging me to the ground.

"Shh! Fay!" Wes hisses. "That's a Lunar unit a couple dozen meters away."

His voice reorients me. *That was the first laser fire I've seen since leaving Base IV.* I open my eyes and press my forehead against Wes's shoulder. Then I raise my gaze to see Finley looking unnerved. I wriggle away from Wes, my head lowered in shame. I could have given away our position and gotten all three of us killed.

"Look at this," Wes says. He brushes some snow off the ground, revealing a patch of tiny white flowers. They have three petals each, all pointing downward, a row of mourners bowing their heads. Snowdrops—the first I've ever seen in bloom. "These flower in the dead of winter. The colder it gets, the harder they fight."

Without speaking, I nod. Then I get my feet under me and brush the snow off my pants.

*   *   *

Low-ranked Pacifian foot soldiers lack anything comparable to the Lunar troops' expensive body armor, and this makes them significantly easier to hit. They're not defenseless, though: they clutch guns the length of an arm and twice as thick. I once read that Earthbound soldiers train with elaborate firearms for so long that they prefer not to use unfamiliar weapons; that's probably why the Pacifians aren't carrying Lazies.

Their loss. Their rigid hands almost invite my aim. When I score a hit, the wolfsbane in the blow dart works quickly, and the soldier drops before I can count to four.

They won't detect us, because we've taken down only the occasional soldier. Other gaps in the ranks have begun to appear too, as soldiers collapse from Punji holes, trip wires, and grenade attacks. Even so, healthy troops cover the field as thoroughly as the Odan farmers' wheat once did.

A loud *whoosh* fills the air; I look to the right and see flames engulfing a nearby farmhouse. "That was Alex and Ive's place," Finley whimpers. The two upstairs windows light up like eyes. A moment later, the first floor caves in, adding the *snap* of cracking timber to the fire's roar.

Wes observes the spectacle, face twisted in a grimace. "Don't dwell on it, Fin. As long as there are trees and people here, there's the possibility of rebuilding."

I clutch my dagger in my hand, wishing I could throw it and stop one more soldier from reaching the Odan hideout. But we've agreed to rush to the Pacifian submarines and board the city, not to try and kill hundreds of enemy troops. That would be a suicide mission. Saint Oda has sent me on enough of those.

Voice commands from the Lunar officers rattle through our stolen helmets. "Remember this, and don't make me say it again," snaps a cold voice. "The natives sneak around. And they're quick. If it moves and it's not wearing a gray or black suit, shoot it. But the original order holds. If you see really good fighters, hand them over to me."

Her tone spurs something in me—recognition, perhaps? The Committee wants Wes so they can question him about the spy teammates he's sure to have on the Moon. I imagine they want to interrogate me about Dovetail, and about Mom, though I know next to nothing about the former topic and have slowly realized how ignorant I was about the latter. They'll torture me anyway, before they kill me in front of the few people I love.

Seeing my despairing expression, Wes lifts his chin and shakes his head: *No, we don't have to suffer that fate.*

He's too optimistic sometimes.

As we near the shoreline, we move behind the Pacifian battalion. In a desperate attempt to stop the soldiers from reaching the Odan hideout, Finley has taken shelter behind a tree. He blows darts into the seats of the Pacifians' unarmored pants as they pass. The victims swat at and scratch their behinds. Wes and I turn to each other and smile through our visors.

Wes beckons to his cousin. "C'mon, Fin."

We run to the beach. The snow isn't sticking here; the sand is too salty. But soon I'll need to adjust my movements to achieve greater traction.

Ahead of us, the Pacifians have tethered their submarines, ranging in size from three to thirty meters long, to large rocks. Half the vessels are being washed by waves, while half flounder in the sand. I watch the Pacifian soldiers guarding the area with narrowed eyes, wondering if we should simply board the submarines like true Lunar soldiers or take out the Pacifians first.

"Phaet, you handle this," Wes tells me, and I know from his tone that we'll try the first option. "I'll pretend to have a sprained ankle."

In my Lunar accent, I shout to the Pacifians, making my voice as deep as possible. "Hey! Injured soldier here!"

My shout is just a few decibels louder than a normal person's conversational voice, so I'm not surprised when only one soldier looks our way—a girl of average height. Supported by Finley, Wes walks forward, faking a limp.

"Three Lunar soldiers running back to Pacifia? That's not part of the plan," says the girl, clicking her tongue.

Her cloying voice turns my blood to ice. *Callisto Chi.* When we were in Militia together, her voice seemed friendly, even sweet—until the first time she tried to kill me. She would've finished the job on the day of Mom's trial if her mother, Base IV representative Andromeda Chi, hadn't revealed her secret Dovetail allegiance to her horrified daughter.

When I look down, I see that even though she's wearing a Pacifian uniform—maybe to mask her identity?—a Lunar utility belt cinches her middle. She lifts a small handheld detector to her face. "Three Militia troops, and no handscreens emitting a signal. Why would that be?"

Fuse, fizz, blast, and damn.

"Please, I need a Medic!" Wes begs in his fake Lunar accent. Because he's out of practice, every word is a struggle. "My arm's hurt, and the circulation's cut off—"

"Team! I've got a treat for you," Callisto calls, ignoring Wes. Her glee alarms me, as treachery is one of the few things that make her happy. "Get over here and take a look at this. Ready your Downers."

A massive male advances toward us, leading five more soldiers, who also wear Pacifian uniforms but carry Lunar weaponry. He holds his arms out stiffly to the side and carries two Lazies, as if one didn't have enough homicidal power. The weapons look comically small in his fists, each of which is the size of a baby's head. There's no question who this is: Jupiter, the privileged son of the General, and Callisto's sadistic boyfriend.

He's uncannily like his father; he liked to call me "little birdy," even as he slammed his massive fists into my body. Even as he tried to kill me during a practice fight. One night during Militia training, he and Callisto cornered me in a dark hallway and cut my legs to the bone with scimitars. And that was before I burned the General with his own laser blast.

Callisto cackles like she's never seen anything funnier. Her hand moves to her belt and closes around the grip of her Lazy.

"Look, team. Wes and Phaet brought a sidekick!"

I never expected high-ranking Militia officers like Callisto and Jupiter to cower on the shoreline while other Lunar and Pacifian soldiers did the real work of attacking Saint Oda. Now my old enemies and their cronies will capture Wes and me and kill Finley—unless we can take them out.

It's not likely; there are seven of them, only three of us. But I *want* to fight, want to hurt Callisto and Jupiter, the Committee's twisted darlings, as badly as they've hurt me. I feel my arms and legs itching for revenge. If I get my way, they'll never laugh at me and mine again.

19

THE BEACH BECOMES A BLUR OF ACTION, with Pacifia's concrete blocks and square windows as a backdrop. I hear the boom of the floating city's engines, interwoven with the factories' churning and screeching. The air smells thick and poisonous, like smoke and gasoline. As I begin to move, Pacifia's lights form yellow streaks in my vision. I duck to dodge Callisto's sedative-filled Downer and fire a laser at another soldier's outstretched hand. Callisto can't shoot anything more dangerous if she wants to capture me alive.

Beside me, Wes isn't so lucky. He twists to avoid a pellet, but it grazes his elbow, surrounding the joint with ropes of electricity. The Militia jacket's fabric is an insulator, but it's not strong enough to withstand this level of shock. Wes's hiss of pain catches Finley's attention, and the younger boy turns, exposing his front to enemy fire.

I toss a dagger, which sinks into another soldier's unarmored hip. As he lets out a scream, I wince as if the dagger had hit me.

Move on. He's an enemy.

At that moment, a streak of violet light from Callisto's Lazy hits Finley in the chest.

"Run, Fin!" Wes shouts.

Finley's stolen armor will protect him until the laser burns through. But instead of moving, he stares in horror at the point of impact, where the armor on his chest is beginning to glow orange. Callisto keeps her finger on the trigger, her visor obscuring what I imagine is a slowly spreading smile.

Three seconds later, the boy wobbles on his feet. Another second, and the wind blows him backward onto the sand.

* * *

It was so easy for her. She killed him, and it was nothing. As the laser burrowed through Finley's armor, I felt his life leave the shoreline. Like Belinda, like Mom, he died at the pull of a trigger. And like them, he never hurt his killer, never even scratched her skin.

I'm going to fight for this boy, though he'll never know it. Fighting won't bring him back, but it'll take away the numbness, the cold inside me.

"Fin!" Wes sprints forward and drives his dagger up and under my latest victim's chest plate. Then he rushes at Callisto, his blade dark with blood.

Callisto stands frozen in place, but I can't tell if it's the cold night or the weight of her actions that's paralyzed her. Her head hangs down as if the helmet is too heavy for her neck. Wes is so close—

Jupiter's lumbering form knocks him sideways.

A Downer glances off my back armor. I twist around to find some idiot private running at me. When he's a meter and a half away, I execute a forward roll to the side, hook my foot around his shin, and yank him down. His head cracks against a rock—not even his helmet can protect him from such an impact.

Immediately, I'm back on my feet, dagger in hand, and running toward Wes, who's grappling with both Jupiter and Callisto. Callisto mostly hides behind Jupiter. At such close range, Wes forces them to drop their guns and engage in hand-to-hand combat, which they don't seem to have practiced since our Militia training days. Wes darts between them, lunging and swiping like a manic animal. Nothing but their armor can stop him from killing them, but will he? Can he murder? The Wes I know is too good for that, but I've never truly feared him until now.

One of the two remaining underlings heads for Wes; the other tries to sneak up behind me. I hear his boots crunch on the wet sand, and I turn and throw my last dagger into his groin. As he looks down, wondering what clipped him, I dash forward, grab the dagger's hilt, and yank upward. Hot blood spatters my hand.

Without thinking, I throw the dagger at the soldier running for Wes. It burrows into the back of his neck. He flops forward and lies lifeless on the sand.

What have I done? What will I do?

The knife—I have to get it. It's lodged in my third victim's body. Dead body. Dead, because of me.

I reach him. My knees hit wet sand.

I hear Umbriel's singsong in my head: *Beater, Beater, the blood gets sweeter.* He used to chant the Lunar children's rhyme, which mocked violent, power-drunk Militia members. I may be fighting Militia Beaters now, but that doesn't make me any better than they are.

I wiggle the dagger out of the dead man's flesh with the same care Mom used when tweezing a splinter from my seven-year-old palm. But I can't bring myself to remove the soldier's helmet and look at his face. A face that was loved by a mother, a father, a friend—a face I don't want to see in my dreams for the rest of my life.

"Phaet!" shouts a familiar voice. Wes. I've been kneeling here too long. I look up in time to see him smash a sizable rock into Jupiter's chest armor, denting the plates. As I rise to my feet, Wes runs, feints, and side-kicks Callisto, felling her.

What's wrong with her? She doesn't fight back as Wes repeatedly kicks her in the stomach. Her movements are so lan-
guid, it's like she's sleepwalking. Maybe the guilt caught up to
her too. Maybe she's "soft" like me.

Wes isn't hitting to kill. Yet.

"How could you?" he shouts. Callisto stops moving, lies
limp on the snow-dusted sand. "My *cousin*! He never hurt you.
He wasn't ever in a real fight! You're *filthy*, you're *worthless*—"

But Jupiter barrels into Wes, knocking him to the ground.
They wrestle, Wes's knife-hand strikes to Jupiter's neck seeming
to have no effect. With his legs, Wes tries and fails to push his
attacker off of him.

"Damn you!" Jupiter bellows into Wes's face. "Don't touch
my girl!"

"Phaet!" Wes hollers. "Get him!"

I jam my dagger into the holes in Jupiter's armor: behind
the knees and elbows, the upper thigh. Finally, it's enough. Wes
pushes Jupiter away and launches into a limping run toward
a nearby submarine, bigger and better camouflaged than the
Tourmalinian one we used to reach Battery Bay. Blood trickles
onto his white skin from a decimeter-long scratch on the side of
his face, blood I want to wipe away.

For a moment, I stare at the dark stains he leaves on the
white sand. Then I sprint after him, every square centimeter of
my skin tingling. I don't feel like myself—my body has become
a charged chemical soup.

The hatch on the nearest submarine is locked. "Agh!" I holler,
pounding on the metal.

A clicking sound as a bolt slides open.

Even as I lift the hatch and help Wes climb in, we hear Jupiter's footfalls behind us.

20

THE PACIFIANS LEFT A HELMSMAN IN THE submarine to make pickup. He's on the round side, with a patchy blond beard and a bald spot on the back of his head. He sits in a small nook, his behind propped up by a black cushion. His head nearly touches the low ceiling, which is crossed by bluish fluorescent lights that make everyone's skin look pasty.

"Mutineers!" cries the helmsman, taking his hands off the tarnished analog gauges he's been adjusting.

Grabbing an exposed, rusty pipe for balance, Wes stumbles into a seat by one of the oval windows. He sucks in breath as he yanks something shiny—a knife—out of his shin.

"Pacifia!" I shout at the helmsman, pointing my bloody dagger at the floating city.

"Wha—"

I hold the dagger to his throat. "Go!"

Hands shaking, the helmsman pushes the submarine off the beach and submerges us beneath the black water. I sit by Wes, but face the cockpit to make sure we stay on course.

Wes has pulled the submarine's medical kit off the wall. He efficiently disinfects his leg wound and binds it, wrestling with the tape. I dip my finger in the gooey disinfectant and, with a shaking hand, rub it into the cut on his cheek.

"Thanks. Jupiter pulled a knife," Wes says. "I should have anticipated that—I was so angry, so stupid." His face contorts in shame.

"At least you punished Callisto."

"She hardly put up a fight. Maybe she felt bad for . . . for Fin." He looks out the window. "Did anyone hurt you?"

I shake my head. My skin feels scratched up, and my muscles are sore, but neither will handicap me—not like my guilt will. "They didn't hurt me. But I killed two of them."

"Oh, Phaet." He raises his hand and catches mine with it. My finger is shiny from the antibacterial cream. "Your first kill . . ."

I couldn't even lift their visors to see their faces.

"I'm as bad as the Committee," I blurt. "Who were they? What were their names? Back on the beach, I didn't even care."

"They would've sent you the same way as Fin if you hadn't—"

"Don't try to make me feel better." I take my hand out of his, and Wes falls silent. I immediately regret snapping at him. I turn away, but instead of leaving me to stew, Wes hugs me tight. It's a kindness I don't deserve. Tears pool in my eyes; I blink once, allowing a few to fall.

"You're still coming on board Pacifia?" I gesture at his leg.

He looks surprised. "I wouldn't miss the opportunity to see another architectural wonder of the twenty-third century. Battery Bay, now Pacifia—soon I can call myself a seasoned globe-trotter."

"If you can't run . . . if you can barely walk, let alone fight . . ."

"I have to. I'll get you on your way home, and then experiment until I can disrupt the attacking battalion's chain of command. Either take out some higher-ups—remember, the General's camped out on Pacifia—or grenade the control tower. My leg isn't that bad. Remember your arm the day we left Base IV? We've fought through worse together."

"Thanks for watching my back," I say.

"You've always done the same for me. Nothing will happen to us, all right?"

"I'd like to believe it."

The submarine's interior vibrates with a series of sudden clangs and clashes, interrupting our conversation. We've arrived. Metal arms lift us into Pacifia's underbelly, where the gray walls crawl with tan barnacles and the water is slick with spent diesel. *Our reception at Battery Bay was far more glamorous,* I think sarcastically. There, we had uniformed escorts—albeit ones that were threatening to deport us—and a whole entourage of glittering followers. Even the trash in the water was shiny.

We rise into one of many submarine-sized rectangular pools in the vast indoor port. Dim overhead lighting illuminates the sickliest tones of every object. Pacifian and Lunar soldiers scurry across the pathways connecting the hundreds of docking stations, skidding into row formation. Even as we watch, many of the troops hop into other submarines. *Blast—reinforcements.*

I push Wes from the hatch. Before I exit the vessel, I shoot a Downer into the helmsman's neck. *Sorry,* I say to him in my mind.

The room smells as ugly as it looks. The slime molds growing between the rectangular, puce-colored floor tiles give off a sour stench. A family of brown rats nests in the corner nearest us. The skin on the back of my neck crawls at the sight, and I swallow bile to keep from retching.

A second submarine docks beside ours, even though there are scores of stations to choose from. *Jupiter.* It has to be. He made good time. Wes and I run once more, blending into a crowd of mixed Pacifian and Lunar soldiers before Jupiter can disembark and spot us. Leaping from his craft, he consults his handheld radiation detector, though it won't help him find us, because our handscreens have been disconnected.

Looking back, I watch as he raises his head, scans his surroundings, and then takes off in the opposite direction, toward another group in which a returning Lunar soldier is doing a worse job than Wes of hiding his limp.

When our group passes a square doorway, Wes and I duck inside. He leans against a wall, standing only on his good leg.

"Is that your version of 'it doesn't hurt so bad'?" I say.

"When I stand like this, I only dirty one shoe at a time." He's joking, but he's also trying not to sound annoyed. "Stop worrying about me, Phaet. I'm *fine*."

I nod, resolving not to ask about his leg again. "Then let's go."

"Don't fall too far behind." Wes grins before jogging lopsidedly down the corridor.

* * *

From the maps we've seen, the naval docks sit at the center and bottom of Pacifia, and a cross section of the city's floor plan looks like an elongated U. The aviation and space center is located high on the stern, so that exhaust from takeoffs doesn't settle into the U's base, where population density is highest.

Along with about twenty other soldiers, Wes and I board a cubic monorail car. It takes us up to the naval compound's entrance, which is accessible from the Pacifian streets. The soldiers disperse, probably to carry out assignments on the floating city itself.

"Where are we meeting your Sanctuarist friends?" I whisper to Wes.

"I don't think anyone else made it to Pacifia." His voice sounds dead. "They must be putting out fires and protecting the shelter."

Except for the military's hustling, the area is strangely silent. Clumsy orange streetlights line narrow walkways between identical concrete buildings. Only about 20 percent of the windows are lit. Through the metal bars installed on the first-floor windows, I see dingy rooms with cloth-covered furniture and cracks in the walls. In one home, three children warm their hands over a gas stove on the living room floor. Occasionally, I catch a burst of beauty—a bunch of dried flowers, a child's sketch of an owl. They remind me of my hidden moss garden in my family's old apartment.

The Militia has surely destroyed my moss by now. Sadness lands on my heart like dust motes. For a time, those little plants were all the beauty I had.

Our feet kick up soot as we run to the civilian monorail station, and I taste the smoke particles in the air. Three Pacifians, all wearing dusky brown, blue, or gray, wait for the next late-night ride. No colorful clothing or private hovercraft here. This city lacks the vigor of Battery Bay, the vigor that comes with endless activity, the movement of people and their clashing opinions.

One of the Pacifians, a sweaty middle-aged man, registers our presence but seems unsurprised; a glance and then he goes back to staring lasciviously at the young woman beside him. She's pretty, with a high nose and pointed chin, but soot and sleeplessness pinch her features. If she had the Batterer vlogger's 3-D clothing pen, I imagine she'd sketch a veil to cover her face. But she can only brush her tangled dark hair in front of her eyes and grip her daughter's arm more tightly. Her hand relaxes the slightest bit when she notices Wes and me.

The monorail arrives, and we board. Dirt coats our car's square windows. The metal floor is so filthy that the occasional drop of blood falling from Wes's pant leg blends right in.

We have no Pacifian money, but I remember from Primary that Pacifia is . . . different from most places. The government collects 80 percent of an average citizen's income, and redistributes that wealth as food rations, transportation, education, and other public goods.

"Stupid," my Earth Studies teacher commented. "Capitalism laid waste to the Earth and left developing countries' economies in the dust. So Pacifia encouraged other city-states to try communism, as several Earthbound states did in the twentieth century. The government guarantees people their survival, but where is their motive to improve? If people don't retain their earnings, why even work? There is about a zero-point-one correlation between their economic output and returns from the government."

What my teacher said seems to hold true for Pacifia: the people here don't seem to benefit from their labor. I press my helmet to the window, looking at the sorry streets, the flickering lights, the gray apartment buildings that rise above and fall away below us. We pass a final gray block, and I catch my breath. On our left is a vast city square of red brick. In its center is the Pacifian alliance's symbol: a white fist punching a yellow sun. At the far end, two rows of soldiers stand at attention before a five-tier scarlet building hundreds of meters tall. Each tier is marked by a sloped golden roof that tilts upward at the corners. The hexagonal tower must house the government offices.

When my amazement wears off, anger sets in. Pacifia's poor live crowded up against this grand plaza. From their underheated homes, they can see the shiny paint and relative cleanliness; likewise, the officials in the tower can see the squalor in which their people dwell. At least the bases are more discreet about social inequality. There, the wealthiest people live walled off from everyone else, as I did in my captain's apartment.

But perhaps the contrast only shows how much Lunars like hiding things.

Beyond the square, darkness descends again. As we pass over a cluster of smokestacks, my nostrils burn; I smell acid and a sickly splash of bleach. The woman and child get off at the next stop; the creepy man slinks away at the one after. Wes and I ride the monorail until the last stop, where the stench of smoke is replaced with something else.

Wes sniffs the air. "Beautiful. Spaceship grease."

"We're in our element at last," I say, feeling lighter.

Wearing half smiles, we tear into the aerospace complex. Soldiers hustle through motion-sensor doors, tracking mud across the scarlet floor tiles. The walls are buttercup yellow, with painted images of a fat white fist punching upward every dozen meters or so. Black disk-shaped lamps hang from the ceiling.

Because the main hallway has the most foot traffic, Wes and I pick that one to jog through. Hopefully, we'll find a hangar or runway at the other end. I hear his breath hitch with every other step, and my ghost of a smile vanishes.

If the Committee sent only Base IV Militia to deal with Saint Oda, as Lazarus said, I can board any Lunar ship and know I'll end up in my home city. What's essential is picking a good hiding spot and selecting a vessel that'll get there quickly. Without access to flight plans, I'll have to eavesdrop until we find out which vessels are suitable, and then sneak on board while no one's watching.

We run through the last set of doors and back into the smog outside. The runways buzz with ships taking off, landing, taxiing. Up close, the command center no longer looks like a toothpick. It's a tower eighty meters tall, covered in flashing red and yellow lights.

The first ship is fewer than a hundred meters away. *Go, go, go!* I tell myself. But Wes starts to fall behind, and I can't help but slow down for him.

"Don't mind me!" He's more hopping on one foot than running. "You're the only one who needs to . . . Oh, *fuse.*"

Some distance away, an enormous figure faces us, holding an Electrostun in each outstretched hand.

"No!" I shout. The soldier can't really be aiming at us, not when we're so close. I can almost smell the greenhouses' black soil, the coffee in the Market Department, the sweetness of my sister's hair. The place I must go to set things right. Home.

My cry falls on ears that welcome my pain. The mountain of a soldier addresses us. "Kappa, Theta, stop right there."

21

HOW DID JUPITER FIND US? OR GET TO THE runways before we did?

He holsters one Electrostun and holds up a metal device the size and shape of a tarantula. "It's a damn pain not to have the LPS tracking you guys. Not that it would work on Earth—they don't call it the 'Lunar Positioning System' for nothing. But the Pacifians have had a GPS satellite around here for a long time, and these gizmos can follow anything that moves. I just"—Jupiter tosses the bug at Wes's helmet, and it adheres upon impact—"stuck one on Kappa's back armor. You guys didn't even notice. Who's clever now, Fat?"

I slip behind Wes to see if it's true. Jupiter's right: we were stupid. I knock the ugly curled thing off Wes's armor with the butt of my Lazy.

"Two things." Wes looks unfazed. "First, my name's not Kappa and hers isn't Fat. Second, how'd you get up here so fast?"

Good. Wes will keep Jupiter talking while I find a way out.

Delighted at having outsmarted us twice, Jupiter answers without hesitation. "My Pygmette." He points at the little space speeder twenty meters behind him. "Dad let me dock it in the Titan we brought—"

A small figure runs toward us. "Sergeant Jupiter, sir!" calls a girl's shrill voice.

I snort. Last I knew, Jupiter was just a corporal; his father must have used his influence to bump him up to the position Wes abdicated when he fled the Moon. *The Militia's as corrupt as ever.* No surprises there.

The girl slows to a trot and stops, lifting her visor. I hold back a gasp. Eri Pi, my classmate from training. The day Wes and I left the Moon, she warned us that the General was on our tail. The favor was probably more for Wes's sake than mine. She's crushed on him since they were in upper-level Primary, and she doesn't care who knows it. I'm so startled to see a friendly face that I simply gape at her from beneath my helmet.

"Can't you see I'm busy?" Jupiter snaps.

"Sir, you look concerned. Anything I can do to help?"

"Fizz off. I've got prisoners here."

Eri's sharp nose twitches with curiosity. She walks closer. "Prisoners? But they're Militia."

"Eri . . ." Wes mumbles, just loud enough for Eri to hear.

Eri's mouth spreads into a smile that takes up the entire bottom half of her face. Strands of orange hair, fiery as a burning city, escape from her helmet and blow across her pale forehead. Her yellow-green eyes scrunch up, and she looks so beautiful that for a moment I'm not even jealous. I can imagine how pleasantly surprised she must be to see Wes (and me?) alive. But doesn't she know how dangerous a smile for Wes could be? At least the silly girl's back is to Jupiter.

A faint whine sounds from above. I check the sky—nothing.

Jupiter lifts his visor and glares at Eri. Even in the dim light, his face looks purple with frustration. "Damn it, help me shoot them or leave me the fuzz alone, you—"

An explosion overtakes my senses. Heat flattens us in waves. I fling myself down onto the runway and throw my hands over my head; even so, I see red behind my eyelids.

"Unmanned Batterer aircraft!" someone shouts. "And there's more coming!"

Another explosion tosses me a decimeter into the air. I flop like a sea slug when I land; my chin clanks on concrete, and my molars cleave through my tongue, spilling salty blood into my mouth. But my discomfort can't shake the wonder off my face.

I turn my head toward Koré Island and see lights of every color dancing in the backdrop. The island is now dwarfed by floating cities on both its north and south flanks. I hear the whine of a hundred or more drones, hidden in the clouds and circling above Saint Oda, and the distant echoes of the blasts that are painting the islands in red and orange. The scene awes me with its sick beauty—the sun rising over the sea, again and again, taunting us with the promise of morning.

Battery Bay's referendum passed. The floating city's forces are here, and that means we—and Saint Oda along with us— are no longer prisoners awaiting execution.

I close my eyes, rub them hard, and open them again. Nothing's changed.

Next to me, Wes breathes, "Thank God."

*　　*　　*

No more explosions on Pacifia after the first two strikes. The command center, once a tower rising from the aerospace compound, has been stripped of its top few floors. It leans to one side, handicapped.

Jupiter's unconscious. Kneeling at his side, Eri pulls a dart from the back of his neck, lobs it across the runway, and holsters her tranquilizing gun. She must have popped him while he was distracted by the drone strike.

Is this the same Eri who cried when she got a blister on her foot? She's changed since Militia training. Her face is tougher; her squeamishness has faded. She hasn't even giggled yet.

"Thanks," I say. "You didn't have to do this."

"It's not a big deal," Eri says. "*Sergeant* Jupiter will think the drone-quakes knocked him out, and then be too embarrassed to own up to it."

"Aren't you worried someone saw?" Wes asks.

"Who has time to worry these days?" Eri says. "I just *do*."

I look out over the ocean and see a host of Pacifian boats, submarines, and planes leaving Saint Oda. It looks like the Pacifians are redirecting their efforts, attacking Battery Bay and defending their home city.

"You're risking everything." Wes shakes his head, bewildered. *"Why?"*

Eri removes her helmet and shakes out her sunburst hair. I remember it being shorn close to her head; it falls to her chin now. *She needs to tie it back before her superiors catch her.* But the Militia's hairstyle protocol is probably the last thing on her mind.

"Well, I heard they were trying to kill you," Eri says. "And I don't want any of my friends to die ever again. So I studied terrestrial protocol real hard and got assigned to Earth." She swallows. "At least . . . I *thought* you were my friend, Wes, after all the time we spent patrolling together. Why didn't you tell me you were from Earth?"

Wes bows his head.

Eri smiles briefly, as if in spite of herself. "I'd never have hurt you, even if I knew the truth."

"I'm sorry," he says in earnest.

He shouldn't apologize; he had every reason to keep his identity secret. I press my lips together to keep from scowling.

Eri looks up at Wes with pleading, watery eyes; flashes of longing shimmer in them. "I wish you'd trusted me. Because I really, really like you. I thought you knew that."

Wes looks bewildered. He had to have known she had feelings for him, but maybe he didn't expect her to confess them, and not in this way. "But you said your parents had already made plans for you, before you even joined Militia . . ."

"So what if they tried to set me up with some colonel's son? They didn't care if I *liked* him; they just thought I wasn't smart enough or strong enough to make a living any other way. But you've had my whole heart since tenth-year Primary . . . Wes, are you even listening to me?"

My eyes dart to him. He's trying to watch Eri, but he repeatedly looks at the flames engulfing his city, breathing hard. "Sorry, I'm listening but not really looking, if that makes sense."

I knew Eri's family was wealthy, but not that they were cruel or old-fashioned. All Lunar citizens are encouraged to support themselves, but a few women still rely on their partners for their survival. If Eri married someone successful from another well-to-do family, she could take an easy, low-paying job and never worry about money. Looking at her now, I wonder if she fell for Wes—a Base IV outsider—partly because he was the opposite of the society boy her parents wanted.

Eri faces me. "Phaet, maybe *you'd* understand why I joined Dovetail. By the time Militia training ended, I was already sick of doing everything people told me to do. But your mom's trial pushed me over the edge. She woke up the rebel in me. I decided to join mostly for me—but also partly for *him*." She looks sideways at Wes, who turns around, looking guilty. "Because I saw you fighting next to Phaet that final day, and I knew you'd taken their side. But . . . but as soon as I made up my mind to be a Dovetailer, you left. Without saying good-bye."

I frown, pitying her but also admiring her. Eri traveled to an alien landscape and risked her life for a *boy*? She didn't even have proof that he liked her back. Maybe this is what self-less love looks like. But it only makes Wes uncomfortable. He squirms, looking at the space above Eri's head instead of making eye contact.

"I wanted to prove to you that I'm not some stupid, giggly girl." Eri's speech speeds up. "That I can help you like you've always helped me."

She takes his arm. His body seizes up, but she holds on tight. Watching them, I find myself wishing I were half as brave as her. Eri's heart has walls as clear as glass. Mine? Iron castings to hide the sludge of emotions inside.

"I'm telling you all this because"—she inhales—"I thought . . . it might be nice to hear that someone loves you, when there's so much hate going around."

Several seconds pass. Wes blinks in confusion before step-ping forward. "Oh, Eri," he says, hugging her. Part of me seethes with jealousy—until he pulls away, and I realize that the em-brace was one of mercy, not passion.

"I'm honored, and flattered, and I wish I could do you jus-tice. You'll make a wonderful companion for . . . for some other lucky fellow."

Eri wipes away a tear, laughing and crying all at once. "I wish you weren't so *nice* about all this. Can't you just say no to my f—"

"*Hey!*" A Beetle, wearing the gold computer chip insignia of a sergeant, runs toward us. "We need more people on the ground. What are you three standing around for?"

"Sir! Yes, sir!" Wes hollers back.

"Eri," I whisper, "find us a ship."

Eri's eyes glint with determination—and, perhaps, animosity toward me. *Can I trust her when Wes isn't around? Or am I imagining things?*

"Yes, Captain," Eri says. Her expression gives nothing away.

*   *   *

"This one!" Eri leads us to a midsize omnibus. "I'm on air crew here, because they decided I was too much of a sissy for ground combat. We weren't expecting so many injuries during the assault. This ship's taking forty people who need medical treatment back to Base IV in the morning."

"Go on up." Wes doesn't look at me. His eyes are fixed on the omnibus; his expression flickers from distaste to longing and back again. That's how I know the sight of it is wringing his heart dry. "This is where I leave you."

My stomach twists as we reach the ladder leading into the ship's belly.

"You're not coming?" Eri cries. "But Wes, Dovetail needs you!"

"Lunars, Pacifians, and now the Batterers are reducing my city to an ash heap." Wes looks over his shoulder at Saint Oda. The flames enveloping the mountains cast one side of his face in orange light. "This is the second time I've seen my home destroyed. I'm going to help get people to safety. As long as some of Saint Oda stays alive, we'll return. We'll build a new city with the ashes if we have to."

He's regal, with his straight back and determined expression, and tattered, with the wound on his cheek, the moving shadows under his eyes and jaw. I study him, burning his image into my memory. This is how I want to remember him. It'll have to suffice until we meet again.

"I only got to see you for three minutes, and you're already going away again," Eri says. She punches him in the shoulder.

"Don't think I'll forget you helped us," Wes tells Eri.

"All right, Stripes." Eri nudges my arm. "Let's sneak you onto this ship."

"Ten more seconds," I say, glancing at Wes.

Frowning, Eri looks from me to Wes and back again. I want to dive under the ship and hide, but I meet her gaze. *Please, please understand,* I beg with my eyes. It seems to work. Disappointment and resignation cross her face. She shuffles to the ladder and begins to climb.

I step into Wes's open arms and hold him so tightly our helmets clack together. Beneath the scents of metallic blood and stinging smoke, I smell on him fresh pine, pure rainwater—these things on Earth that I've grown to love.

"Good-bye," I whisper. What else can I say? Should I throw a sweeping declaration at him? Speak words like Eri's?

"Just for now," he says. "Phaet."

Because I don't know how else to get my feelings out, I kiss his cheek. It's rough, like sandpaper.

As I pull back, shaking, I don't open my eyes. I'm too scared to see what he's thinking.

His hands remove my helmet. His fingers brush sweaty hair away from my forehead.

I feel the warmth of his breath on my face.

Our lips touch, long before I'm ready. Our surroundings fall away, leaving me, and him, and our happiness, alone. We press our faces together, wrap our arms around each other, commit to memory everything we can about this moment—before the time comes to let it all go.

22

THE WALLS OF THE CRATE ARE COMING closer, and I'm sweating as if someone's snuck a slice of sun inside the cargo hold with me. My thoughts make for unpleasant company; they distort the space and generate heat of their own.

With a sorry little smile, Eri stuck me into this empty metal container, which had been filled with the preserved food that the crew consumed on the six-hour trip from Base IV to Pacifia. I don't know how long I've been floating, weightless. There's no room to stretch my legs and nothing to eat or drink—but what does it matter, when I'm feeling too green to swallow? My head fills up with blood, because my heart thinks it must still work against gravity.

My heart. *Wes.* We felt the same way about each other all along.

The euphoria lasts until I realize that with that kiss, we've acknowledged the hold we have over each other's lives. We can't take that back. In the midst of war, with our families clinging to life, we've declared some sort of allegiance to each another. But like Murray and Lazarus, one of us is staying on Earth while the other flies off to the Moon. Will we inherit their misery?

Murray. An image of her scarred face, her sparking eyes, seems to fill the container. Have I seen her for the last time? Does a half-blind girl with a frayed mind stand a chance if she's caught in the cross fire of the battle I left behind?

May her god keep her safe. It's not enough, but it's all I can wish for.

And again, Wes occupies my mind. On the runway, I lost control—*we* lost control.

Now more blood rushes to my face.

Think about something else, something that's important, Wes would tell me.

If Yinha were here, she'd add, *Yeah, you want to pop an artery?* Finley.

No, don't think about Finley. Or the soldiers on the shore. They were enemies, but I'm sure they didn't want to fight any more than I did. I haven't gotten over Mom, Belinda, and my friend Vinasa—why add more people to the list of those I must mourn?

My forehead pounds, and rage simmers within me. *Anka and Cygnus could be next.* I'm going back to help them, but I can't guarantee their safety.

When will it end?

Focus.

Yes, but on what?

Not Wes, not on the dead or on the fate of Saint Oda. It wouldn't be wise to cry and congest my sinuses in zero-g. Determined to occupy my mind, I pick a practical topic, an issue that has chafed my brain since the first drone strike: Why has Battery Bay decided to start a war with Pacifia?

With Pacifia's outright attack and Wes's unprecedented offer of oil and aid, perhaps the Batterers saw the island as fair game. Parliament can always call their involvement another attempt to protect the weak from Pacifian malice.

"Get enough Earthbound politicians together," my Earth Studies teacher always said, "and they'll find a way to justify anything."

That statement applies to *any* celestial body's politicians. The Committee must have its reasons too for allying the Moon with Pacifia, far beyond my capture—they've put in too much effort.

Does the Committee see the Batterer bloc as a threat to their rule? Do they fear another democratization attempt? Or do they want revenge for the one thirty years ago? The Committee loathes anyone who asks them to change. When my mother pointed out the bases' flaws, they poisoned her, tossed her in Penitentiary, and put a laser through her head. It was nothing to them—*she* was nothing.

There's a familiar surge of anger. I let it come. I will make sure the Committee remembers and regrets what they did. But how?

My temples pound. Until I have more facts, all this cognitive effort is a waste. I need to find whatever Dovetail members I can and bombard them with questions.

I'm not sweating anymore—in fact, it's gotten terribly cold—but too much blood is still rushing to my head. Dizzy and exhausted, I doze off, using nothing but air as a mattress.

*　　*　　*

With a *whoosh*, the lid to the crate opens into an unlit part of the Defense hangar. Thank the sun and stars, I once again know which way is up.

"Welcome home," Eri whispers, leaning over the crate. The skin around her eyes is pink and puffy; she's been crying. *Get it together*, I wish I could say. There are times for feeding a broken heart, but the middle of a smuggling operation isn't one of them.

I attempt to stand. My limbs feel so *heavy*, I end up sitting where I was, with a sorer tailbone.

"Let me help. We have to be quick." Eri grabs my wrists, tugs me up, and flips my visor down. She's behaving like a mother or an older sister, despite what happened between Wes and me on the Pacifian runway. Did she see us? Regardless, her goodness makes me regret my impatience with her. I lost Mom, and I don't know if I've lost Murray, but somehow I've found another person who will care for me.

And Anka's waiting.

Eri slides her visor down and leads me away from the ship. Together, we jog toward the hangar's exit, her left hand in her pocket to cover her handscreen's audio receptors. Out of habit, I mirror her gesture, even though disconnecting the handscreen from my blood flow has rendered its every function useless.

"Sorry you were in there for so long," Eri says as we duck behind another ship. "I had to wait until they moved us away from the unloading slot. More ships came in, and they ended up putting this one further back, into storage."

Through her visor, I can see her eyes. They look at everything but me. "I'm sorry, Eri," I say.

Her smile turns to a grimace. "For what? Let's not start fighting over nothing." She strides away from me and ducks behind another ship without looking back.

I follow, concerned about the passive-aggressiveness in her body language.

"Okay, you did kiss the guy I've liked for years just a minute after he rejected me." With her flat tone, Eri might as well be talking about what she had for lunch. But that doesn't mean she's not angry. "And I never saw it coming, since you pretended you didn't care about him. For all I knew, you thought of him as your personal trainer, but you were really too scared and emotionally constipated to admit how you felt. Both you and Wes lied to me, Stripes."

Hearing my old nickname stings. "I should've been honest back in training."

Eri finally raises her voice. "Didn't I just say that?" she snaps. "I didn't want to hurt anyone."

Awkward silence stretches between us. Then Eri's expression softens, and her eyes meet mine. "What am I talking about? This is ridiculous."

Again, I wait for the silence to grow uncomfortable—and she elaborates, as I'd hoped.

"I used to think that just because I wanted him so much, he'd want me too."

I think of the time in training when she bought two-hundred-Sputnik boots on the spur of the moment. "Are you used to getting what you want?"

Eri chews her bottom lip. "Maybe. Nothing really got in my way when I was a kid." I don't reply, and again she keeps talking. "I mean, I had a supercomfortable life. Whenever I met people through my family, they wanted to be my friends."

"Why do you think that was?"

"My father's the Primary Education Superintendent. Makes it hard to tell whether people really like me or not."

I gape at her. Her dad runs the Base IV school system for everyone under age eighteen; as an administrator, he has direct contact with the Committee and a hefty salary to match.

"But you know, Wes didn't give a nuke's fart who my dad was. Or what people thought of him. He did his own thing. It's why he's special to me. Now I know that he was too busy trying to save the world—literally—to think about all that."

I underestimated her, thinking she was shallowly infatuated with Wes's looks and fighting ability. Suddenly, I regret that I didn't try to get to know her better during Militia training.

"I see why he picked you, Stripes. You're the one girl who

can keep up with him. I'll stop being mad at you, eventually. I think. I can't hate someone Wes cares about."

I feel as if I've ducked a punch that was never thrown. *Could I have forgiven her if Wes had rejected me?* "I—thanks."

She cuts me off with a nonchalant wave of her hand. "Whatever. Neither of us can be with him now, so let's look out for him and his people together. That sound all right?"

I nod. "Even from a few hundred thousand kilometers away."

Eri gives me a quick hug, and once again, I'm filled with admiration for her.

"What happened to the Odans after you hid me?" I ask.

Eri looks around the corner, checking to make sure the corridor is empty. Then we break cover and move toward the exit. "The battle wrapped up quickly. The Militia and the Pacifians couldn't figure out how to break into the Odan hideout without getting zapped; there was some kind of electrical cannon hidden up on the mountain."

I smile, a wave of relief passing over me. The Sanctuarists must have weaponized the electrochemical battery in the Carlyles' basement. "The Odans in the hideout . . ."

"Their caves and farms got wrecked, but most people should be okay. They ran for Battery Bay when the enemy started pulling back. But I think a lot of people made it."

Longing burns in me like a sore muscle. *Wes and his family escaped, surely.*

"*All* the people?"

Eri sighs. "Check your hopes, Phaet. We set Saint Oda on fire."

23

AFTER ERI LEAVES ME, I SET OFF FOR SHELTER, Anka, and Umbriel. But I must take a new route, because wandering about the base's closely monitored hallways, even with the lights off, is sheer idiocy. I'd be asking for capture and torture—the Cygnus treatment.

After some careful searching, I find a Sanitation manhole in a remote corner of the hangar, slip my thumb into Wes's fake fingerprint sleeve, and press the digit to a tiny groove in the floor. The manhole cover slides back, revealing the tunnel beneath, and I jump in feetfirst. Even as the stench of bleach mixed with sweat and feces hits my nose, I feel immensely powerful. Almost free. Not a soul knows my blood pressure, body temperature, heart rate, or hormone levels. They can't hear what I'm saying or follow where I'm going. In the dark sewers, I'm invisible. To the eavesdroppers, the Medics, the Militia, and every other person on Base IV who would care, Phaet Theta is in limbo, neither alive nor dead.

It's an eerie freedom, though, and a limited one. The rare security pods in the tunnels could still record my movements. And a stray nighttime worker might think it awfully strange to find a Beetle wandering the tunnels. With these thoughts in mind, I tiptoe carefully—when all I want to do is run. Scum sticks to the bottoms of my boots, and they squelch with every step.

I keep the Sanctuarists' maps in my mind as I approach Shelter.

A few dozen meters from my destination under the dome, the Sanitation lane ends at a sealed door. I tap my knuckles on the impenetrable block of metal, unwilling to believe it's real.

The Committee probably sealed Shelter off, to keep Dovetail sympathizers from sneaking in and out.

I push the metal door, throwing all my weight behind my hands. Then I ram my shoulder against it—once, twice, three times. Tears spring to my eyes, not because of the pain, but because I'm so close to Anka and Umbriel. To feeling my sister's wispy black hair against my cheek; to the old security of my best friend's arms.

I hold back shouts of frustration. At such a high-security juncture, anyone or anything could be listening. I tiptoe back the way I came and find a meter-high door in the tunnel wall. It opens into a closet used to store cleaning supplies. There's just enough room for me to curl into a ball on the floor, shut the door against surveillance, shut my heart against sorrow, and plan my next move.

*   *   *

"High knees!" someone's shouting on the floor above me. "They should reach your chest with every step!"

After a brief rest in the maintenance closet, I set off for the Defense complex to look for other members of Dovetail. From my conversation with Lazarus, I've guessed that Shelter serves as the organization's home base, but Defense houses several of their moles, one of whom I'm sure is on my side.

On Saint Oda, I studied the Sanctuarists' maps of Base IV until my mind could reproduce my home city dome by dome. I know more now than I did when I lived here, and it's paying off. I find my point of exit from the tunnels by listening for Yinha's Militia-instructor roar. A smile creeps across my face as I remember how much she once intimidated me.

"Sixty more seconds until your lunch break! Is that motivation enough for you? Those knees better touch the *ceiling!*"

After a minute, a timer buzzes in the training dome, and the trainees dash out to get food. Hoping I'm making the right move, I press the fake fingerprint sleeve to a groove in the wall, and the circle of floor beneath my feet rises like an elevator, lifting me up to the training dome. I surface in the shadow of the rock climbing wall. With my helmet's visor down, I peek out and see that thin frame, those severe features, the hair slicked back in a bun.

Yinha's berating two abashed trainees. "I've seen vines creep faster than those feet of yours!" she shouts.

It's her, it's really her! Yinha Rho, my teacher and friend. She egged me on and kept me strong when all I wanted to do was wallow in pain and frustration. But she also kept her involvement with Dovetail a secret from me—I'm not sure she even knows I'm aware of it. I can needle her about it later. Right now, I need to slip back under her wing. I break cover and approach.

"Pop some caffeine pills before the afternoon session, cool?" Yinha trails off as she notices me. The two trainees slink toward the exit, shoulders slumped and heads hung low.

"Looking for something, Private?"

"I just landed, Captain." I adjust my throat muscles to create a deep-sounding tone. Everyone on the base has heard Phaet Theta's high warble; ambient sensors will be primed to detect it. "Passed the ISS on the way. It's all torn up now, but someone told me that it used to shine."

Yinha's face passes through shock and wonder before settling on barely suppressed happiness. "You . . . I . . . Yes, it did."

The night after I had a terrible fight with Umbriel, Yinha dragged me out of my Militia captain apartment, fixed me up with a Pygmette, and raced me to the International Space Station. Someone had ripped away its solar cells and metal plates, leaving it a decrepit skeleton, but Yinha told me she'd visited the ISS with her brother when it was whole and beautiful. The experience was something she never forgot, and she passed her wonder on to me.

"This way, Private," Yinha says, walking us both out of the training dome. "I have urgent new orders for you."

24

"I HAD NO IDEA YOU'D LANDED!" YINHA whispers. "None of my bosses saw anything on the LPS monitors."

We lean against the sloping white wall of Defense's main hallway, which bustles with foot traffic. Yinha's left hand is in her pocket to hide her handscreen, but mine dangles by my side, freeing us from suspicion. No base resident attempting to keep secrets would have her handscreen receptors uncovered, and no one knows mine's useless.

"Wes disconnected my handscreen and took out the LPS chip," I say. "Technically, I don't exist."

Yinha laughs. "Smart kid, that Kappa. Is he . . . is he all right?"

She's asking if he's alive. I shrug. If Wes went back to Koré Island during the Batterer bombardment, who knows what happened? He could've been burned or captured or shot through with a laser beam like Finley. At the thought of his glorious heart stopping, my insides turn to ice.

Please let him be alive, and safe, and free.

"Huh." Yinha rocks back and forth on her toes, looking at her feet every time she pitches forward. She seems to understand that I don't want to talk about Wes.

All around us, overeager soldiers are returning from their lunch break. We have a few minutes at most.

"Yinha, I need your help. I tried to visit Shelter via the maintenance tunnels, but—"

"To see Anka and Umbriel?" Sympathy flits across her face, but the expression is quickly replaced by blankness. "That's sweet. But stupid. They've sealed the underground entrances to that sinkhole. Everyone in Dovetail got their LPS chips removed—"

"That many people?" I say. "How?" Wes told me that he'd studied handscreen diagrams for weeks before figuring out how to do the procedure without injuring my hand—or worse.

"Our Medics accidentally paralyzed a few people before getting the job done correctly." Yinha grimaces, and I feel my fists clench. "Some people got mad; a whole lot ditched Dovetail. We wanted to knock out people's audio receptors too, but that involved rerouting blood vessels." It's miraculous that Wes managed to do that for me without causing adverse side effects—but then, he always was a skilled Medic. "Too risky to try en masse. After the LPS removal, we thought things were going well. Then the Committee found out." The memory of whatever punishments they doled out briefly silences Yinha. "They couldn't have hundreds of people going around untracked, so they fenced Dovetail in with Militia soldiers and bars in the underground tunnels. Dovetail's been completely cut off."

"There has to be a way in. I need to see if my family's all right—"

"They're alive, but they're being held under Penitentiary-level security, Stripes. You'll only put them in more danger if you try to sneak in. Speaking of the Pen—they threw Sol in there. Locked her up a month after you left, which is why I've had to take over some of her to-do list—"

"Wait, wait," I splutter. "Rewind to Sol Eta getting arrested." I have little love for Sol, but her arrest still disturbs me. Sol was a witness for my mother during her trial, and claimed on the stand that Mom didn't write the "Grievances and Propositions" that lambasted Committee rule. She took up the mantle of lead-ing Operation Dovetail after Mom was executed.

How will Dovetail move forward if the Committee contin-ues to decapitate its leadership, to cage it in? They'll be like a tree confined to a tiny pot, trying to grow while choking on their own roots.

"Sol aired the footage of your mom's trial on the other bases," says Yinha. "Count 'em—I, II, III, V, VI. Everyone knows about you now—and about Dovetail. I've got to say, you looked pretty awesome telling off the Committee. 'I don't know better, but I may know more'—you come up with that on the spot?"

"Hold on," I say. "How did this happen? I thought the Com-mittee was trying to keep knowledge of Dovetail confined to Base IV."

Yinha shrugs. "Even though the Committee generally tries to keep each base isolated from the others, the six Journalism Departments have always been allowed to collaborate. The Committee wanted to make sure they all told the same lies. My guess is that Sol sent everything to her contacts, people she knew would be sympathetic or intrigued, and they aired the segments: your mom's trial, Belinda's death, Shelter residents in the Atrium, you and Wes facing down the General."

"And you stabbing him with your visor down?" I ask. When the General cornered me, a mystery soldier stuck a dagger into the junction where neck meets shoulder.

Yinha wears a naughty child's grin.

"Of course," she says. "Sol added a clip of herself saying that you and Wes had crash-landed on Earth. She told everyone that he was an Earthbound agent all along, and used that info to put a nice spin on things. Lunar girl and Earthbound boy, united in the fight for freedom!"

Not quite. We were fighting for *survival.* At the time, we had zero concern for base politics. But Sol spun the threads of our story into a yarn that's entirely hers.

"How'd Sol know Wes's real identity?"

Yinha shifts uncomfortably, stepping away from the wall and walking toward the training dome. "Militia put me on his case, and I found out about his voice samples. I had to tell Sol. She thought it was great ammo, so she, uh, shared it with the entire *Moon.*" She huffs, frustrated. "I wish Mira and Sol had given us Dovetail underlings a warning before they started dropping news bombs all over the place. Led to their capture, and we've been a mess without them. There's still no real plan—but we're secretly backing one of our members in the elections next month. His name's Asterion Epsilon."

The name stirs something in my memory. "The medicinal chemist who earned the Committee Medal of Achievement?" It was three years ago, I think. He discovered ingestible chemical compounds that protect astronauts from the long-term effects of cosmic rays. At the time, I dreamed of becoming a titan among scientists, like him.

"Yeah, he's still mixing potions in a Committee lab. But he's a great guy—lots of influence in the Chemistry Department— and he doesn't care that the Committee's going to steamroll him in the official tallies, no matter how many people vote for him. Says it's the standing up that matters."

I hope he's right. Because those six monsters might kill him, like they killed my mother. Panic for any family this man might have courses through me.

Yinha glances at the time on her handscreen, rolls her eyes, and begins walking toward the training dome. "Look, Stripes, I have to get back to those green-faced newbies."

I follow her, murmuring over her shoulder. "But Shelter—"

"Sometimes I go in to evaluate my underlings—Dovetail's got a few moles in the Shelter Assistance Program, by the way—but not today. Corporal named Cressida Psi has the 14:00 patrol. You can try your luck, but don't take that as encouragement. Cressida's . . . difficult. If you need help—and let's face it, you probably will—keep this name in mind: Tarazed Pi. Psychology assistant working in Shelter—a recent transfer from Base II. Goes by 'Zee' around the kids he experiments on. He's pleasant enough, though he's got a really prim way of talking. But don't let that annoy you—you can go to him in a pinch."

A trainee ahead of us calls Yinha's name. Before he can ask who I am, I beeline for the Defense lobby, hoping I can catch Cressida's unit on its way out.

A Base II transfer with prim speech habits—named Pi. . . . Could it be Penny? I wonder if this mystery man is indeed Lazarus. Yinha apparently trusts "Tarazed," so he's on Dovetail's side. Why *wouldn't* Lazarus oppose the Committee, anyway? He seemed to hate them when we last spoke.

If it is Lazarus, and if he has access to Shelter, I need his help to reach my family. My instincts tell me to rush to him right away, but I can't blindly trust that he'll act in my best interests, knowing his top priority is the Odan collective good—and that he broke off his engagement to Murray. I wonder what reasons he had for hurting her so badly.

I'll only ask him for aid if no one else can help me.

These thoughts carry me within a few meters of the Defense doors. Five Pygmette speeders crouch near the wall. Four privates and a corporal occupy the first two, and several other privates are running toward the remaining vehicles. I check the lobby clock: 13:38, a little more than twenty minutes before Cressida's unit's shift. But could these people be . . .

The corporal straddling the first Pygmette in line looks up from her handscreen, upon which she's furiously typing. Perhaps a command to call in her troops? I start lifting my left hand to look her up on my handscreen—and then stop, remembering that it doesn't work anymore. Losing access to the wealth of information I used to have makes me more frustrated than scared. *I should be scared.*

The mystery corporal flips up her visor, revealing a pallid face, arched black eyebrows, eyes violet and piercing like laser fire. I shrink back in fear despite the distance between us. There's something familiar about her, but I can't place it. Then her red lips pull back in a sneer, and she screeches, "There's trouble in Shelter! Patrols need reinforcements—move move move!"

Trouble? Could it involve Anka and Umbriel? Unlike me, my sister never learned to filter her words, which once conveyed only a little girl's universe: explanations of her inventive drawings, diatribes against Primary bullies, swoons over a first crush. But in the weeks before Mom's trial, Anka got frustrated. Angry. For her own sake, I hope that Shelter has dulled her light. On the Moon, only the dimmest people remain safe.

A fifth private now occupies the front seat of the third Pygmette. This is my chance—in the heat of the moment, Cressida, if that's who the violet-eyed officer is, won't be taking attendance. I sprint forward and sit behind him. The private looks panicked, ready to hit the accelerator before a higher-up calls him out.

Indeed, four soldiers board the last two Pygmettes within seconds, and we lift off, leaving one private running and waving her arms behind us—the private whose spot I stole. She jumps onto a sixth craft, all by herself, tries to fire it up with fingerprint access, and fails. Dumb idea. Whomever it's been assigned to will be annoyed to see that she tried to take a joyride.

The private sitting in front of me twists around, causing the ship to jerk. "Hey! You're not in our unit!" he yells.

"Corporal didn't like *her* performance," I say, referring to the private we left behind. "Obvious reasons. So she sent me instead. Keep your eyes on the hall or you'll get the boot too."

"Oh . . . whoa!" Unwilling to question a superior's judgment, the private faces forward and narrowly misses crashing into a zucchini display in the Market Department. We both exhale.

We reach the end of a hallway, and the Atrium, Base IV's expansive central hub, opens up before us. The private whose waist I'm holding steers our Pygmette over the crowd's heads, which allows me to watch the wall screens, each of which shows something different.

PHAET THETA: REWARD = 10,000,000 SPUTNIKS, blares the scrolling text on one screen. GUILTY OF DISRUPTIVE SPEECH, INSUBORDINATION, ASSAULT, BRIBERY, THEFT, CONSPIRACY, AND TREASON. In the background is a picture of my face in washed-out gray scale; shadows cluster under my eyes and cheekbones. I look malicious and exhausted all at once, exactly the way they want.

The next screen shows an image of WEZN KAPPA. He's got a similar list of crimes—except he's committed ESPIONAGE and HACKING instead of BRIBERY. Eight crimes, not seven. He always did one-up me during training.

The dull ache of missing him takes me over. It doesn't retreat until I notice a screen showing Representative Andromeda Chi's glowing silhouette against a backdrop of black and white, the colors of the Lunar flag. REELECT ANDROMEDA CHI AS COMMITTEE REPRESENTATIVE, reads the notice. APRIL 1, 2348. I shake my head. Andromeda was never *elected* in the first place. As Yinha said, the Committee has kept its promise to hold democratic elections across the six bases, despite the supposed risk of losing power. But they still haven't revealed their faces, as the persistence of Andromeda's silhouette shows.

An ad for HARTLEY NU appears on the next screen over. He's an old man I've never heard of, with three chins, a hooked nose, and indifferent eyes. ARE YOU TIRED OF WAR? asks the text of his ad. I am, but the bases are in it so deep that I doubt Hartley could stop it even if he were elected.

As if mocking him, the screens across the Atrium show the flag of our Earthbound ally: a white Pacifian fist punching the yellow sun. The image's red background lends the Atrium the glow of early morning light. *Has the Committee publicly admitted to working with Pacifia?*

TOGETHER, WE WILL SLAY THE BAY! says the ad. *Apparently so.*

My thoughts spin in tight circles. An upcoming election, a war on Earth, Militia involvement in Shelter—none of it quite fits together, but I know the Committee's planning something sinister. Someone, or something, has to depose them before those plans reach fruition. Otherwise, no place on the Moon, the Earth, or the space in between will be safe from their lethal reach.

25

SHELTER SOUNDS LIKE A BEEHIVE. ALTHOUGH this place is full to bursting, it's half as bright in here as I remember. Many of the ceiling's fluorescent lights have lost power, and the gloom makes everything seem older, filthier. Near the center of the vast dome, Militia patrols from the last shift are firing Downers at hundreds of restless, dirt-smeared people—I assume they're Dovetail members. Residents who moved in before the rebellion must also be here, but they're probably the people cowering on the periphery.

We zip toward the chaos, my eyes checking every figure we pass for a hint of familiarity. Where are Anka and Umbriel? I can't reach them soon enough, though I don't know what I'll do when I get there.

Within seconds, the stink of Shelter creeps under my helmet, threatening to gag me. The Shelter Assistance Program, which the Committee instituted in the wake of Mom's arrest to improve the residents' quality of life, has put up tents for what appears to be a Psychology study. The clear plastic Medical tent is in its old spot, off to the side. Wes worked there before he joined the Militia, dashing out once in a while to help kids like Belinda.

Our Pygmettes reach the edge of the Dovetail crowd. Every rider save one dismounts and points a tranquilizing gun at the Shelter residents. I imitate them. Our leader, the tall corporal, stands atop her Pygmette's seat so that she towers over everyone.

Silence falls. It's as if someone has pushed the mute button on the entire dome.

"You are nothing!" She lets out a sharp laugh. It's like a dagger to my eardrums. "*Scum!* The dissident you saw beaten today was scum!"

CORPORAL CRESSIDA PSI appears on the nearby Shelter residents' handscreens.

Cressida raises her arms, daring anyone to contradict her. "In exchange for the right to congregate here, you Dovetailers promised the Committee you'd behave. But you've broken that promise—for the thirty-ninth time in six months."

Oh. Dovetail made a deal with the Committee—that's how so many people ended up living here. The Committee couldn't disband or eliminate them because of their sheer numbers. Word would get out, and after Sol's mass broadcast, they probably couldn't afford more bad publicity.

"You!" Cressida points her Lazy at a hunchbacked old woman. "Let's see if your ears still work. What right do you have to dispute the Committee's rule? What is Dovetail, compared to the rightful government of the Moon?"

"N-nothing, ma'am," the woman stutters, clutching her chest. She looks like she might collapse from fear. But then she straightens and clears her throat. "But the Girl Sage is more than *you'll* ever be."

"Yeah, the Sage'll come for us," says a young boy standing near the old woman. "My mum told me that a comet fell on her when she was a baby and turned her hair all silver."

I inhale sharply, causing one of the privates to glance my way. *Me? A sage?* Have the rebels turned me into a ridiculous legend? If so, I'll have a harder time hiding; someone might recognize me and alert the Militia to my presence.

A Beetle scurries toward the boy, truncheon in hand. "I'll shut him up, Corporal."

"Not yet, Private—stay right there." The little color remaining in Cressida's face drains away. She turns again to the crowd. "Phaet Theta is a coward. She and that traitor boy fled to Earth. They're either dead or in hiding. Your *Girl Sage* didn't give two grits about you. If she did, she'd have come back by now."

If only they could know I have. I seethe silently as the people around me murmur among themselves. I scan their dirt-covered faces, looking for two in particular.

Cressida shakes her head. "When the Militia took Mira Theta into custody, do you know what Phaet did? No? Well, I was there. She hid behind her scrawny friend and cried for mommy. Your Girl Sage did *nothing* to stop us. Even when we smacked her *mommy* in the head with our truncheons. Even when we dragged her out by her arms."

My entire body trembles, and I can almost feel the hot fury rolling off my skin. Cressida was there, hurting Mom, and she laughed as she did it.

She started everything.

"Yes." Pride suffuses Cressida's voice. "I helped put away Mira Theta, one of the most heinous criminals in base history."

Silence. I can almost see a wave pass over the crowd as everyone takes in her words. Then—

"Shut up!" The scream is like glass breaking.

Cressida's violet eyes narrow. "What did you say?"

"You heard me." The girl pushes past the Dovetail members in front of her, shoving them aside in her haste to reach Cressida. Her skin hugs her bones; her hair is a hopeless mess of tangles and grime. But even in her anger, her face is fixed in a stern, powerful expression. "I told you, *SHUT UP!*"

Anka! I stop the scream before it can escape my body.

"Get back!" A boy, taller than I remember, chases after her. *Umbriel!* Someone's hacked off the wavy black hair that once dangled into his eyes, revealing a pronounced widow's peak and strong brow. What's left of the fuzz on his scalp looks like velvet. His face is square, his jaw a hard line. He looks more like Atlas, his father, than the friend I knew.

Anka doesn't stop. "Get out, *Corporal*, and take your stupid lies with you. No one talks like that about my family!"

Cressida sneers. "I just did."

Order implodes. Dovetail members scatter, some trying to push Anka forward, others struggling to pull her back. Forgetting my Militia disguise, I sprint into the mass of people and see with a spike of dread that Anka's evaded the well-intentioned Dovetailers. She expertly dodges the melee, sprinting forward to a position beside Cressida's speeder.

"I see." Cressida looks down her nose at Anka, who stands two and a half meters below. "Just like her sister."

She leaps from the Pygmette, drawing a glass truncheon from her belt. "Did Mira and Phaet fail to teach you a lesson?" she shouts at the ragged crowd. "Then let this Theta be an example to every last one of you!"

"No," I whisper.

I try to push my way to Anka, but the mass of people is too dense. Through the gaps between bodies, I see Umbriel burst from the crowd and try once again to pull Anka to safety. But it's too late. Cressida and three of her underlings club my sister with their truncheons, the grace of their movements making their brutality all the more horrifying. Umbriel tries to shield Anka with his body, but this only earns him blows as well. He looks like a flailing stick insect, brown-robed and horribly thin among the well-nourished soldiers.

Lying on the floor beside him, Anka's transformed by a kind of dignified fury. "I'm not my sister, Umbriel—I don't need you to protect me." Her eyes are wide and perceptive, not clenched shut.

I manage to come within an arm's length of them. *I need to end this—*

"Private!" calls Cressida. She means me. "Get to work! Where's your truncheon?"

She wants me to beat my own sister. My hand drifts to my utility belt, wraps around the glass rod, lifts it out of its restraining loop of fabric. If I don't start soon, Cressida will pull off my helmet, discover Phaet Theta's face underneath, and send me straight to the Committee. The thought of their looming silhouettes fills me with fear, and I nearly drop the truncheon.

Do it, I tell myself. *You can't help Anka if you've gone the same way as Cygnus.*

The saliva dries in my mouth. The rod rises, almost against my will—

"That is enough!" shouts a man's voice.

The truncheon falls from my hand, glances off my foot, and rolls away. A tall, straight-backed figure emerges from one of the white tents and strides toward us. He has wavy black hair parted down the side of his head and wears a Psychology Department badge—the letter Ψ, with two snakes and angel wings crawling up the central tine—pinned to his cobalt Pi robes.

Cressida backs away from my sister, staring at the newcomer. Color rushes to her pale cheeks.

The man pivots to face different sections of the crowd, taking his time. What seems to have affected Cressida as much as his authority is his beauty: he has dark, sloping eyebrows and a face like a perfect ellipse, its smooth curves disrupted only by the corners of his jawbones. His lips are bow-shaped, his light brown skin clean-shaven and glowing.

His eyes, the color of new summer leaves, slide to mine. They're brilliant but patient, as if lit by the late afternoon sun. His lips twitch almost imperceptibly, and then his gaze moves onward.

"I'm—I'm sorry, Mr. Tarazed." The pitch of Cressida's voice rises with every syllable. "I forgot myself. Captain Yinha said to discuss possible punishments of prominent Dovetail members with . . . with either you or Dr. Biela."

"Yes, Cressida," the man says softly. "Would you remind our kind spectators why approval from one of us is necessary?"

That voice . . . I scrutinize the newcomer, remembering the pain that suffused it when he warned me about the impending attack on Saint Oda, and then said he needed to reveal my identity to Wesley Sr.

Tarazed Pi—the man I'm now sure is Lazarus Penny—makes a fluid gesture with one hand. Cressida regurgitates something she's obviously memorized: "We don't want the punishment of one to lead to the uprising of a thousand."

"Precisely." The Psychology worker smiles with one side of his mouth, revealing a sharp canine. It's the only aggressive-looking feature on his face. "In addition, it seems to have escaped you and your Militia entourage that I am performing biweekly obedience experiments on Anka Theta and her ilk. The Committee is expecting results, and I cannot claim statistical significance if you insist on introducing extra variables. A short clarification:

do not strike her again. I will speak to Anka now, and I require one of your soldiers as an assistant—this one, perhaps."

He takes my arm, and I tense up involuntarily.

"Relax, little one," he whispers in my ear. "My office is a sanctuary for all."

His voice is a sedative for my nerves.

Blushing, Cressida slides her visor down, straddles her Pyg-mette, and motions to her other troops to move out. *She didn't even check my identity.*

As they zip away, Anka and I follow the Psychologist toward the cluster of tents. He bends and whispers in my ear, his tone as smooth as I remember from that fateful conversation in the Carlyles' basement. I feel as if my entire body has been sub-merged in warm liquid soap.

"I never anticipated our first interaction occurring like this," Lazarus Penny says. "But I am pleased to meet you, Girl Sage."

26

ANKA'S HAND IS WARM IN MINE, HER CHEEK pressed against my shoulder. "I knew you'd come back!" she says in a hoarse whisper.

On the emptier side of Shelter, we enter a tent that Tarazed Pi shares with his lab's principal investigator, Biela Upsilon.

"I knew it," Anka goes on, "and I told everyone, even though the Beetles said again and again that you were dead. I knew they were wrong! They could've sent all six base Militias after you, and they'd still never catch you."

Lazarus lifts the front flap of the tent and touches my shoulder with the fingertips of his other hand, guiding my sister and me inside. He scans his thumbprint by the door, and a recording of my sister's screams begins to play, horrifying in their volume and intensity. I can hardly focus on Anka's words, on my joy at seeing her. Screams of my own threaten to burst from my lips.

Lazarus tucks his left hand in his pocket to hide his handscreen's audio receptors. "Please, do not panic; these cries of distress are a mere recording. After I sampled Anka's voice, I used the HeRP here to manipulate the pitch and volume until it sounded like the product of my alleged sadism. Everyone believes that you—not the Sage, but a random private—and I are performing an Electrostun-aided obedience experiment on her as we speak. I guarantee that no one will intrude upon us."

"Tell her about the HeRP issues," Anka says.

"Yes, that. I am lucky the Committee let me keep mine as a Psychology employee," Lazarus says. "They took possession of most privately owned HeRPs after they saw what your brother did with his. My Sanctuarist colleagues and I mostly use ours off-line, with multiple firewalls—thus far, we are still safe."

We move through the empty anteroom, where people waiting to be evaluated would ordinarily sit on the floor, into a tiny chamber with three chairs, a square table between them, and foam on the walls for soundproofing. A HeRP sits on the table. Anka's fabricated screams must come from the speaker in the waiting room, to which the modified machine is likely connected.

Lazarus shuts the door, points us to two chairs, and sits on the table's other side. Now that we're in relative privacy, Anka throws one arm around me, nearly tipping over her chair, but continues sitting on the other.

"What happened, Phaet? Where did Wes take you? When can we get Cygnus back? Dovetail hasn't even tried, and it's making me crazy." Anka speaks with total abandon, even though Lazarus Penny is patiently waiting for us to finish so that he can talk. He may have earned Anka's trust—and Yinha's—but I can't forget how he almost single-handedly caused Wesley Sr. to assign me that suicide mission to Pacifia.

". . . you have to tell me about Earth too, Phaet. Does water really fall out of the sky? Did you see weird things and scary people?"

"I'm afraid I must disrupt this happy reunion." Leaning backward, Lazarus starts rolling up his right sleeve to display a muscled, veiny forearm. Then he rests his fingertips on Anka's shoulder. "Anka, your sister and I must speak privately, which I hope you understand. I have already called upon the Militia to return you to Umbriel Phi—if they so much as disturb a hair on your head, you must inform me straightaway."

I shudder, even as Anka's fake screams fade away.

The real Anka sits quietly, holding me. She only budges at the sound of someone approaching the door. When a private enters to hustle her away, I want to shove him out of the tent. He shouldn't be allowed to touch her, to take her from me again.

"I'd shock her harder if I were you," the soldier says to Lazarus, seizing Anka's upper arm. I wince; she bares her teeth. My sister's eyes never leave mine as they depart—the private eagerly, she grudgingly.

"Before we proceed, Sage, I must first apologize for the ordeals you have endured since our last tête-à-tête." Lazarus pats the back of my hand; although his tone is warm, his fingertips are room-temperature cold. "I failed to anticipate that Coordinator Carlyle would react so unfavorably to your identity, even though I implored him to exhibit the mercy central to our Odan faith. But I am beyond ecstatic that you have returned home safely." The left side of Lazarus's mouth pulls back in an asymmetric grin, exposing that same sharp canine.

I can't help but smile back.

"My colleagues' messages tell me that with the younger Wesley's cooperation, you transformed your intended exile into a heroic rescue mission. Wesley Jr. has been transmitting messages to *them* from Battery Bay, but frustratingly, he has left me to receive these communications secondhand. Perhaps he has encountered technical difficulties in that foreign city."

Wes is alive. I'm massively relieved—he's once again proven that he's invincible, at least in body. I keep my expression neutral.

"Odans have contacted you," I say. "How are they?"

Lazarus shakes his head; his back curls into a defensive slouch. "They are conducting proceedings against me for licentious behavior."

"Oh no," I say.

"This is due to Wesley's testimony regarding my interactions with his sister—testimony which, in my view, is deficient and fragmentary. The Sanctuarists are debating whether to expel me. It is undeserved, especially considering that young Wesley all but bartered our islands to corporate Batterer interests, and mining operations will begin the moment they declare the archipelago habitable again."

Wes and Lazarus both want to help me, but they will need to work together—which they apparently are refusing to do.

"But let us return to the present dilemma," Lazarus says. "All the Odan survivors have heard some version of the Marina narrative, though mine is not among them. Whether their information is thoroughly validated or not, they are taking part in the discussion over my possible expulsion from the Sanctuarist force. If they remove me, I will be stranded on this godforsaken nugget of space rock, with the other agents monitoring my every move. And I will be stymied if I attempt a return to Earth."

"Sounds awful," I say. "What have they gotten wrong?"

Lazarus looks at his lap, cringing. "They perceive me as a predator, because Marina was several years younger than I was, and damaged to boot. . . . But I have never desired anything but the best for her. . . . I apologize for my inability to elaborate at this moment. It causes me profound pain and regret to discuss the past."

I nod quickly. If the realm of repressed memories had a queen, it would surely be me. *Maybe he broke the engagement for*

Murray's good, I think. He seems as private a person as I am. Because he hasn't told his side of the story—and doesn't want to—all the Odans must have the wrong idea.

"But it is not too late to transcend these circumstances. Mark my words carefully." He leans toward me. I can smell hints of citrus and sandalwood, a reprieve from the usual odors of Shelter. "I can help you rescue your brother. If we succeed, I will have contributed enough to the Sanctuarist cause that they will allow me to retain my post. And I will have demonstrated that despite my supposed violation of propriety, my heart remains pure. Do you agree? I will need you to vouch for my character, but that is a small matter."

"Of course," I blurt without thinking. Lazarus's physical presence has brought on a weightless feeling in my lower belly. I lean backward in my chair to clear my head. Lazarus breathes deeply, sits up straight, changes the subject.

"I regret introducing additional unpleasantness into our discussion, but I must ask: what is a life to you, Sage?"

Someone else is dead. I know it with sickening certainty. Why must the destruction go on and on, and why is it always somehow my fault?

Lazarus walks back to his desk and taps the HeRP. A video begins to play. On the screen is a young man dressed in Rho gray. He has a long face full of freckles, thin blond hair, and a dark birthmark that covers the right half of his chin. A patch showing the golden scales of justice is pinned to his robes: the Base I Law badge, I'm assuming.

"This is footage recorded by a Penitentiary security pod," Lazarus says, shifting his weight from one leg to the other. The word *Penitentiary* makes me shiver.

We watch the man walk through white hallways, passing identical black metal doors. The doors lead, presumably, to prisoners' holding cells. When the man reaches the one he wants, he stops. I look closer—the door is blank, marked with no letters or numbers. The man grabs the security pod that's filming him, and the video goes blurry as he fits it into a lock of sorts.

The security pods in the Base I Pen are keys? My mind spinning, I watch as the door slides open, revealing a bare cell, white and brightly lit.

A heap of grimy cloth leans against the wall.

"I've got you, Cygnus," the man says. "You're going to be safe."

With great effort, my brother raises his head, blinking. One eye is swollen, cloudy, and infected. There are bald spots on his head; clumps of black hair litter the floor like downy tumbleweeds. A metal ring with red lights winds around his neck, making him look like a wolf pup caught in a trap. *What have they been doing to him?* He's even thinner and dirtier and more *hurt* than in the video Tourmaline played on Saint Oda.

I've forgotten to breathe. My lungs open violently; they suck in air as if absorbing Cygnus's suffering. As if to compensate for my waiting so long to come back. When I exhale, I let out a whimper.

Cygnus shakes his head.

"What?" The man kneels next to my brother and strokes his skeletal face. "Cygnus, don't worry. I have everything under control."

My brother parts his cracked lips as if to speak, but only air emerges. Instead of trying to get up, he yanks a dagger from the man's belt with surprising deftness.

"What are you doing?" the stranger says. "I've got to get you home!"

"You can't," my brother whispers. The security pod, released from the man's grasp now, flies closer to pick up their conversation. "My collar. Take me out that door and it'll constrict. Until I'm dead."

"You've got my knife—we could cut it off. Right now," the man says.

"It's carbon fiber and tungsten. It'll bend your knife in half. Got a laser blaster? That might burn through it."

The man shakes his head.

Bracing himself, Cygnus makes a deep gash in his left hand—into the shiny surface of his handscreen. Blood and colored dye burst from the wound. I almost retch as my brother pushes the dagger further in and wiggles it, his face a mask of agony.

When it's over, a tiny blood-covered square of metal is balanced on the dagger's tip. I'm impressed that Cygnus didn't damage it with the knife. The man picks it up, looking bewildered.

"My handscreen's memory chip. Find a HeRP," Cygnus says.

He collapses. Pounding footsteps approach. I know that sound—Militia boots.

Lazarus's HeRP blacks out.

27

"NO! WHAT HAPPENED TO CYGNUS?" I demand, my chest heaving.

Lazarus shushes me with a finger on his lips, and then taps the screen. The next video clip shows the blond, freckled man sprinting down a hallway lined with offices, half a dozen soldiers in hot pursuit. Sweat drips down his forehead; his gray robes are damp from the exertion. He reaches a door labeled ARCHIVES MANAGER MIKKO RHO, ducks inside, and closes the door before the security pod can follow him inside. Through the glass, the pod films him as he feeds Cygnus's handscreen chip into his HeRP and fiddles with the screen. An instant later, he ejects the chip, pops it into his mouth, and swallows it.

Wielding truncheons, the Militia members smash down the door. Shards of glass sparkle and spin. The man pulls an Electrostun from his desk drawer, but it's no use. A scream, a burst of purple light, and it's over.

The video fades. Lazarus's HeRP displays the profile information: MIKKO RHO, age twenty-four, of Base I. In the photo, his eyes are pale blue and watery, betraying none of the fierce determination I saw in the video.

I cover my eyes, and soon my palms are wet. Before I know what's happening, strong arms enfold me, and I'm sobbing into Lazarus Penny's shoulder.

My skin is so dirty—or numb—that I can't feel the wetness

of the tears on my cheeks. Lazarus's hand strokes the top of my head, smoothing my matted hair.

"Oh, little Sage," he murmurs.

My arms tighten around his neck—although I might choke him, I refuse to let go.

"Shh." He rubs the back of my neck.

I pull back, and in a hoarse voice demand, "Who was that man? He died for Cygnus. I have to know."

Lazarus sighs. "His name was Micah River. Perhaps you heard of him during your time on Saint Oda? When he saw the . . . torture footage, he gave himself an extraordinary assignment. He told not a soul. Yinha only became aware of it when Base I security sent the footage to the premier Defense officers."

I remember Larimer, Micah's brother, who gave me the snowdrop bulbs. His small, smiling mother, who brought vegetables to welcome me to Saint Oda. *Micah came to the Moon to protect them, and he died for a boy he didn't know.* I imagine Larimer's joyful eyes filling with tears, his wife Willet's hands wiping them away.

If I'd returned home earlier, Micah might not have gone after Cygnus. But I didn't even try. I sit still as a cliff face, hardly breathing, feeling unworthy of the air around me.

"Utterly reckless," Lazarus says. "Courageous, but reckless."

Wes's words ring in my ears. *He wanted to be different. To be a hero, whatever the cost.* And he was.

Why must things happen this way? I'll never meet Micah, let alone show him how grateful I am.

Lazarus opens another document on his HeRP. The word BLOCKED takes up the entire screen; at the bottom, in small letters, are the words WATCH THE TORTURE VIDEO AGAIN.

"Before his death, Micah distributed the document he found on Cygnus's handscreen chip to all Odan agents. Because of our jail-broken equipment, we have managed to keep it confidential. As you saw, Micah ingested the chip to prevent our enemies from reading it. His stomach acids broke it down irrecoverably. Even in the event of an autopsy, the document will not come to light."

"But there has to be another way to read it," I say in desperation.

Lazarus nods. "The file is protected by a text password. In Cygnus's compromised state, that must have been all the encryption he could come up with. Although we do not yet know his location, the document may reveal it. It is essential we know, Sage. We cannot go in blind."

Cygnus wrote that we should "watch the torture video again." I stare at the screen, my mind whirling.

"The password is in the clip that Tourmaline played on Saint Oda." I jump to my feet. "Cygnus wasn't speaking nonsense. He was giving us clues! I need to see that video again. Do you have a copy?"

"Yes, but you should not subject yourself to further horrors. I have the transcript written down. It is more palatable that way."

"No. He's my brother. I'll read him better if I can see his face."

Sighing, Lazarus taps his HeRP several times, and the jail cell that's haunted my dreams appears. As the video plays, I only watch Cygnus's mouth. *"T two A one G three omicron C-E-T alpha C-O-L alpha P-H-E dodeca-chordata T two A one G three . . ."*

"Have you got it?" Lazarus shuts off the HeRP.

I nod, repeating Cygnus's mantra in my mind. The numbers and letters take shape: *T2A1G3 OCETACOLAPHE dodeca-chordata T2A1G3*. Maybe there's a pattern, but I don't see it.

"You don't seem to recognize his meaning." Lazarus looks

deeply disappointed. "Yinha has provided me with intelligence that may help. It seems your brother froze an image from your mother's trial on his handscreen in the seconds before his capture. An image of you, facing the camera. He zoomed in on your left eye until it covered his entire screen, which was in a jailbroken state at that time."

I frown. How will a blown-up picture of my eye help us save Cygnus? And for all I know, the string of characters could be something a toddler punched into a HeRP.

If this is all we have to recover the password, a rescue is impossible. But I'll lose my mind if I don't act soon, knowing Cygnus is still strapped to that chair, screaming.

Lazarus watches me struggle for breath, and gives me a playful kick to the shin. "Look alive, Captain Phaet. We will operate together, as I said before. You attempt to decipher that password, while I sift through the logistics of travel to Base I. Cygnus's rescue will reunite you and your brother, and reconcile me with my colleagues. Within a matter of weeks, our lives will return to normal."

"But what if it doesn't work? What will you do if the Sanctuarists expel you?" I ask.

He presses his lips together. "Assuming they do not reveal my identity, I will ascend to a prominent position in Lunar society and continue to work toward a democratic Moon with Dovetail. But I fervently hope my expulsion will not occur. If I narrate all the experiences Marina and I have shared, perhaps the Odans' minds will bend in my favor. . . ."

I blink, ready to hear more.

"I first encountered Marina when she was a jubilant schoolgirl, running wild with her cohort of companions. In my early twenties, I was a guest speaker in the Odan Academy and delivered monthly philosophy lessons to the schoolchildren. The girl was taken with the Confucian idea that man is born good and is corrupted only by experience. She displayed a formidable optimism about humanity."

"That's not the Murray I know," I say. *She's a world away now.*

"After the Lunar attack, she abruptly changed," Lazarus continues. "She dragged her feet, withdrew from society, allowed her stunning voice to fall into disuse. We saw each other sparingly, the demands on my time from Sanctuarist duties preventing me from lecturing. However, she sought me out at mass and after my meetings with her father—she clearly admired me, but as an older man, I did not reciprocate her affections. Three years passed in this way. When she was sixteen, she had grown beautiful despite her defects, and I succumbed to emotion. We carried out a secret but loving courtship. Because she laughed and danced and even *sang* in my presence, I believed that I had done right, that I had saved her from her own ghosts."

His words rush into me and fill me with the joy Murray must've felt.

"This does not end well, Girl Sage," Lazarus says, shaking his head. "So you must not smile just yet. The time inevitably came for me to leave. I informed her I would not stop her from saving herself for me—to clarify, I never explicitly asked for her hand—and she swore she wanted to. On the Moon, however, I realized that my mission was thornier than anyone had anticipated, and that I might die before seeing my girl again. How unfairly I had treated her—and any Odan man who might desire her. I had knocked the apple from the tree, with no ability to consume it. So, through her brother, I told her to run free, associate with other men, for her own benefit."

My head bobs in time with his words.

"Murray said there were Lunar women," I say. "She implied you left her for them."

"The words of a woman who believes she was scorned," Lazarus says. "Her accusation has no basis in fact. But young Wesley, her brother, could not help but believe her and nurse a prejudice against me."

A voice from outside pierces the tent—Corporal Cressida's. "Mr. Tarazed, sir! Major Skat Yotta's here to collect today's notes."

Lazarus looks as if he'd very much like to swear, but he holds his tongue. He grasps my shoulder and pulls me toward an open manhole. "You will receive communications from me when it is time. Until then, I beg you to stay underground, where it is relatively safe. The tunnels should be devoid of Militia until to-day's moonquake ceases. I am distressed that I cannot provide additional assistance."

Bewildered and afraid, I stumble. It's partly due to the force of his hands—and partly the tremors of the moonquake that's just begun.

Inertia pulls me forward; with Lazarus's hand around my wrist, I drop a meter and a half into the tunnel and bend my knees when I land. Still, the impact jars all my joints.

"Tarazed, the major's *waiting*!" Cressida calls.

"All the best, Sage," Lazarus whispers, letting go of me. I wish he wouldn't. "Good-bye for now."

The manhole seals above me, cutting off all light.

28

I PRESS MY BACK AGAINST THE TUNNEL wall and jam my head between my knees. Pipes clang above me, and dust, invisible in the pitch dark, blankets my skin and clothes. My memories rattle and shift like pebbles overturned by a rip current. Wavering impressions of Dad, of his tough hands and soft voice, pass before my eyes.

I was five when Geology sent him to the Moon's far side; a moonquake shook his faulty excavation vehicle until it sprang a leak. *Decompression* is far too pleasant a word to describe the way he died.

He's my first ghost, the only one for whom I feel no guilt. I won't let Cygnus join him and the other dead.

T2A1G3 . . . *dodeca-chordata* . . . The video begins to loop through my head.

By the time a beam of white light shines between my knees, onto my face, I almost welcome the distraction.

Who's that? If I'm found, it's over. I struggle to stand, trembling.

"I knew it was you back there. . . . And what Beetle wouldn't talk *or* hurt Anka?" The whisper is hoarse, familiar. "I got my ex-Sanitation-worker friend to let me into the tunnels."

My pupils contract enough to make out Umbriel, squatting next to me with a bowl of Shelter mush in his right hand. The light is emanating from his handscreen; he promptly sits on it to prevent anyone from eavesdropping on us. At least he only blots out some of the light. Our eyes lock for an instant, before the next tremor knocks him sideways.

Laughing at his annoyed expression, I throw my arms around him. His skinny body nearly buckles—I forgot that I'm the stronger one now. Still, I don't let go. "Aren't you worried that the Militia will notice you're missing?" I whisper. Because of his relationship with me, Umbriel must be under extra surveillance.

"I was more worried that I'd never see you again." Umbriel's rough hand leaves my back to take my wrist.

Men want different things, Murray said to me once.

I pull away and lift the bowl of mush to my mouth, pour in the brown lettuce and watered-down wheat. The lukewarm liquid slips into my esophagus without leaving any taste in my mouth.

Umbriel's hand falls away, and his tone shifts. Months of frustration manifest in his words. "While you were off having *adventures* on Earth, Anka and I were stuck in that grit-pit Shelter, wondering if you were alive or dead. I blamed myself for not trying hard enough to stop you from blasting off with *him*."

Part of me had expected Umbriel to be so happy to see me that he'd forget our parting interaction: me choosing to run away with Wes, leaving Umbriel to watch over my siblings. "It can't have been easy," I say. "Sorry."

He gestures with his chin at the bowl of mush in my hands. "Easy? Try *grueling*. Literally." Then he points to the top of his head, where his thicket of black hair used to grow. "Got a bad fever last month. They put me in quarantine and shaved me bald."

Oh. In such a dirty place, infections must run rampant. Has Umbriel's family helped him? Where are his father and brother?

"Back in Shelter, I didn't see . . ."

"Ariel and my dad are living at home." Umbriel can still

answer my questions before I finish asking them. "They've disowned me, as far as the Committee's concerned, but they only did it to keep their jobs in Law. And Mom . . . the Committee kept her for interrogation. She's probably given them megabytes' worth of dirt on your family. All the memories, even the embarrassing ones."

I picture Caeli Phi's face, and almost instantly, my head begins to throb. *The rat.* If not for her, Mom wouldn't be dead, Cygnus wouldn't be a captive, and Anka wouldn't be in Shelter.

What did Caeli hope to gain by turning in my mother for her rebellious writing? Money? A better job? Whatever it was, she discarded her relationships with Atlas and the twins to get it. It's a terrible punishment, but somehow I don't feel it's enough.

"Don't worry about her," Umbriel says. "I don't know how she contributed half my DNA. It's half, right? I'm starting to forget all the bio we learned in Primary. Give me a brain here, Phaet."

I swat his bony shoulder. Even after all these months apart, Umbriel knows how to crack my shell open, no matter how tightly I've sealed myself inside. No matter how upset he's been.

"You're even more beautiful when you're happy." Umbriel studies my face.

My smile inverts into a frown. *Not now.* Reuniting with Umbriel has brought up so many other emotions that I've nearly forgotten how uncomfortable he can make me. My appetite disappears. I put my half-eaten porridge on the floor, hunch my shoulders, and tuck in my legs. My mind is a void, the space in my skull a cavern.

Umbriel gives a long, melancholy sigh.

On the tunnel floor, the liquid surface of my leftover porridge vibrates with new shudders from the moonquake.

"Talk to me, Phaet. I didn't think it would come to this, but this time you've got to tell me what you're thinking. I can't figure it out."

There's a new phenomenon: me, a mystery to him. Umbriel sighs again, but it's a quick, anxious breath. "For a few months, I . . . I thought you wouldn't come back. That was stupid, because I know you'd do anything for Cygnus and Anka. But what about me? What I mean is—blast it—you spent half a year on Earth with *him*, so does that mean you didn't miss me? At least not the way I wish you did? What . . . what does Wes mean for *us*?"

When we were twelve, Umbriel tried piloting a Pygmette speeder through the greenhouses with me on board. He slammed into a treetop, and it felt like my head would topple off my neck. He's given me a similar shock, nearly four years later, with his words.

Me and Umbriel. We never said it, but we grew up assuming that we'd start a family and spend our lives together. He was my favorite person, excepting Mom and my siblings, and we trusted each other entirely. As his mother proved, trust, even within a family, is rare here.

I thought it was enough. But that was before I trained in Militia, before Wes helped me stand on my own, before he set me on fire somewhere deep beneath my skin.

I shake my head. "Sorry."

In the awkward hush, I remember Wes letting Eri down easy, with kind words and a hug. But Eri wasn't Wes's best friend; they didn't share toys, get into petty fist-swinging arguments, or concoct their own sign language. This is more complicated.

Umbriel's mouth opens and closes; he looks like a fish gulping at dry air. We're both speechless—a situation neither of us knows how to handle. "Did anything . . . happen with him?"

I remember my last moments with Wes. *One type of happiness,* I muse, *like rain and pine needles.* It's nothing to be ashamed of, so I say loud and clear, "Yes."

Umbriel scowls. "You fell in love."

I nod once.

He crosses his arms. "I know Wes is mysterious and strong and all, but can you trust him? Does he know the real you? The real reason, for instance, that you haven't really talked for ten years, and how hard it was to watch you go through that?"

Ten years—*since Dad died.* I turn away, horrified that Umbriel would use that dark time as a guilt trip.

"You completely shut down, Phaet. Remember, I had to tell people what you were thinking and feeling, since only I knew! After you started staring blankly at *nothing,* even during science lessons, everyone thought you were dead inside. Everyone but me."

I can't look or listen to him anymore. I avert my eyes—and what I see makes panic seize me and hold on tight. Deep in the tunnel to our left, there are three bobbing handscreen lights.

"I went on loving you anyway," Umbriel goes on, oblivious. "Will Wes ever understand you like I d—"

"Shh!" A tremor rocks the confined space; the lights move frenetically, revealing heavy black boots that pound the floor as they approach us. The authorities didn't wait for the moonquake's end before chasing after Umbriel.

". . . the infrared signal's coming from somewhere near here," we hear one soldier say.

Umbriel springs to his feet. Out of habit, he reaches down to help me—but retracts his hand at the last instant.

I stand on my own. I'm used to it now.

"Wonder which of the Dovewailers tried to run away this time," the soldier is saying.

Because Umbriel and I don't have LPS chips, the Beetles don't know our identities. Yet.

"I need to get back before they realize it's me missing." Even as the moonquake tries to knock him back down, Umbriel stays standing. "The tunnels under Shelter are sealed off, but if we're lucky, a Dovetail-friendly Beetle might leave the doors open while the squad's on rounds. Wait it out; get around them, and you can go to the greenhouses, somewhere like that."

We shuffle along the wall, away from the soldiers and Lazarus's secret manhole entrance into Shelter. As the tunnel rattles, my shoes slip and slide on the floor's coating of detritus. I breathe through my mouth so that the stench won't affect me.

We take three right turns, each navigated by Umbriel, and end up behind the soldiers. Then we sneak farther out and find the metal slab of a door through which they entered, open just a crack. A Dovetail mole in the squad must have left us an exit. *Won't always be this lucky,* I tell myself.

Umbriel and I throw our body weight against the slab. The bottom edge scrapes along the floor as the slab gives way.

The soldiers must have heard that.

Time to go. I fumble to find the words with which to tell Umbriel good-bye—and then the Militia's lights sweep across the hall, passing alarmingly close to my head. A farewell nod suffices. Umbriel takes off down a side tunnel, possibly heading back toward the manhole that leads to Lazarus's tent. I slip through the metal door, slam it shut with a mighty *clang*, and slide the bolt into place. The Beetles will need time to unlock it from the inside and force it open again.

Strange, I think as I sprint through the still-quivering tunnel. I squirmed out of Umbriel's arms a minute ago, yet I'd do anything short of sacrifice my freedom to bring him back to me now. But protecting that freedom will require hiding, waiting, surviving, away from him and Anka. Away from their light.

29

THE CEILING UNLEASHES ANOTHER TORRENTIAL downpour into Greenhouse 17. Filtered "rainwater" fills the half-eaten, hollowed-out mango in my right hand, and I force myself to drink. My left hand clasps a branch, lest I fall from my perch in this broadleaf tree.

How long have I been here? More than twenty-four hours, surely. The sunlight has been incessant, as daylight lasts for over 200 hours at a time. Decades ago, Bioengineers made sure the bases' genetically modified plants could handle the Moon's extended cycle of light and dark, saving the Agriculture Department vast amounts of power.

With such exposure, I dare not touch bare soil until nightfall. I'm about to burst with frustration, split apart like an overripe fruit. Stuck in the canopy, I'm not getting any closer to my brother. As soon as the sun sets, I'll head out, find a HeRP— maybe Yinha has an extra?—and download a set of computer science textbooks. Cygnus's message may be in a programming language. Greek autocode, perhaps.

My food, which consists of raw fruit and the occasional nut, seems to go in through my mouth and straight out via diarrhea and vomiting. I'd have preferred to hide in Greenhouse 22, where Umbriel and I used to tend berry bushes, apple trees, and salad greens, but the security pods there would find me easily. InfoTech hates sending pods into the tropical greenhouses like this one; the heat and humidity cause them to malfunction, and the liters upon liters of artificial rain can knock them to the muddy ground.

It's so hot that I've ditched my helmet, hanging it on a cluster of bananas, and rolled up my sleeves and pant legs. Raw scrapes mar my skin, injuries sustained while crawling between trees to hide from the Agriculture workers, some of whom I recognize. I'm horrified to see the bloody skin around my wounds turning scarlet and even yellow. It burns in some places and itches in others.

I have to leave. Every new wound, every creeping infection, will make it harder for me to help Cygnus, whose pain is immeasurably worse than mine.

Navigation in this greenhouse was difficult at first, as the plants here aren't partitioned by species. Rather, in any given area, the overstory consists of a tall tree species and the understory of various shrubs, many of which produce edible fruit but have poisonous leaves. Some plants, whose ancestors were saved before Earth's rainforests disappeared, have healing properties, most of which base scientists are still exploring. Because of this greenhouse's importance—and its dangers—only experienced Agriculture workers are assigned to work here. Umbriel and I were never allowed in.

Day finally shifts to night, and I shimmy down to the base of the tree. When I hit the ground, my legs crumple underneath me, and mud soaks through the seat of the Militia trousers I'm wearing. I'll be useless until I've rested for a few hours.

Sleep, then find a HeRP.

Inching on my elbows like a worm, I find a nook sheltered by a fig tree's spreading branches and bounded on the sides by a clump of weedy vines with scarlet seeds. *Red: aposematic coloration. A warning sign to potential predators.*

Poison. The panic I feel is cold. My heartbeats come quiet and slow like distant waves. *Could it already be too late? Maybe I'm just exhausted. . . . A few hours' rest, and then I'll go ask Yinha for a HeRP. If I don't touch those plants, I should be fine . . .*

I grow dizzier by the second. By the time I admit that I'm deluding myself, my consciousness has all but drifted away.

*   *   *

"What on this side of the sun are you doing here?"

My sleepy pulse picks up, and sweat beads on my face— which, I realize in a rush of dismay, is exposed to the air. *I've been discovered.* This could end my career as a fugitive and begin my new one as a prisoner. I force my eyes up. The tiny movement taxes my ocular muscles and takes far longer than it should.

A middle-aged man stands before my hiding place, his nitrile-gloved hands in the air. His handscreen's light shines through the rubbery purple covering. He wears airtight laboratory goggles and a transparent face mask over his nose and mouth. A thick black mustache, quivering like the rest of his body, blankets his upper lip. It's the most prominent feature of his round face.

"Get away from those jequirity, miss!" he says, pointing to the vines at my side. I take another look at them: they're weighed down by scarlet seeds with black stripes. The clear plastic bag dangling from his hand is filled with them. "Inhaling just milligrams of the fumes could kill you!"

He's more concerned about my safety than my identity? Puzzled, I gather my strength, roll like a log away from the jequirity, prop myself up on my elbows, and take a better look at the man. His skin is bronze, his small eyes a light shade of brown that borders on gold. He wears robes dyed black, a color not associated with a civilian residential compound. Haphazardly pinned to his chest is the flask-shaped badge of . . . the Chemistry Department?

So. He's as much of an intruder here as I am. I can almost feel a cool breeze blowing the sweat off my skin.

Looking anxiously back and forth, the man kneels, facing me, and stows his left hand in a pocket to cover his handscreen. "I know you," he whispers. "Sage." Slowly, he flashes the Dovetail sign, thumbs interlocked and fingers spread. "You're alive."

Barely. A wave of nausea rolls through me, and I scrunch my eyes shut.

"I'm Asterion Epsilon." The man pats my shoulder with a big, soft hand, the way I imagine a father would comfort his daughter. But my body seizes up nonetheless. I've never liked physical contact with strangers.

Is Asterion a stranger, though? Something about him seems familiar, and it's more than Yinha's hasty words in Defense about him running in the next election.

He goes on: "I've wanted to meet you ever since my daughter told me about a sagacious fifteen-year-old in her trainee class. Possibly the youngest Militia recruit in history."

History. An icy sensation creeps up my spine, vertebra by vertebra. "Vinasa," I whisper. The first girl who showed me kindness in Militia training, brilliant and beautiful; she aspired to learn from the past and improve our society in the future. But she lost her life in a needless spaceship crash. It's been more than a year, and I don't think the shock has ever faded.

"I'm her father. Let's get you cleaned up and better hidden. You're not safe here." Asterion helps me to my feet. "Don't worry. This won't be the first time I've turned the lab into an infirmary."

I hesitate, unsure. What if he's not really a Dovetailer? Will he turn me in?

His eyes shift as they scan for intruders; the skin around them is bunched with concern. Suddenly, I feel silly for suspecting him. If he were a Committee crony, he'd have put a Downer in me by now.

Tiptoeing across the ground, screening ourselves with the jungle foliage, we reach the glass dome's wall. In this region, it's embedded with circular metal grates. "These lead to the CO_2-O_2 filtration system," Asterion says. "It's a quick crawl to Chemistry from here."

Our combined strength is required to heave me into the canopy and through the vent's mouth. I wait to move farther inside until I've thoroughly scanned the tunnel for security pods. Asterion secures the grate behind us, and we move off on our hands and knees. The tunnel's steel floor rubs me the wrong way, but I crawl quickly behind Asterion, eager to leave the suffocating greenhouse behind me and see the Chemistry lab where he made his groundbreaking discovery.

Soon, we reach the huge, humming filters, porous metal cylinders that extend upward several stories and produce a sound like wind buffeting a stony cliff. Because the walkway around the filters has no guardrails, we scuttle sideways. Acute vertigo from looking over the edge makes me feel as if I've left my body. Keeping my eyes focused on the way forward, I make it to the other side: another narrow tunnel.

Finally, Asterion kicks away a grate below us, and we drop onto a black lab bench, which is dusty with dried mud. From his previous trips to the greenhouses, I assume.

His award-winning lab differs from what I expected to such a degree that I nearly laugh out loud. The room is only ten meters long and eight meters wide; an interactive, colorful periodic table with the 124 known elements takes up half a wall.

Mountains of unwashed flasks, beakers, and test tubes fill two of the four sinks. A rust-colored concoction in a conical Erlenmeyer flask sits on a switched-off hot plate in a closed hood.

On a side bench, there's a plastic bag labeled "$NaHCO_3$"— sodium bicarbonate—and another "$C_6H_8O_7$"—citric acid. As I remember from Primary, adding these compounds helps reduce solutions' acidity or alkalinity before disposal. The sight makes me miss spooning the powdery substances into corrosive liquid and watching it fizz. Above the bench, someone has scrawled, *Neutralize excess H^+ and OH^- ions, or we'll have to charge you.*

I laugh to myself at the pun, even as jealousy jabs me in the gut. I would've loved to work in an environment like this one— after tidying it up a bit. If I hadn't left Primary for Militia last year, my future might have held discoveries, not destruction.

But there's no going back now, and I'd pick reuniting with my family over all the discoveries in the world.

Asterion steps out of the lab while I stand in my undergarments under the emergency showerhead and pull the lever. Forty liters of cold water land on me like a pile of stones, but I feel strong enough now to handle it. I scrub the dirt off my limbs with hand soap and a washcloth. After drying off, I put on an extra set of yellow Epsilon robes, tie a cleaning rag around my head to hide my hair, and cover my nose and mouth with a disposable face mask. Then, painfully, I wash out my wounds at the only clutter-free sink. Asterion returns with a bottle of hydrogen peroxide and disinfects them while I squirm.

"May I ask you something?" I murmur.

"You don't need to whisper," he says, after sitting on his handscreen. "We have security clearance from the Committee—no pods allowed. Airborne objects could disturb our experiments, you see."

"Why were you sneaking around the tropical greenhouse?"

Asterion sighs. "I'm trying to isolate the jequirity toxin, abrin, in quantities large enough to run multiple replicates for a study. Exposure inhibits ribosome function and therefore cell protein synthesis—frightening, but fascinating too. Among other things, abrin may have applications in treating neurological disorders." As he speaks about his research, childlike excitement lights up his round face—and I could almost hug him. I know the feeling. I've missed picking apart the workings of the world.

"Unfortunately," he says, frowning, "I can't say any more, not even to you. I'm sure you understand."

"I *don't*. I don't understand why someone with a Medal of Achievement would join Dovetail. You have security clearance! You can work in peace."

Repressed rage contorts Asterion's face into a mask. His gaze is distant, though, so I decide his anger isn't directed at me. "Vinasa died in a Militia evaluation, aboard a Militia Destroyer. And yet when Defense sent my younger daughter Chitra and me a notification, it said, 'Militia assumes no responsibility for Vinasa Epsilon's death. We sympathize with your loss.' When I asked to see her body, they told me they'd already given her organs to the Medical Department and burned the rest, as per usual, for greenhouse fertilizer."

I want to sob, to scream, but I dare not interrupt her father.

"I'd known for a while that the Committee's rule was no good," Asterion says. His voice sounds sad, and very old. "When I was a green Militia recruit fighting against Battery Bay and Pacifia, an older soldier—he was twenty, almost done with his service—gave speeches to the rest of us. Said he *respected* the Batterers! Told us they held fair elections, let the people make decisions. That they changed policies when they weren't right."

"But that was so long ago," I say.

Asterion shrugs. "I thought about his beliefs often, even after he died. I knew of Dovetail's formation, but I was too timid to risk joining, too comfortable in my career, too protective of my family. Until I lost Vinasa. She used to ask, 'What's the use of the past if we don't learn from it?' In the wake of her death, I've learned. And I volunteered to run for Base IV representative. No one told me they wouldn't give me a spot on the ballot or let me air ads on the news. As a write-in candidate, I've had to campaign by word of mouth, in secret. . . . Fairness, openness, accountability, and unity. Cooperation, not war, with the nations of Earth. I've made all these promises to people, and I must win to keep them."

He sighs. Looks away.

"In all likelihood, I can't. My supporters and I will suffer horribly for even trying."

It astounds me, the effort he's put in to achieve an impossible outcome. "If you know you'll lose, why do you fight so hard?"

"My other daughter. Chitra. She's sixteen, like you. I want her, and every other child on the Moon, to grow old with smiles on their faces. You love your family so much. You must want the same thing."

He's right. I ache with longing for it. But will Anka ever let go of her rage? Will Cygnus ever recover and be . . . normal?

"I don't know if it's possible for my sister," I say. "Or my brother."

Asterion sighs. "Until we try with everything we have to change things, the answer is always yes and no."

That reminds me of the basic quantum theory we learned in Chemistry class. I almost grin. "Schrödinger's rebellion," I mutter.

"No," Asterion says. "Ours."

30

ASTERION'S LAB IS A WELCOME HAVEN after doing time in the greenhouse. My digestive system has responded well to the barley crackers and hazelnut butter he's given me. While he performs extractions and reactions with the jequirity seeds, humming to himself, I rearrange the pieces of Cygnus's message in my head, muttering the snippets of code aloud and typing them into the programming database installed locally on Asterion's HeRP. As an added precaution, I wear gloves so that the system can't register my fingerprints.

OETACOLAPHE, I type into the Greek autocode database. **NO MATCHES FOUND,** says the screen. My thoughts keep time with the whirring of the state-of-the-art nuclear magnetic resonance machine in the corner. *T2A1G3* didn't turn up a match either—not for any programming language. Those same letters and numbers are repeated at the beginning and end of Cygnus's mantra. If it's a computer command, surely the initiation and termination codes of a program wouldn't be identical?

Nothing clicks.

"Phaet?" Looking anxious, Asterion stands in front of me, left hand and handscreen stowed in a pocket. His goggles have left owl-eye imprints on his face. "I'm sorry, but the head lab tech will be coming in to finish up some spectroscopy soon. I trust her, but only with chemistry."

He places food, water, a first-aid kit, and a tattered length of stained yellow cloth in a small satchel. I'll use the cloth like a scarf, to cover my hair and most of my face. Since my hand-screen can no longer emit light, he adds in a small flashlight.

I shoulder the satchel, reassured by the tangibility of these supplies. Together, Asterion and I detach the grate covering an air vent, and I crawl inside.

"Thank you, for . . . for all of this," I say. "How can I ever make it up to you?"

Asterion grins. There's a gap between his front teeth. "Kick open the box, take a risk. See if our rebellion's alive. Then come back and tell me about it." The smile drops off his face as suddenly as it appeared. "On a more serious note, stay away from Shelter, at least for the rest of the day."

"Why?" *Are Anka and Umbriel in danger?* "Is something happening there?"

"Girl Sage." He looks at me like a nosy child, then sighs, his expression apologetic. "Remember how I said I've had to campaign as a write-in candidate? That's . . . not allowed as of this morning."

My eyes bulge in their sockets.

"It's repugnant, but true." Face darkening with anger, Asterion shows me the official messaging application on his handscreen.

Trembling, I lower my eyes and read the Committee notification: IT IS DECREED THAT WRITE-IN VOTES FOR COMMITTEE REPRESENTATIVE IN THE ELECTION ON APRIL 1 WILL NOT BE COUNTED.

"Any Dovetail member could have unintentionally leaked my candidacy," Asterion says. "Just one overheard conversation . . ."

I inch backward into the air vent. So much for Asterion's "secret campaign"—the Committee must have found him out, and are taking any and all steps to diffuse the threat he poses.

Asterion stows his handscreen. "People can still write my name on the ballot, but the votes won't be tallied. Dovetailers in Shelter might hold a protest."

As they have a right to do. But that would endanger so many lives—including Anka's. I can only imagine her indignation at the news; she won't be a bystander in a demonstration, if there is one, but will actively participate.

"Now I have to go," I whisper.

"Don't!" Asterion says. "Go to Nanoengineering, or some other small department. To another greenhouse. I'm going into hiding myself." He fits the grate onto the air vent's opening, sealing me inside. "Stay *away* from Shelter."

He'll be in hiding—for how long? I realize with horror that I might never see him again. And what about his daughter? Will she feel the way I did when Mom was in the Pen?

Breathless, I crawl through the wind tunnels until I reach the whirring filters. Now that I've slept and eaten, they no longer look so intimidating—or perhaps in my haste to get to Shelter, I'm immune to fear. I swing over the edge of the walkway and drop down onto a lower level.

In the next tunnel I pass through, the sucking noise of a vacuum robot behind me reaches my ears. There's a faint backdrop of tired, clomping footsteps. *A Sanitation worker!* And he's traveling in Shelter's general direction. Willing myself to calm down, I inch along the wall until I feel the outline of a squat set of sliding doors. With the fake fingertip sleeve, I press the scanner and duck into a closet that smells like bleach—it's unpleasant, but still better than the tunnel's mildew-and-rot stench.

Faint sounds are audible now: a chorus of people, cheering intermittently. The noise from Shelter must be loud if it can carry all the way here. In the gaps between applause, there's a voice—the gravelly one of an old man. I can't make out his words, but it sounds like an organized event. A rally? That means Anka might throw herself in, and Umbriel will run after her. It also means . . .

Militia will be there soon.

Outside, the footsteps fade. I exit the closet, holding a suction mop; quickly, I smear dirt from the tunnel walls on my face and clothes, and run on my tiptoes behind the worker. At the next manhole elevator, he steps inside, and I do too, turning away to hide the fact that I don't have a Sanitation badge. At least I'm wearing a face mask similar to his. He looks away with the gruff introversion of a typical tunneler.

We surface in a base hallway near Shelter. The doors are open, and a tide of Militia soldiers rushes past us, heading inside. The Sanitation worker goes the other way. Ditching the suction mop behind a two-meter-high security mirror, I head straight for the Beetles. As I run, I wrap Asterion's length of tattered cloth over my face mask for extra coverage.

I shove past Beetles, standing on my tiptoes, hoping for a glimpse inside the dome. But all I can see over people's heads is Shelter's blotchy brown ceiling.

Someone lightly strikes my back with a truncheon, and I cover my eyes with my hands, trying to hide whatever the rag doesn't. *Need to move faster.*

"Sneaking out of Shelter?" barks my assailant, a faceless Beetle with his visor down. I'm so filthy from the tunnels that he thinks I'm a resident. "Get back in there!"

Thanks for the invite, I mentally say to the Beetle. Still shielding my eyes, I sprint into Shelter amidst the rush of soldiers.

My Militia-honed agility allows me to slip through the web of bodies before they have the chance to physically abuse me. In fact, they hardly seem to notice my passage. They're distracted by what's ahead.

In the dome's far interior, at the heart of Dovetail territory, a small crowd has gathered. They hardly pay the Militia any attention; someone else occupies their eyes, ears, and minds.

An elderly Shelter resident stands atop a rickety chair, addressing a motley assemblage comprised of people his age, young children, and a group of chain-smokers in their late teens. Even that final group listens intently. One girl raises a joint to her mouth, but misses; it hits her upper lip, and she's too stoned to notice the cluster of glowing orange embers that fall to the floor.

". . . unacceptable. We cannot stand for any more cheating from the Committee!" the old man is saying. His robes are barely recognizable as Xi orange. Under its layer of dirt, his hair might be white. Despite his dishevelment, though, his wrinkled face radiates a sense of purpose that's more rare in Shelter than cleanliness. "Asterion can change the Moon from the inside out—but he needs to be *voted in* first."

Near the front of the crowd, I make out Umbriel and Anka; they scoot closer to the old man. Umbriel hovers behind her, arms slightly extended on either side—as he did when he wanted to shield me from Primary bullies and the like. Without me to look out for, has he shifted all that attention to my sister?

Fighting back dread, I pull my scarf tighter around my head and follow Umbriel and Anka forward.

"When you cast your vote in two weeks, the Militia will threaten you," says the old man. "They'll track the ballots to see who voted for write-ins. But you must walk past the truncheons, the faceless helmets. Do not vote for anyone you do not believe in. I tell you, write down Asterion's name! If we stand together, they cannot and *will not* ignore us!"

The crowd cheers, drawing the attention of other Shelter residents—and the Militia patrols, which are gathering silently around the perimeter. *Stop, please*, I beg in my mind. *Don't turn this into a bloodbath.* If violence breaks out, my sister and my best friend will be on the front line. I push through the crowd, diving between the people around me, trying to reach my loved ones.

The old man flashes the Dovetail sign, thumbs interlocked and fingers spread. I hold my breath. *He shouldn't do that, not if he values his life. All our lives.*

"Asterion Epsilon. Reform and Equity Coalition," he says. "Around here, we're all for Asterion."

"All for Asterion!" choruses the crowd.

The old man ducks his head in a small bow.

An amplified screech fills the dome. We reel away from the sound, covering our ears. Small children cry out and burrow into their parents' robes.

"Quiet!"

While the old man hypnotized the Shelter residents with his empowering words, the Militia patrols—and reinforcements from Defense—silently surrounded the audience. Once again, Corporal Cressida Psi's in charge. She gives a stiff nod; three privates step forward and drag the speaker to the dome's center. I recognize Ganymede Zeta, Jupiter's crony, among them. He's smiling cruelly; his long, skinny tongue darts out like a snake's to lick his lips.

Sneering, Cressida flips over an empty tub, which would ordinarily hold the Shelter's meager supply of mush. Her subordinates push Asterion's supporter down on top of it. He struggles against them, his movements sporadic and crooked. The tub resounds with brassy bangs and crashes—until the soldiers secure the man's hands and feet.

I scan the room for a friendly Militia member—Eri, Nash, Yinha, anyone. My eyes come up empty. And where is Lazarus?

Heart pounding, I slink up behind Anka and Umbriel. Instead of hugging my sister, I tap her on the shoulder. She turns around and gives a happy squeak of surprise, but then whirls and immediately faces the old man again, lest other people notice me. To make up for the distance, she reaches back blindly and grabs my hand. Umbriel looks over his shoulder at me and nods, but he doesn't smile. *Ouch.* But what was I expecting?

I pull Anka backward to a safer spot. To my great relief, Umbriel follows.

"You lot can't keep a bargain, can you?" Cressida is shouting. Her violet eyes gleam. "The deal was that if you behave, we won't use the truncheons."

With obvious pleasure, Ganymede snaps magnetic handcuffs around the old man's wrists. "Get up, geezer!"

A few able-bodied Shelter residents advance, their faces furious. "Linus didn't disrupt fizz!" shouts the girl who held the joint.

In response, five more privates surround the upside-down tub, forming a ring around Ganymede, the corporal, the tall private girl, and the old man, Linus. They point their Electrostuns outward, and the Shelter residents back down. With a chilling smile, Cressida whips out her own Electrostun and shoots Linus. He collapses, screaming, as the electricity sends his arms and legs jerking like puppet limbs.

I squeeze Anka's hand harder, horrified. Out of instinct, Umbriel brushes my shoulder with his fingers. It's the first time he's touched me since we talked about Wes.

Cressida stops electrocuting Linus, puts her foot on his chest, and turns to address us. "This filth is deluding you," she says. "Asterion Epsilon doesn't stand a chance against Andromeda Chi. So what if you vote for him—you are *nothing*. We killed Mira Theta. We threw Sol Eta in the Pen. Your precious Girl Sage abandoned you—and for all we know, her bones are rotting at the bottom of the Atlantic. We will put this Asterion away before you even know it's happened. You keep throwing people at us? We will keep destroying them."

I feel Anka's hand form a fist. Her arm begins to shake.

"Stay calm," I say in a fierce whisper. The idea of Asterion in Penitentiary—or worse, in an electric chair—makes me tremble. "Don't let Cressida hurt you again."

"I hate her!" Anka screams. Thankfully, the crowd's shouting drowns out her voice. She tries to run forward, but Umbriel grabs her and holds her tight. Anka's harder to safeguard than the Phaet of old. "She deserves to die!"

Cressida electrocutes Linus again. His body does the same contorted dance atop the tub. This time, the old man doesn't even have the strength to scream. A plainclothes Dovetail guard leaps to defend him, but Ganymede electrocutes the man with a flick of his trigger. He falls to the ground, limp. After that, nobody tries to help.

Cressida's going to kill him. Only when I feel liquid dripping from my chin do I realize that I'm crying. What if I ripped her weapon out of her hands and turned it against her? I'm strong and fast enough to do it. But her underlings would kill me in seconds.

Some Girl Sage you are, I scold myself. *You're a coward who'd rather shelter yourself than do what's right.*

Micah River would be disgusted with me. He gave up everything to help my brother, and for what? So that I could hide in the greenhouses and cower in Shelter, making zero progress toward protecting Dovetail and saving Cygnus?

At least I can watch over Anka, make sure she stays out of trouble. . . .

But as I learn a few hours later, she doesn't *stumble* into trouble. She creates it.

31

THE WHITE WING STANDS OUT IN BRIGHT
relief against the filthy Shelter floor. Every feather is visible—
even the barbs on each feather. Three Militia troops guard the
drawing, which is next to the Psychology tent, and one of them
has my sister by the wrist. Umbriel and a majestic older woman
stand nearby, talking heatedly.

As I crouch behind the Medical tent, my breaths come fast
and heavy. After I overheard some Dovetail teenagers whisper-
ing about Anka Theta acting out again, I left my things in the
spot where I'd hidden, alone, mulling over Cygnus's message,
and frantically searched out my sister.

"Unacceptable," the helmeted male corporal says. "This is
Anka Theta's fourth infraction in as many weeks. It's got to be
genetic. Her DNA codes for trouble."

The Shelter residents' dinner mush contained millet, making it an off-white color significantly more appetizing than the
usual stuff, which comes in varying shades of brown. Maybe
someone was trying to appease the population after Linus's violent death. My sister took that gift and made a painting with
it. And what's more, it was a confrontational, illegal one that all
but shouts "We're still standing!" at the Committee.

The majestic woman, who wears her white hair in a braid,
puts one hand over her Psychology badge. This must be Biela
Upsilon, Lazarus's boss. "I apologize sincerely," she says, her

tone soft but reassuring. "Please understand, my assistant and I have collected enough data to know that the imprisonment or killing of a child, especially one as well known as Anka, will only lead to greater disorder in Shelter."

"I'm not a child." My sister's voice rings with vitality, and it's all I can do not to break cover and hug her. "Children will believe anything people tell them. Haven't you noticed how none of the Committee's lies stick to me? If you want to compare us, Ms. Biela, I'd say I'm more grown up than this corporal here."

"Shut up," snaps the corporal. He turns back to Biela, who's regarding Anka with astonishment. "I'm sending a message to my superiors."

Anka crosses her arms. Umbriel, who hovers behind my sister like a bodyguard, advances—then halts abruptly. Heads turn at the clack of another pair of boots approaching.

"Dr. Biela will address this, Anka." Lazarus's voice seems to pass through my sister like warm wind, and her posture relaxes.

"On your knees, girl," Biela Upsilon says.

Anka complies.

"Tidy up this mess." Biela raises her eyes, regarding the others with indifference. "That will be all. Leave us."

Anka's hands push the mush back into the bowl. Her face shows no hint of disgust—only sadness. She's squeezing that beautiful white wing out of existence.

When everybody but Umbriel has departed, I approach my sister at last. Silently, I fall to my knees beside her and hold out my arms. She collapses forward, clings to me. Her chest heaves, but her cheeks remain dry.

I'd rather she cry—I have no experience with this new Anka, who speaks her beliefs without flinching and sheds no tears for the consequences. She's gone from crying when bullies insulted her math skills to eloquently contradicting base professionals. It makes me proud—and scared.

She puts her left hand in her pocket to prevent eavesdropping, which relieves me just a bit. "I'm sorry I got in trouble again. I was so angry. You saw what Cressida did. She killed that old man! And she said such horrible things!"

"We shouldn't let words hurt us," I say.

"We shouldn't let anything they do hurt us," my sister says.

Umbriel reaches for Anka's hand, and she squeezes his fingers until the tendons of her forearm stick out.

When my arm brushes Umbriel's, his dark eyes find mine, and he gazes down at me with a neutral expression. Not happy, but not angry either. I wasn't expecting anything more.

"What kind of election are they running, anyway?" Anka asks. "Why take out Linus? He didn't say anything bad about Andromeda. He only said good stuff about Asterion Epsilon."

I tighten my arms around Anka. The Committee has outdone itself. Last year, it promised free and fair elections; less than twelve months later, its representatives are committing murder to win, again. I imagine taking all the suffering they've caused and feeding it back to them; they'd probably burst.

"If Linus can't give speeches anymore," Anka says, "I will. Mom would want it."

"What if *I* don't?" I whisper. *I can't lose you too.*

"I can't just keep sitting around with Umbriel." She glances sideways at him, and then puts her lips near my ear. "At least I'm never lonely, but he can be so *annoying.* He treats me like I'm you, and won't let me go anywhere alone."

It takes all my restraint not to give Umbriel an apologetic

glance. I didn't know he missed me that much—enough to try and replace me with my sister.

At normal volume, Anka says, "I have a voice, and I want to use it."

Pulling back from her, I marvel at the defiance in her shrunken face. Unlike me, my sister says what she thinks and shows what she feels. Her heart influences her mind, rather than the other way around. There's something heroic about her—and something persuasive too. She's inherited Mom's willingness to look evil in the face, no matter how unlikely it is that she'll win.

Anka and Umbriel head back to their "campsite," and I crouch behind another family to avoid revealing myself. I'll need to head back underground soon. . . .

Three more minutes, and then I'll leave them.

From a distance, I watch as Anka lies down, tosses left and right on the hard ground. She can only fall asleep on her side, just like me, which I know from ten years of sharing a bedroom with her. Those days are no more. Does she miss them too?

Eventually, Anka projects her old three-dimensional star map from her handscreen into the air above her, tracing the lines of the constellations with her forefinger. She lingers on Cygnus, the Swan, and Mira, a star in the constellation of Cetus, the Whale.

In another part of the night sky is the Phoenix constellation, a diamond and a triangle that roughly resemble wings, with the star Anka glowing on its right-hand side. Each star is labeled with both its proper name and an astronomical abbreviation consisting of a Greek letter and the first three letters of the constellation's name.

Lying there, looking at her, I come upon the truth: Anka—

not me—is Mom's true heir, a girl who'll fight for justice with all the fury of her firebird namesake. Meanwhile, I've hidden in the bowels of the base and the tangles of Greenhouse 17. If I can keep my sister alive until she's no longer a child, she'll become the young woman the rebels need. But that's no small feat.

Why was I born without her courage? Was it a matter of chance, which sister came into the world meek, and which inherited her mother's strength? I wonder if Mom ever considered naming her rebel group Operation Phoenix instead of Operation Dovetail.

If only Cygnus were here to see the person our sister has become.

Cygnus. T2A1G3.

Her DNA codes for trouble, the Corporal said.

DNA contains four nucleotides: adenine, thymine, guanine, and cytosine, which are commonly abbreviated as A, T, G, and C.

T2A1G3 . . . TTAGGG.

In a frenzy of hope, I recite the pieces of Cygnus's message to myself; simultaneously, I rake my eyes over Anka's star map.

Alpha P-H-E: Phoenix. Omicron C-E-T: Mira. Alpha C-O-L: Phaet, the Dove.

32

"GOT IT!" I BLURT AS SOON AS LAZARUS opens the door to the examination room.

His jaw drops practically to his collarbone. After a few seconds, he seems to realize how absurd he looks. His teeth clack when he closes his mouth again.

"$T_2A_1G_3$," I whisper as he shuts the door. "Two thymines, one adenine, three guanines."

Lazarus tilts his head to the side, puzzled.

"The repeating nucleotide sequence in vertebrate telomeres."

"Pardon me?"

How could Lazarus not know what I'm saying? This is basic science, the biology I studied in Primary. I suppose that as a Psychologist, Lazarus's research deals with behavior and cognition, not molecular biology.

"Telomeres cap DNA strands," I recite from memory. "They don't code for proteins. They protect the strand from damage during multiple cell divisions, and they shorten as we age."

"Enlightening," Lazarus says, smiling faintly. "But how will we mobilize this revelation to decode Cygnus's message?"

"We won't." I grin. "$T_2A_1G_3$ begins and ends the message like telomeres begin and end a strand of DNA. They encode for nothing and protect what's between them. Cygnus said '$T_2A_1G_3$' to throw people off."

My brother must have ruminated for days about this message,

knowing that at some point he'd be filmed in an attempt to draw out Dovetail—and me. He knows how I think, and he created a code that only I could break.

"The real message is made up of stars." I bounce on the balls of my feet. "*Omicron C-E-T* is shorthand for Omicron Ceti, or Mira. *Alpha C-O-L* is Alpha Columbae: Phaet. And *Alpha P-H-E* is Alpha Phoenicis: Anka. So Cygnus's password has to do with Mom, me, and Anka."

A genuine smile breaks across Lazarus Penny's face. He walks closer to me and, when he's only a meter away, shifts his weight to one hip and crosses his arms. "Impressive, and yet— not a surprise, given his affection for the three of you. Do you also know what *dodeca-chordata* could mean?"

"I can guess."

Lazarus types furiously on his handscreen. Reading upside down, I see: *Dear Yinha, an emergency of the most pleasant variety has arisen. Please notify other relevant parties and find me immediately.*

"Before the arrival of our audience, I am impelled to discuss the proceedings against me on Battery Bay." Lazarus leans in, entering my personal space, but my back is pressed up against a wall, leaving me nowhere to go. "Every hour, they are moving closer to my expulsion not only from the Sanctuarist force, but from the citizenry of Saint Oda. To Wesley and his father, you are now a heroine, one of the city's saviors. Your word carries clout with the Sanctuarists. I have legitimately contributed to the attempt to extricate your brother from danger, so, in the name of equity, I beg you to vouch for my character. Please, Miss Phaet—"

"Not now," I blurt. I like him, and we *did* make a deal, but if I do as he asks, I could lose my good standing with the other

Sanctuarists. "It's too soon. I'll speak to Wesley Sr. after Cygnus is safe."

"But the Sanctuarists will likely have expelled me by then." Looking down, Lazarus plays with his left sleeve, rolling and unrolling it with his long fingers. "This cannot wait for a more opportune time—the only time is now! I cannot continue to help you if we do not clear my name together."

"You've helped me so much," I say. "But I hardly know you."

His nostrils flare, and then his mouth curves into a one-sided smirk. "Then do you consider me a scoundrel—at best, a reformed scoundrel—as the other Odans do?"

My knees begin to wobble, and it's all I can do to stand my ground.

"As you have noted, Sage, we hardly know each other. But that can change." Like a house cat, he straightens and takes a step toward me. But some unidentifiable feeling—fear or nervousness?—liquefies my legs, making them numb and useless. I stumble on one of the low chairs, and his hand catches my wrist.

Up close, I see faint creases around his nose, his eyes. The patience in them has disappeared; they're all too eager now, and magnetic. Since I met Lazarus, I've admired him the way one would a distant star, never expecting or wanting to travel all the way there. But now he's right here, and the nearness is blinding.

The instep of his right foot brushes against mine, and the contact seems to burn me.

I leap back, twisting around in midair. An overreaction to contrast with his smoothness. "Got to go."

"Wait! Don't leave."

Lazarus comes into a kneeling position two meters from my feet. I'd thought him incapable of blushing, but the red blood has flown to his cheeks. Now I almost regret fleeing from him—but he advanced too quickly, and all at once. What I thought was a distant star turned out to be a comet hurtling directly at me.

"I apologize, Sage," he says. "I had hoped you would see something, *anything*, in me, just as I saw wisdom and a beautiful sort of . . . of resilience in you."

What?

"Since Marina, I have not encountered another girl so . . . inspiring. The ordeals you have endured bring out the best in me and draw me to you. But believe me when I say that if such advances are unwelcome, I will not make them again. I am truly sorry."

Maybe he's telling the truth. His eyes droop at the corners. I pity this man, who seems to need a younger, "damaged" girl in his life to make it worthwhile. To make him feel like a savior.

But I don't need him to carry on with my existence. I don't need anyone.

"Please," he adds. "Forgive me?"

My anger ebbs away. As a reward for his earnestness, I give him more than my customary silence.

"Apology accepted. Now, let's pretend this never happened. Yinha's coming soon."

*   *   *

Lazarus's office was not built to hold five people. I can almost feel everyone's pulse through the parts of my body that touch theirs. And I can detect Lazarus's discomfort, even though his face is guarded. He's apologized several more times, and I've assured him that I'm not angry, but I can still feel my skin puckering into goose pimples where he touched me.

He and Yinha hide their handscreens in pockets or under

crossed arms; in their company, it feels odd to leave my left hand dangling by my side.

While we were waiting, Lazarus programmed the sign on the door to read, KEEP OUT—PSYCHOLOGICAL EXPERIMENT IN PROGRESS. The speaker on the outside wall is playing An-ka's fake screams to further discourage intruders. The room's soundproofing makes conversation possible, despite the alleged torture proceeding within.

We've tried several passwords to unlock the attachment to the video, but each has been denied. Cygnus wouldn't have chosen something as obvious as *MiraPhaetAnka* or our favorite colors.

"We can figure this out tonight," Anka says. "I know it."

Yinha sips fragrant matcha from a metal thermo-proofed mug in her right hand. She stands between Lazarus and me as if she has some idea of what transpired before her arrival. "Remember what your mom used to password-protect her 'Grievances'?" Yinha says. "Your birthdays."

"Too easy," I say. Caeli guessed right away, and that guess led to Mom's capture. Besides, we've already tried it.

"The odd-sounding thing at the end bugs me," Yinha says. "*Dodeca-chordata*. We haven't picked at that yet. Any ideas?"

"Dodeca . . . like a dodecahedron," I say. "A twelve-sided die. It's the prefix for *twelve*."

"And *chordata* is a certain group of animals, right?" Anka says. "I remember that from Primary."

"Right," I say. "The phylum includes anything with a spinal column, and a few more clades besides."

"So, *twelve animals*," Umbriel says. "Which ones, though? Loads of animals have spines. It's gotta be a superlong password if he used a dozen species names."

"Phaet, did your family celebrate the Lunar New Year?" Yinha says. "I don't mean the crappy light show the Committee puts on in the Atrium on January first; I mean the ancient Earthbound new year based on the Moon's phases."

I frown. Will my answer help at all? "No . . ." Observing Earthbound holidays is illegal, and she knows it.

"Hmm. Well, my family did." Yinha grins at the secret memories. "We made tofu dumplings every January or February, depending on when the holiday fell. The Chinese zodiac changes by year, not month, and it's a twelve-year cycle. Twelve animals. And *they* all have backbones, I think."

Excitement zips through my spine—the kind I feel when I've got a good problem to solve.

"So your conjecture is that Cygnus's password consists of the daemons of their birth years?" Lazarus says.

Anka shrugs. "Sounds like something he'd do."

I nod. My brother loves puzzles and obscure information; Yinha's idea unites both.

"What year were you born, Phaet?" Yinha asks me.

"2331," I answer.

"You're a pig," she says, and a smirking Lazarus promptly types PIG in the password box.

Umbriel snorts, sounding slightly like an Odan hog.

"Hey, hotshot," Yinha scolds him, "if you were born the same year as Phaet, the pig is your zodiac animal too. And that means you're supposed to be honest and gallant but also really naive."

Umbriel is silenced, for now.

"On what grounds . . ." I trail off, shaking my head. How could Umbriel and I, who are so different, fall under one zodiac symbol and supposedly have the same personality traits? No wonder the Committee banned astrology. Not only does it strip away individual agency; it's the opposite of scientific.

"Take it easy, Phaet," Yinha says. "The zodiac's not supposed to be an exact science. Anyway, *pig* should really be translated as *boar*. Sounds mightier, yeah?"

Lazarus deletes PIG and enters BOAR into the password box.

"Let's figure out Mom's animal next," Anka says. "She was born in 2298."

"Yeesh. I don't remember which animal matches up with that year." Yinha punches some numbers into her handscreen's calculator function, and then nods. "Your mom's a tiger. Brave, but often in conflict with authority."

Anka hugs herself, curling into a ball. When she speaks, her voice is tiny. "That's why she's not a tiger anymore. She *was* one."

Lazarus, bowing his head out of respect, enters TIGER into the box in front of BOAR. It now reads, TIGERBOAR.

"Now it's my turn," Anka says. "I was born in 2336."

"Hm . . . that makes you a dragon," Yinha says.

"Great!" Anka says. "I hoped it would be something fierce. Well, Lazarus, you can add *dragon* to the password."

"Gladly, as always," he replies. "Here we go." He types DRAGON and hits Enter.

PASSWORD INCORRECT, the screen says in red letters. My heart sinks deeper in my chest, and my face flushes with frustration.

"This grit hasn't gotten the best of us yet," Yinha says. "I forgot something. Do any of you have a birthday early in January?"

"Me," Anka says. "January tenth."

"Well, that explains things," Yinha says. "The Lunar New Year usually falls a couple of weeks after the standard new year. So that makes you"—Yinha scratches her chin—"a rabbit. Easygoing and organized."

"Seriously?" Anka makes bunny ears with her first two

fingers. "The zodiac creators got it all wrong."

"They didn't see you coming," Yinha says. "A roaring rabbit."

I tamp down the anxiety and watch as, instead of **TIGER-BOARDRAGON**, Lazarus types **TIGERBOARRRABBIT** into the HeRP.

The document opens.

My sister throws her arms up; they land, one around Umbriel's shoulders and one around mine. I squeeze her back, harder than I meant to.

We did it. We found a way in.

"Brilliant," Lazarus says. He touches Yinha's hand, his face brightening.

Pretending not to notice, Yinha tilts up her mug to chug the rest of her tea, blocking her face. When it's empty, she slams it down on Lazarus's desk with a clang.

"Read the blasted note, people."

And we do.

> *This is the fourth or fifth time I've tried starting this letter, Phaet. I can't even count to five anymore. They've shorted out every circuit in my brain. I've seen you rescue me so many times. I'm scared that if you actually come, I'll think it's another hallucination.*
>
> *When I woke up in this cell, I realized that they'd bugged my handscreen. But they left it jailbroken so I could send out distress messages. Theoretically, they could use those to find my accomplices.*
>
> *I tried to disable the bug, but it failed. Maybe because my head was messed up. So I played stupid. Sent messages to people who didn't exist. While they sniffed down the wrong trails, I hacked into some security pod feeds. Then I flew the pods around until*

I found the Law exit. I programmed them to help. If you show up, they'll take you to me.

They beat me bloody when they found out about the fake messages. They filmed themselves shocking me. They sent the tape to you guys to make you come get me.

I know you, Phaet. You'll come running in a second. That's why I'm writing this. So that when you show up, you'll know what to do. I have no idea how to get you this document. I can't send it through cyberspace or the Committee will get their hands on it. But I have to write this down before I forget.

When you get to Base I, go to the Law lobby. Find the pod that hangs around the third seat in the first row of the waiting room.

Don't try to find me without the pods. It's a labyrinth in here. This isn't the Base IV Pen.

They put a tungsten and carbon fiber collar on my neck. It'll suffocate me if I leave my cell. Bring something that can cut or burn through it. Bring guns. And people—but not too many, for nukes' sake.

Sometimes, I see you and Anka and Mom. Even Dad. All of you, lined up in a row. It's in my head, but it feels real. I've got to remind myself who's alive and who's dead. It shocks me worse than electrocution every time I sort you all out. But it keeps me from going crazy.

I know you probably won't listen to me. So if you need to come for me, come prepared. Don't make me put you with the dead people.

The message ends. I feel my fingers turn to ice.

It's okay, it's okay. He can still form coherent sentences. Still, I can't shake the numb panic creeping through my limbs. While Cygnus doesn't sound broken, he doesn't sound like himself either—there's no laughter between his words, only jagged shards of hope. It's like he's aged twenty years in mere months.

But he's left us a trail. He found a way, even under the worst conditions imaginable. Although he hasn't given us his exact location, we can find it if we follow his directions. Cygnus may have discouraged me from coming after him, but that evidence of his love for me makes me want to help him even more.

I feel the eyes of Yinha, Anka—even Umbriel. They're watching me, waiting for me to tell them what to do next.

I throw all my weight behind my next words: "It's time. We're going to Base I."

33

"ANDROMEDA'S STUFFED HER BODYGUARD team full of Dovetail-friendly Mili—" Yinha stifles a yawn. "Militia. Me, Nashira Phi, Eri Pi. Callisto Chi will be on board too, but that can't be helped; it would look suspicious if Andromeda's own daughter didn't come. Colonel Arcturus Theta will remain on Base IV to advise the General and keep him from going berserk if the election gets crazy. Which I think will happen."

Lazarus blinks away sleepiness, opens his mouth wide in a yawn. His black hair points in a couple hundred different directions, and he's developed a pimple under his bottom lip. With the approach of our mission, chinks in his impeccable appearance have started to appear. I like him better for the imperfections. "Should we be concerned for Asterion?"

We've already discussed Lazarus's plans. He'll arrive on Base I several hours before we get there, under the guise of preparing for the presentation he and Biela will make to the Committee about the Dovetail situation in Base IV's Shelter.

"Asterion went into hiding the day Linus was killed," Yinha says. "His LPS chip was already out; now he's disconnected his handscreen too. After Militia sacked his lab, they gave up on finding him. Making a big deal of the search would be too embarrassing. He's too famous, you see."

"We've already embarrassed them," Anka says fiercely. "If the

Militia or the Committee tries anything on Election Day, I'll—"

Lazarus puts a calming hand on her shoulder to cut her off.

"Anka, we would all prefer it if you stayed in Shelter without making a spectacle of yourself."

"Knew you'd say that." Anka twists her mouth and gestures at Umbriel with her chin. "What about him?"

Yinha sighs. "Umbriel should stay in Shelter too."

"I'm coming on the ship." Umbriel straightens up. Now that he's no longer slouching, he towers over everyone but Lazarus. "Andromeda can stow me away with Phaet."

"Do I have to *order* you to stay back?" Yinha points to her captain's insignia. "Look, I like your enthusiasm, but you haven't had any Militia training. You could mess everything up."

Umbriel lifts his hands, palms outward, but it's not a gesture of surrender. He turns them over in the dim light, as if showing off the long, dexterous fingers; the nails, slightly overgrown; the double-jointed thumbs. "You want anything? I'll pick it out of someone's hands without him noticing. A security pod? I'll snatch it from the air and stick it up my sleeve. If you get hungry . . ." Umbriel shoots me a small smile, the most welcoming gesture he's made since our brief, torturous conversation. Even though it hurts, I look away. "Think. If Lazarus is with Biela, and Yinha, Nashira, and Eri are with Andromeda's bodyguards, then Phaet will be alone. Cygnus said it in his letter: working alone on Base I is tricky, maybe idiotic. I could go with her into the Pen."

"Okay, I get it!" Yinha stomps her foot. "You're coming too. That's six of us! I'm half expecting Kappa to fly up from Earth and make it a party."

Wes. Why did Yinha have to mention him now? I'm more

than willing to sacrifice everything for Cygnus, but I haven't let myself think about one particular repercussion of our mission: *I might never see Wes again.*

Umbriel scowls at me, as if I were the one who said his name.

"Wesley sent me a message last week," Lazarus says. I shift my weight forward, attentive. "The displaced Odans are adjusting poorly to Battery Bay. His older sister in particular. The Batterers have put on a fireworks display every night, but all the Odans can hear are the sounds of cannons and exploding grenades."

Yinha's eyes dart between Lazarus and me, her face serious. "Sorry, Zee. I wish we'd left Saint Oda alone. Then and now. The raid, all those years ago? That's what made this mess, right? It . . ." Her face closes off. "It was the worst thing I've ever done."

"But it had some positive outcomes, Yinha," Lazarus says. "I wouldn't be helping to depose the Committee, and you wouldn't have become my friend, if the invasion hadn't—"

"Yeah, and I'd still be an active soldier." Yinha turns away from Lazarus. "After my unit plowed through your city, I told myself I'd never return to Earth."

Yinha's words jog my memory. *If she helped raid Saint Oda . . .*

"Do you remember a girl with thunderclouds in her eyes?" I say.

Yinha's face crumples as though I've kicked her. Her cheeks turn pale instead of pink. Beside her, Lazarus frowns and averts his eyes. Anka and Umbriel observe their reactions, confusion clouding their faces.

"So she lived," Yinha murmurs. "I didn't say anything, not to anyone. For ten years. But somehow you met her. What's her name?"

My breathing quickens. More and more pieces fit together:

Murray said the soldier who injured her had a thin frame and eyes like mine. Yinha can't bear to fight; now I've learned why. It was her. She cut Murray that night, and spared her.

"Murray Carlyle," I say. "Wes's older sister. You saved her life."

Lazarus's boot slaps the ground hard, and he straightens stiffly, running a hand through his already ruffled hair. *This is a revelation for him too.*

Yinha sighs, rubbing her forehead. "Wes always did seem familiar. How bad is the girl's scar?"

I shake my head.

"I thought so." Yinha's voice hitches. Is my former instructor about to cry? "Has she forgiven me?"

"No." I don't see why I shouldn't be blunt. "She doesn't understand why you did it. Maybe someday you can explain it to her."

"I do not believe that meeting you would be healthy for Marina." Lazarus gestures—it's more of a twirl—with his right hand, and then places it on his forehead. "Due to circumstances beyond her control, of course, she has recently grown as unstable as the Juan de Fuca tectonic plate." He shoots me a knowing look.

I confirm Murray's condition with a nod.

Umbriel takes advantage of the silence to excuse himself, taking Anka with him. Yinha, who's presumably had enough of Lazarus too, leads me toward a deserted spot in the Shelter dome. She sits on her left hand, over her handscreen, touches my arm with her right, and begins talking, quickly and urgently.

"Stripes, all you've thought about lately is saving your brother, and that makes perfect sense, but you should know that Dovetail has . . . bigger plans for you."

What? My mind has no room for anything more than traveling to Base I and returning with Cygnus.

"You've seen how people talk about you. The Girl Sage. They don't know for sure if you're alive, but the *idea* of you has kept them going. I hope that your involvement in this group doesn't end when you get your family back. What if you rescued Cygnus, and *then* took a stab at the Committee? Something dramatic, bigger than them losing one prisoner, one election. Something to scare them gritless."

I can't imagine the Committee being scared of a teenager, let alone a silent one.

"You'd be like a girl from a story my grandma used to tell."

My arms hug my knees closer to my chest. "Go on," I say in a tiny voice.

"It's just an old folktale, but okay. There's a peasant girl, Si'er, and she lives happily in a village, until the local landlord kills her dad because he can't pay his rent. Crazy, huh? But it escalates. The landlord kidnaps her. She's his slave until a servant boy falls in love with her and frees her. She hides in the mountains, living off her garden and offerings from a nearby temple. Months go by, and shock and sadness bleach her hair all white."

Her diet was probably missing copper and a couple of amino acids, I think.

"The landlord comes to pray at the temple during a thunderstorm, and *bam!* Si'er shows up, with her ribbons of white hair, and he thinks she's some goddess sent to punish him. He's so freaked out that he's literally paralyzed. She takes the incense burner, sets fire to the temple, and runs off into the night. She returns to her village, which is now free of the landlord's cruelty." Yinha laughs. "Mind-blowing, yeah? All the parallels? Proves that revolution's been around as long as the human race."

She calls Dovetail's fight a *revolution.* As if she's confident we'll succeed. *Kick open the box*, Asterion said. Yinha thinks she knows what's inside.

"I'm not saying you should burn the Committee alive, but maybe you could throw them off enough to make a difference. You get your revenge, your family gets its security, and all of us get democracy. How does that sound?"

I'm not sure. So I say the only thing I'm certain of.

"Cygnus first."

*　　*　　*

And before that, the maintenance tunnels. I've stayed aboveground far too long. I plunge back into the murky maze beneath Lazarus's office, not looking forward to being confined again. But this time, I have food in my satchel, a source of light in my hand, and more than a bit of hope in my soul.

34

THE NIGHT OF MARCH 31, 2348, I SNEAK back into Shelter.

It's not easy. I wait inside a maintenance closet, listening to dozens of Militia patrols pass through the metal door into the blocked tunnel. Every time, they open the door, shut it, and slide the lock into place. Always, the *click* feels like a rejection.

Hours later, I finally hear the door shut freely. I tiptoe into the blocked area, sending a silent *thank you* to the Dovetail mole who's given me access.

With every hair-raising clatter or clang that reaches my ears, I curse my decision to return. But I can't stay away. What if I lose Anka—or Umbriel—in the next twenty-four hours? I don't want to regret having spent the last few hours before this mission cowering beneath the surface of Base IV.

With Asterion's flashlight on its low setting, I crawl across the dome floor until I find their campsite. Umbriel lies on his back, his arms spread, snoring gently through his open mouth. The scene takes me aback: he looks so boyish and unthreatening, so . . . kind.

But he hasn't forgiven me, and he shouldn't have to wake to the sight of me. To put distance between us, I step over my sister's sleeping form, which is curled into a ball, lie down next to her, and close my eyes.

Just before I begin to dream, Anka gives my shoulder a gentle shake. She was awake all along.

"Phaet? You're here? I thought they'd catch you if—"

"Shh," I say.

She stops talking, but only for a moment.

"I've wanted to ask you something. . . ."

I nod.

"I know I'm too old for bedtime stories, but will you tell me more about Murray? Why doesn't Zee like her?"

"He doesn't have a problem with her," I say. *Only a whole lot of memories.* Perhaps he doesn't want to remember how he breached Odan mores. But how to explain that in a manner appropriate for a twelve-year-old? Funny that I'm still trying to shield Anka after all she's seen and done for Dovetail in my absence. But . . . she's my little sister.

"They're very different people," I say haltingly. "They used to be . . . friends. But they had a misunderstanding. Murray remembers everything about their time together. Zee doesn't, or he tries not to."

"That's dumb. If Murray gave half her memories to Zee, they'd be even, right? Maybe then they could make up. Meet in the middle. Like if you talked more and Umbriel listened more, you guys would've fixed *your* misunderstanding earlier."

Could it be that simple? Anka laughs at the surprise on my face. "He wants you to say something first. Your fight's getting old."

She's so wise sometimes; I can't believe she's four years younger than me. The dark obscures her features, all but her wide, gleaming eyes. *They see much more than I've given her credit for.* Who's the real girl sage here?

"But what if he doesn't . . ." I can't get the words out.

"Forgive you? You have to try anyway. You're going on that rescue mission together, and if you're not mad at each other anymore, I know you'll make it out alive. Both of you, and Cygnus too. I just know it."

Anka's optimism is infectious. I imagine her speaking to a crowd, inspiring them to take action; this phoenix, encouraging the struggling members of Dovetail to rise up from the ashes. Mom would be proud.

"You're going to be awesome," she says. "It's time I had all of you back."

*   *   *

April 1, 2348, arrives. Today, Lunars age eighteen and older will congregate in the hallways to receive instructions and cast their votes via handscreen. Voting will remain open until 18:00, when the votes will be counted and the Committee will broadcast the results.

Lazarus leaves early in the morning with Biela Upsilon. Left in charge, Yinha is restless. She seems to doubt her own memory, incessantly reminding Umbriel and me about details in our plan and clucking around us like a mother hen. "Remember, you don't *have* to, but if you guys want to avoid fingerprint checks, Umbriel needs to swipe a Law badge. Ariel and Atlas can't give him theirs—the Base I badge is gold, not silver like Base IV's. The Law secretary on duty tomorrow is a fellow named Sulzer, and he's tough on security, but you can use that to your advantage, like we discussed."

Though I know it's foolish, I can't stop thinking about the two-hour transit to Base I. I'll be trapped in the tiny cargo hold of Andromeda Chi's ship with Umbriel, and I'm dreading it more than I'm dreading what might happen once we reach our destination. But rescuing Cygnus will be worth it.

Journalism has mobilized all its resources to cover the first Lunar election in thirty years, dispatching employees to interview candidates, campaigners, and voters alike. Huddled near a dark wall, I spend the morning watching the live news broadcast—Yinha told me to stay in Shelter so that she could usher me and Umbriel out together. For election day, a sizable section of the ceiling has been converted into a screen, with images beamed from a projector near the Medical tent. The Committee must be trying to prove something, or maybe intimidate Dovetail. Are they trying to win people back?

"This is a picture of the ballot," the announcer says, and a simple text file appears. There's a checkbox next to Andromeda Chi of the Lunar Democratic League; I smirk at the irony of the name the incumbent Committee members have chosen for their party. Below Andromeda's name is Hartley Nu of the Lunar Asylum Party—a fringe group of radical isolationists.

Today, many people, at least in Shelter, will write *Asterion Epsilon* in the ballot's top margin as a gesture of defiance. By some miracle, he hasn't been found yet; he might have taken to the greenhouses, like I did. But the Committee won't count the votes he'll get, and that might enrage people even more.

In the early evening, Yinha arrives to pick up Umbriel and me. Anka says good-bye with hugs so fervent her arms go rigid. "I'd better see you later," she says, smiling through the pain.

"Let's move. You're under arrest." Yinha handcuffs Umbriel and me, grimacing. "Sorry for poking you," she adds under her breath. But to keep up the ruse, she prods us with her truncheon all the way to Defense.

We arrive before Callisto, as planned, but after Nash and Eri. We'll separate from them when we reach Base I, but they'll meet us outside Penitentiary after we've gotten Cygnus out. And we *will* get him out, however tough it might be. I can't afford to think about failure.

Nash does a double take as we walk in. When she recognizes me, she grins, causing her eyes to crinkle, and runs toward us so fast that her curly black hair starts to loosen from her bun. It's a lopsided run, because her left hand is in her pocket to prevent the Committee's eavesdropping. "Stripes! Gah, I've waited half a year to get you back in my life! How *are* you?"

Nash's expression is eager and open—until Umbriel shoots her a disapproving look. He clearly finds her question insensitive, given all that's going on.

"Sorry, wrong question?" she asks.

"Don't worry about it," I say.

"So, I'm guessing you're Umbriel," Nash says quietly, "the best friend with the quick fingers, yeah? Stripes told us about you in training."

"She talked?" Umbriel looks surprised, almost happy. "About me?"

"Said your record's clean, with zero infractions on account of stealing," Nash says. "You've never been caught, even though Stripes claims you nicked an apple a week since you were seven."

While Nash talks to Umbriel, Eri raises an eyebrow at me. Back in training, when she discovered my nightly workouts with Wes and asked me if there was anything between us, I countered by dropping Umbriel's name. Of course she's wondering what's going on now.

Wes . . . The thought of him makes me feel lonely, even though I'm surrounded by friends.

The sound of clacking boots grows louder.

"That'll be Andromeda and her nutjob kid." Nash grabs Umbriel's right elbow and my left and leads us to the back of the Titan ship. "Umbriel, sorry to cage you up thirty seconds after meeting you."

Umbriel gives her a strained smile. "Could've been five."

I catch one glimpse of Andromeda Chi before Nash seals Umbriel and me inside the cargo hold. Finally, I can see the Base IV representative as more than the black silhouette I know from the Committee public addresses. Andromeda can't be much older than Mom, but she has drooping jowls, a thick waist, and eyebrows that slope downward, probably from years of wearing the defeated facial expression she's sporting now. Thirty years ago, she likely had brown and yellow curls like her daughter's. Now her hair is gray and slack.

Beside her, Callisto, my old nemesis, thrums with nervous energy. She's a land mine, that one. It's impossible to predict what'll set her off—whether she'll spare my life like she did after Mom's trial or try to kill me as she did on Earth.

* * *

We take off, and I chafe against the strap across my hips. Two hooks on the ends hold me down to rings on the floor; they're meant to keep cargo from sliding around. Moon-grav doesn't make the ride any more stable than my journey from Earth; the ship tosses me to the right, then the left, like a piece of undigested food in an empty stomach. Yinha should've stuck me in the pilot's seat instead. With my former rank, I could be steering—and doing a better job of it—not cowering in the hold with Andromeda's luggage and Umbriel's resentment.

Sunlight glares in through the little window next to us; I

slam down the shade so that we don't overheat or get radiation sickness. Still, I feel as if someone's stuck me in a microwave. Perspiration drips into my eyes and pools under my armpits. During the lunar day, the Moon's surface temperature can reach 360 Kelvin, and despite our well-sealed spaceship, some of that heat energy inevitably makes it in here.

The second human body in this cargo hold doesn't make it any cooler. A tense, sweaty Umbriel is strapped down next to me, so close I hear a faint growl whenever he exhales. The ship lurches again; the pilot's probably swinging the controls to dodge space debris. My head smacks into Umbriel's bony shoulder.

"Yeow!" He leans away from me, but then instinct takes over and he pats my head. "How badly did I hurt you?"

The double-edged question knocks the breath out of me. The bump was nothing, but his sullenness, the absence of his laughter, the worry that I've lost him yet again—those have hurt me more than he'll ever know. "I've missed you," I say.

"I know," Umbriel says.

Silence.

I lean my chin on my clasped hands and watch my best friend's face. Eyebrows up—he's expecting something. A slight frown—he's disappointed that I'm not going to deliver. A shake of the head—he's trying to start afresh. As usual, he opens up when my silence unnerves him.

"We've kidded ourselves, haven't we? You went to Earth—I knew it was for your own good, though I never admitted it to myself—and then you came back. But since then, we've avoided each other, pretended that we didn't care, in the tiny bit of time we had. Who knows when things will be peaceful again?"

In the dark, only his teeth and the whites of his eyes stand out. Even from those, I can tell that he wants permission to embrace me. He's acknowledging at last that such contact has made me uncomfortable before.

Taking the initiative, I hug him. *We*, he said. Our standoff was my fault too. I failed to show Umbriel that I love him, just . . . differently.

Umbriel sniffles. The ship dodges another piece of debris, and I keep him from tipping over.

"I spent years waiting for you to . . . to like me. I knew you didn't, not really. And I know you tried to be nice about it, even when it made you twitch like an earthworm. One of the panicky ones we'd dig up in the greenhouses."

I smile into Umbriel's shoulder. His words remind me of sunlit gardening days in our childhood.

"But I was sure you'd come around," he continues, "no matter how much Ariel said you wouldn't. It hurt to clear stuff up with you the other day, but I'm glad we did. I don't want to keep wondering if everything you do means something, or keep trying to convince myself of stuff that isn't true."

I'm so relieved I could cry. Umbriel knew all along. He just couldn't believe that I didn't share his feelings until I told him directly.

"Come to think of it, I can count the guys you've ever really talked to on one hand," Umbriel says. "Me, Wes, maybe Orion, that Lazarus, who's twice our age . . . oh, and Ariel."

I grimace.

"Ugh, my brother. That would be weird." Umbriel chuckles. "Take me off that list, and out of everyone left, I guess Wes is . . . okay. If not for him, you wouldn't be sitting here now, right? Maybe if you didn't like him so much, I'd want to know him better."

Wes. I conjure up the image of him that I burned into my memory: on the Pacifian runway, fire illuminating half his face, starlight shining on the other.

I can't hide the sweltering blush from Umbriel, even in the dark. He pokes my cheek, and then shakes out his hand as if I've burned him.

"I heard Andromeda's luggage contains some pretty flammable stuff, clothes and whatnot. You sure you won't set this place on fire?"

A snort escapes my nose. Umbriel shakes his head, sadness lurking behind the amusement in his eyes. "Phaet, I've missed this too. Laughing and talking and being together. I'll try, really try, not to pick a fight with you again."

"And I should start explaining myself better."

Umbriel blinks twice. Close, open, close, open. "Yeah, but not just to me."

35

BASE I WELCOMES ANDROMEDA CHI WITH A parade fit for a returning conqueror. As she and her escorts make their way to the Governance Department, cheering citizens join the procession, massing behind them. Everyone wears a palm-sized Lunar flag pinned to their robes. Their elbows pump as they march in time, jabbing Umbriel and me in the ribs. If the crowd didn't offer protection from security pods and Beetles, I'd elbow them back in annoyance.

"Why does the Committee ever leave Base I?" Umbriel whispers in my ear, sarcasm turning his words to acid. "Looks like everyone pops caffeine pills whenever they go out in public."

We lag about five rows behind Andromeda, Yinha, Nash, Eri, and Callisto. To hide my hair, I've taken someone's extra HYDRUS: THE ONE FOR US banner and wrapped it around my head. Though it's necessary, I hate to advertise for an incumbent Base I Committee representative. Yinha also gave me a medical mask to conceal the bottom half of my face; I'm supposed to pose as a patient fresh from Medical treatment. Thanks to Sol's broadcast, everyone on the Moon knows what I look like. I'm no safer on Base I than I was on Base IV.

Beside me, Umbriel sports a vicious smirk and an ugly, cylindrical black hat, which is tipped over his eyes to hide his features. As an open member of Dovetail who's spent lots of time with Anka Theta, he's on file too. For additional coverage, he's wrapped a silver banner around the hat's brim. It reads, HEART,

HONOR, HYDRUS. To complete the farce, Umbriel periodically waves a small Lunar flag in front of his face.

We both wear clean civilian robes—the olive green of Lambda—that Yinha left for us in the cargo hold. Umbriel and I tugged on the robes and Yinha's other presents with our backs to each other. We could easily fit Militia chest, arm, groin, and leg armor, as well as utility belts, beneath the baggy tunics and pants. My sturdy boots hold three daggers apiece. I've also tucked a small diamond-bit drill, borrowed from Yinha's Militia mechanic friend, into my left boot. It should cut through Cygnus's tungsten collar. Even without gloves and a helmet, I feel like I can defend myself again, as I did in my Militia days.

A row of Militia soldiers marches in front of us, raising one foot to knee height with every step. Their black dress uniforms have been designed more for show than camouflage. Silver and gold piping runs across their chests and down their arms and legs. The soldiers wear no helmets, but they wave Lunar flags taller than they are. The fabric threatens to smack Umbriel and me in the face with every ripple.

"Isn't Election Day exciting? An opportunity to show the Committee how much we love them!" shouts a middle-aged woman to my right, her voice cutting through the majestic din of "Luna," the national anthem. She stands on tiptoe and beams at a young male Beetle. "Silver mountains, blackest seas," she sings. "Only here is mankind free."

Without breaking stride, the Beetle grins, his face transformed by manic patriotism.

The Committee murdered my mother! I'd yell it out loud if I could. *What if they do the same to yours?*

"Yeah." The woman's teenage daughter watches the soldiers

march past her—then grits her teeth as a security pod buzzes in front of her face. I turn my head the other way so that it can't film me. "And no one stands a chance against Hydrus. The other candidates don't know what they're talking about."

They're more loyal here on Base I. But then, this is the first Lunar macro-structure, built a hundred years ago. It shows. Base I has a less efficient design, one heavily influenced by twenty-third-century architecture. Instead of seamless interconnected domes, the structure is made up of domelike shapes with triangular or hexagonal facets—polyhedra that resemble cut gemstones. Black-and-white streamers cross the ceiling, intertwining before racing along again, parallel to each other. Lights shaped like cut diamonds hang from them, catching and throwing white light.

Instead of a central Atrium with hallways branching in four directions, Base I has the Colonial Circle, a cul-de-sac at the end of an immense walkway called the Main Lane. As we march down it, surrounded by cheering citizens, the Governance Department comes into view. The Pillars of Liberty, six colossal hexagonal columns of black-veined white marble, serve as sentinels for the Committee's stronghold. Flanking the Governance Department are InfoTech and Journalism on the left, and Law on the right. Real glass, clear or tinted with black, white, silver, and gold, adorns the doors.

Even the wall screens on Base I are different. The square facets in the ceiling each serve as a screen, so I see about fifty images of the same Journalist talking to Andromeda about the election situation on Base IV.

"Support seems strong, despite efforts from the opposition," Andromeda's silhouette says in a monotone. "My campaign looks forward to the final vote count. Thank you."

Behind Andromeda's dark shape, Yinha glowers at the camera. Anyone unacquainted with her might think it's just her stern Militia face, but I know that she's fed up with this whole election debacle.

I pull Umbriel to our right as we move closer, my eyes fixed on Law. My little brother is in there, and he needs us. We walk into the lobby, keeping our heads down, and beeline for the third seat in the first row on the waiting area's left side.

The space is mostly empty. No one wants to miss the festivities outside, and out of a hundred or so chairs, only four are filled. Black-and-white stars and lines decorate the polyhedral room. I hear a low thrumming from carbon dioxide and oxygen filters somewhere behind the walls, like the growling of an undersea monster in Odan folklore.

Again, Base I is decades older than Base IV, so the imperfect insulation and soundproofing shouldn't come as a surprise. Still, it sends a jolt down my already tingling spine. Scanning our surroundings, I see the security pod, about half the size of my fist, just as Cygnus promised. Although I could lunge desperately in its direction, I shuffle slowly toward it instead. At the last second, Umbriel grabs my shoulder.

Despite our efforts to hide, the man at the front desk has noticed us. He beckons with a forefinger. Sulzer.

"Check-in is here," he calls.

He's about a head shorter than me and seems absentminded, but Yinha warned us otherwise. The bottom half of his face pooches out like an Odan hunting hound's. His robes are the rust color of Nu, his frame so small that the fabric's slipping off his shoulders. The badge of Law, a gold scale, gleams on his chest.

Umbriel and I walk faster. I deepen my breathing to quell my nerves. He's only a secretary, I tell myself; he doesn't know who we are, and he can't see my face.

"You must check in *now*."

Umbriel taps the back of my hand and pushes ahead of me, toward the front desk. I guess he'll try to swipe a Law badge while we're here.

At each end of the desk sits a good-sized Lunar flag. Sulzer straightens the one on the right, his thick lips twitching. When he turns to me, his face is a mask of boredom, but his fingernails drum a frantic rhythm on the table.

"Thumbprints."

Umbriel withdraws his hand from his pocket. Though it's invisible to Sulzer, his thumb is sheathed in a mold of someone else's fingerprint, made by a Dovetail-affiliated Medic. The execution is excellent; the line where his skin ends and the bioplastic begins is barely visible.

"My cousin and I are here for a walk-in appointment. She just finished alveoli replacement therapy for her lungs. The Medics are worried she'll inhale debris and mess up all their work, so that's why she's wearing the mask. The first available Law counselor would be great." In his days of thieving, Umbriel developed excellent lying technique. The secretary nods and presses his thumb to a circular scanning plate.

I offer Sulzer my own thumb, also encased in a soft mold. I'm not one for speaking, let alone lying. As Sulzer scans me in, my uncovered and quivering index finger brushes against the plate—but so quickly that I'm sure it won't register.

Be brave, I tell myself. *Showing fear could cost us the mission.*

"Adria and Adry Lambda."

"Have a seat." Sulzer leaves his desk, gesturing to the

waiting area with his other hand. As he passes, he grabs my arm, sending a zap of anxiety up my spine. "Standard procedure: I need to see the rest of your face."

Before Sulzer's other hand can reach up to take off my medical mask, Umbriel lays both hands on the secretary's chest and pushes him away from me. "Sorry—don't want to get in trouble with Medical, sir."

Sulzer looks up at Umbriel, who towers half a meter above him. His lips tremble, and then he backs away, eyeing us with suspicion. A small family waves him over, and as he answers the mother's rapid-fire questions, Umbriel and I sneak off.

By the time we near the first of Cygnus's security pods, Sulzer's shouting at the woman. Umbriel opens one of his clenched fists. Shining against his palm is the gold badge of Law.

The security pod flies over to greet us.

"Did Cygnus say what to do when we found the first pod?" Umbriel whispers.

I shake my head. My brother assumed I'd know. But then again, was he capable of lucid thought? Even when he was well, my brother often forgot that not everyone thinks on the same frequency as him. He would always skip steps when explaining things.

Thinking back to my first meeting with Lazarus, I recall another piece of information. It wasn't part of Cygnus's message, so we didn't use it—we hardly talked about it.

Your brother froze an image from your mother's trial on his handscreen in the seconds before his capture, Lazarus said. *He zoomed in on your left eye until it covered his entire screen.*

Umbriel sees my face change and looks at me with frantic anticipation.

"Retinal scan, left eye." I sound more confident than I am. If I get this wrong, we'll both end up in a torture cell like my brother's.

Umbriel snatches the security pod out of the air and holds it to my left eye. A light flashes, and the pod comes alive. It spins in a circle, and then jets toward the lobby's leftmost exit.

Before we follow, I look back. Sulzer's still occupied with the inquisitive mother, whose small children are tugging at her robes, begging her to leave.

We follow the pod through a set of doors, staying a few meters behind so that we won't attract attention. The doors have no fingerprint scanner, another Base I quirk, but open instead when they sense the golden badge in Umbriel's hand. He pins it to his robes after we pass through.

"Your brother," Umbriel whispers, "is my hacker hero."

In spite of the danger, I give him a thumbs-up and a grin full of pride for Cygnus.

We walk past seven pods, some of which fly toward us curiously, but the pod we're following disregards them. When we reach an eighth—funny, eight was Mom's lucky number—the first slows down and the second scans my retina.

In this manner, we follow a string of pods along twisting and turning hallways, through intersections, and down three different sets of stairs. Cygnus told us not to try to find him by ourselves, and now I see why. We've burrowed deep underground. Without the pods to lead us, we'd lose our way or become prisoners ourselves before reaching Penitentiary's entrance.

Several Law workers look up at us from their desks, or from the eyes of the people they're questioning, but they disregard us when they see Umbriel's stolen badge. With each encounter, my nerves stretch tighter. How much longer will this tranquility last? It won't be long before Sulzer tries to get through a door and realizes his golden badge is missing.

Soon the air becomes cold, and so dry it burns my nostrils.

The patriotic decorations grew scarce long ago. My blood hums in my ears.

Finally, we follow yet another security pod—at this point, I've lost count—through the entrance to Penitentiary. The walls are gray and peeling, crouched and cramped from the weight of the floors above. As I remember from the video of Micah River, the cells have no numbers.

We turn the first corner, only to see a figure in a black suit about ten meters away. To hide that we've been running, we pat the sweat off our faces with our sleeves and deny our lungs the air they crave.

"Stop right there!" A helmeted private holds up his Electrostun. "Only Militia in Penitentiary."

Umbriel grabs my hand and squeezes hard.

Please think of a good lie, I beg silently.

"Very sorry, sir!" he shouts, saluting the private. In Defense, *nobody* salutes privates. "We're . . . we're new here, and my boss sent us in to see what happens to people who break rules. It's a new method of training assistants, you see."

The private shifts his grip on the Electrostun. "Really? Who's your boss?"

"Leo Xi," I say. Leo's the most popular male name in the older generation. I've met at least five on Base IV.

But we're bluffing, and the private knows it. "Turn around now, and I'll march you out of the Pen. That's an order. If you disobey me—"

I whip out my tranquilizing gun and fire a Downer into his neck. The private collapses. Exchanging a worried glance, Umbriel and I dash after the security pod as it rounds another bend.

Five seconds later, the alarm blares.

36

"GET BEHIND ME, PHAET!" UMBRIEL HOLLERS. "I don't want you fighting everyone we see!"

But we don't have any other options. We've as good as locked ourselves up. Even though we have no LPS trackers, the private I just tranquilized does, and his comrades will flock to the site where he fell. They won't miss two frantic teenagers in olive-green robes.

I breathe in hard; my medical mask sticks to my mouth. Nevertheless, I run faster, moving to take the lead. Umbriel's never been in a real fight, and his hands are better suited for pilfering than punching. Glancing behind me, I see that he's pulled out his Electrostun. Does he know how to adjust the settings, let alone aim it?

If Wes were running beside us, we'd . . .

No.

"Hands up!" A female private and her male comrade approach us head-on. "Weapons down!"

I hear a zapping noise beside me. Electricity clusters uselessly at the muzzle of Umbriel's Electrostun. It's in short-range mode, only good for incapacitating victims with whom one can achieve physical contact.

"We have to open fire!" the male private shouts. "There's no other way!"

"Slide the white switch!" I yell to Umbriel, aiming and firing at our adversaries. Their ballistic shields block my darts.

Umbriel presses his back to the tunnel wall to make himself a smaller target. *Apparently, experience in theft isn't 100 percent useless in a fight.* I jump as an Electrostun pellet—*their* weapons are in long-range mode—sizzles over my bare head. Another hits my chest and crackles, but my armor's insulation protects me. I send a dart into the female private's outstretched, thinly gloved hand. Seconds later, she collapses.

"This switch?" Umbriel points to something on his Electrostun, but I'm moving too fast to see details.

"Actually, don't!" I scoop up the fallen soldier's ballistic shield and throw it over myself. The male soldier's closing in. I press my back to the wall. Electrostun pellets splat against the shield. When he's close, I thump his head with it, fit my tranquilizing gun between his legs, and pull upward. He emits a squeal and collapses.

Jamming the soldiers' helmets onto our heads, Umbriel and I run onward.

"You're . . . you're really good," he says. It sounds more like an admission than a compliment. This is the first time he's seen me fight, seen that the girl he protected from jibes and jeers in Primary grew talons in Militia. Talons Wes helped sharpen.

Stop it. Move! Although my lungs are burning, I run harder. *If I survive this, I can see him again.*

"Those two *should* have been easy pickings for a former captain," I say to Umbriel. "They were privates." I hear more footsteps. "Behind us!"

Five soldiers approach. Their Electrostun pellets hit the backs of our robes but splat uselessly against our armor.

"Forget the pellets!" shouts a male soldier. "Lazies out!"

We have to keep going—even faster. But side stitches sear my abdomen, and I curse those days I spent creeping around the base, getting little exercise and less food. Umbriel's breathing is growing labored too.

"Go!" I holler. His freedom and his life depend on me. In this moment, Umbriel's not only my best friend; he's a soldier under my command.

The Militia troops stay on our tail as we race after the pod, skidding down two more flights of stairs. *Where is my brother?* It makes sense that the authorities would lock him up far away from the entrance. *I can't do this anymore.* My calves sear, but thinking of Wes, and of Cygnus, I push through the pain.

On and on we run, until the pod slows and stops by a black set of doors. It fits itself into the lock and twists. The doors slide open.

Umbriel and I tumble into the tiny cell.

It smells like Shelter, but with a metallic edge. I struggle to breathe while my eyes adjust to the light—or the lack thereof. Dark bloodstains spot the gray stone floor, and torture instruments line the walls: a faucet near the floor for waterboarding, shelves and shelves of needles, a chair with straps and electrodes—the same one I saw in the videos, the one I see in my waking nightmares. The machines look like perverted Medical equipment. But the worst thing about the cell?

Cygnus isn't here.

His metal collar lies abandoned on the chair, its clasp half open, like a pair of jaws.

This is his cell, though. He wouldn't have rigged the security pods or sent a secret document to lead us to the wrong room. All his effort, gone to waste. Too much effort for someone holding on to the last slivers of life.

Umbriel puts his arm around my shoulders. "Phaet . . ."

"Where's my brother?" I demand, pushing him away. *Is Cygnus still breathing?* I fall to my knees in front of the electric chair and cradle the tungsten collar against my chest.

The doors to the cell slide open again. Boots stamp; guns click. There's no hope of fight or flight. Behind my visor, I begin to cry.

What will the Committee do to my brother now that they have me?

*   *   *

"Handcuffs," says a tall female sergeant.

Two privates click magnetic sets of jaws around our wrists. "Gags."

My lips pull back painfully to accommodate the sour-tasting rag they stretch across my mouth.

"Upward." The sergeant seems to enjoy talking as little as I do.

The jail cell *moves*, taking me, Umbriel, and our captors with it. It's a decoy, a podlike elevator with glass walls. The Committee's rigged Base I more thoroughly than anyone in Dovetail anticipated.

Our surroundings go dark as we rise through the depths of Penitentiary. Where are we headed? And toward what? I feel my heartbeats as a fluttering in my throat and realize that I may not have many left.

Unlike me, Umbriel hasn't been rendered useless by terror. I hear his handcuffs clinking softly as he executes various maneuvers to try and remove them.

Today wasn't a rescue mission. It was a death trap. Some sadist loyal to the Committee used everything, from Cygnus's torture video to the programmed security pods, to lead us into the center of a maze and watch us run. He's laughing at us, and I can do nothing but cry and rage and tremble in response. There's no way that turmoil isn't showing on my face.

The sergeant points at two more of her underlings. "Magnets."

An older male special private gives a low chuckle and presses a series of buttons on a handheld remote. My handcuffs pull me into a nosedive; I hit the floor, grunting in pain. Umbriel follows a second later. Then the cuffs yank me two and a half meters upward, the electromagnet between my wrists gluing me to the ceiling. Like Earthbound fish out of water, Umbriel and I flop around the cell, our bodies smacking against the walls. Trying to focus on anything but the pain, I recite in my head the names of the bones that are sustaining damage: cranium, patella, fibula, scapula, other scapula . . .

Every Beater except the sergeant laughs maniacally.

"Some Girl Sage," one of the women sneers. "Time to snap some of those twigs!"

Or that's what I think she says. The universe flips over itself every second; I can feel new bruises blooming across my body. My teeth have cut my tongue in several places.

Not soon enough, everything goes still. Umbriel and I lie on the floor of the cell, panting.

Rough hands draw us to our feet. They strip off my helmet and pull the ties out of my hair. It falls over my shoulders in a sheet of silver and black. Lunar colors.

"When we show you to the Committee," says the sergeant, "we want them to recognize you."

The Committee. My breath rattles in my lungs. I *knew* the tyrants would be our final destination, but I didn't allow myself to think about it. What's the point? I've already lost. Again and again, I've lost. Why keep struggling? Why not lay down my hopes? They're nothing but a burden now. Cygnus will remain in captivity. Wes will have to find another girl. Someone else must honor my mother's memory.

The glass doors to our cell open, letting in a blast of cool air. Our tormentors step out into a large hexagonal room, leaving us alone. I hear the rhythmic whir of a cranked-up air-cooling unit above us before the doors close again. *We're on the top floor, so the sun's directly overhead.* I imagine shutting off the cooling unit, letting the sun heat this place up to a couple thousand Kelvin, and watching the Committee members try to deal with being inside an oven.

Militia soldiers line the hexagon's perimeter—including Nash and Eri, who look scared stiff, and Yinha, who tilts up her chin and wears an inscrutable expression. Beside her, I see Callisto, who tries her hardest to look unruffled.

Interspersed among the soldiers are Journalists, who poke at their handscreens to direct the video cameras hovering in the room's center. Lazarus lounges against the wall behind Cassini, the Base II representative with the long, crawling fingers.

What's a Psychology worker doing here during an election? I stare, bewildered, until I realize that he's staring back, exposing one canine in that asymmetrical smile of his. *And why is he smiling?*

They're *all* staring back. Even the six Committee members seated at the conference table, which is raised high off the floor. And after sixteen years of seeing only their shadowy silhouettes, I can just discern the outlines of their features.

They're six normal, everyday faces, stained sallow by indoor living. It's a letdown and a relief; I'd half expected them to have razor-edged teeth or slits for pupils. There, a round, dimpled face; here, a sagging old one. A long one shaped like a sunflower seed, and a perfectly sculpted one. One with prickly eyebrows and hair. And Andromeda's. The five men look smug; Andromeda wears an expression of barely concealed alarm.

Although the room's center is dark, the perimeter is brightly lit. The lighting creates the threatening silhouettes that the populace sees during Committee addresses, and I realize that heavy editing must obscure their faces even more on-screen.

Above us, the ceiling is divided into six enormous equilateral triangles, one for each base; each of these is further divided into sixteen smaller triangles, showing a total of ninety-six video feeds of people listening to the election results. Base citizens are watching wall screens, HeRPs, or handscreens in the bases' public spaces, in their living rooms, in their offices, in the corridors. I can hear the muted hum of their conversations. Presumably, each base's InfoTech Department sends the Committee the most relevant security pod footage in real time. *The six of them watch us through the watchers*, I think, my skin puckering with goose bumps. *And they never, ever stop.*

Another screen, this one a massive rectangle, makes up the hexagonal room's rear wall. Currently, it's covered by six pie charts and sports the heading, **LUNAR BASES' VOTE PERCENTAGES**. Each chart has a large black wedge representing the incumbent's portion of the vote. Presumably, the same image is showing up on people's handscreens on all six bases. Across Base I, heads bob up and down. On Bases II, III, IV, V, and VI, though, scattered individuals look restless. Frowns pull at their mouths; I can hear the buzz of conversation.

The person reading the results out loud to them is looking at me too. Sitting by Andromeda's side, a stream of meaningless words issuing from his mouth, is my little brother.

37

I SHOUT INTO THE RAG GAGGING ME, BUT only garbled mumbling comes out.

". . . Base II's Cassini Omicron, 68.3 percent of the vote." Cygnus continues to stare at me. His skin looks flawless, his infected eye has healed, and he wears Theta robes of unblemished white. But when I look closer, I can see swathes of makeup caked over his face. It doesn't match his skin tone. The Committee's trying to show people that they've treated him well; that he belongs to them and supports their mockery of an election. "Janus Lambda of Base III, 63.2 percent. Base IV's Andromeda Chi, 73.9 percent. Nebulus Nu of Base V, 75.5 percent. Finally, Wolf Omega, Base VI, 53.7 percent. . . ."

Watching Cygnus among my enemies hurts me almost as much as witnessing his torture. His feet periodically jerk—he's clearly uncomfortable—but magnetic rings around his wrists and ankles bolt him to his chair. *This is torture too.*

A sweet, slimy male voice that I know all too well picks up where my brother left off, passes through the speakers in our glass cell, and raises goose pimples on my bruised skin. "Yes, yes. Incumbent supermajorities for every base. We are honored that you have once again entrusted us with leading the Moon." *Hydrus.* The tyrant who rules Base I. "There are your election results, fellow Lunars, which even Cygnus Theta, a former rebel, cannot deny. The Committee candidates have won, and that is the whole truth."

No, I silently correct him. *You eliminated the write-in candidates' chances.* How many uncounted votes did Asterion get?

He sees me and Umbriel, smiles maliciously, and nods to his colleagues. They all sit up straighter in their high chairs.

"Where are the real results?" shouts a man on Base IV. A crowd has gathered; the people murmur and mill around the Atrium, watching the Committee's election broadcast on the wall screens.

"These results *are* real." Nebulus Nu's perfectly chiseled jaw twitches as he speaks. "If we had not apprehended the so-called Girl Sage in time, she and her cohorts might have succeeded in falsifying them. She was caught lurking in InfoTech on Base I, near the polling databases."

I lunge forward, handcuffs chafing my wrists, indignant at his lies. The bases flare up in discussion, and Nebulus gestures for one of the Journalists to lower the volume on the feeds. Cygnus blinks obliviously at the scene, the makeup on his face obscuring his actual emotional state.

The voices of the people get quieter, but their faces are still before us, hopeful, expectant. I think of Yinha's suggestion that I astonish them. That's all a fantasy now. The best I can do today is surrender my pride—and my life—with dignity.

"Some of you puzzle me, my fellow citizens," Nebulus says. "This little upstart abandoned you in your time of greatest need, fleeing to planet Earth. Welcoming her back is illogical, when she has been nothing but selfish."

His words only enrage the Dovetail supporters more.

Janus Lambda, the ancient, hunchbacked Base III representative, addresses me directly. "Phaet Theta. Adding electoral fraud to your list of crimes, and so soon? Have you no shame?"

I fight back an angry hiss. By twisting the facts with that aged, rustling voice, he could probably persuade the Moon itself that I'm guilty.

"We would have the man who brought you here teach you a lesson in serving the public—if it were not already too late to reform you," Cassini Omicron says. His long, arching fingers tap out a spiderlike dance on the conference table. "Tarazed Pi. A Lunar citizen of the highest order." *Lazarus.*

"You honor me, Representative. But I was motivated by personal considerations as well. For some time, I've longed to see this brat get the thrashing she deserves." Lazarus slithers into the light. Wolf Omega begins applauding. Nobody, aside from the Committee members, joins in. Their lonely claps echo off the high ceiling.

Stupid, stupid, stupid . . . It's the last thing I want to be, but no adjective describes me better. His smooth words and handsome face prevented me from seeing the truth about him—the truth Wes and Murray already know too well.

Striding up to our cell, Lazarus whispers through clenched teeth. "Little Sage, you have decimated my career and inserted your pug nose in places it never belonged. Due to your actions, I have been shunned by the Odan people and evicted from my Sanctuarist post. If you had decided to help me recover my reputation, I might have spared you. However, you have failed to show me the respect and admiration I deserve. No matter the outcome of these elections, I will sleep soundly knowing that you have been eliminated. And that your extermination will torment Wesley Carlyle unceasingly until he meets his own end."

The snake. Unable to stop myself, I smash my fists, handcuffs and all, against the shatterproof glass of the cell. But the chamber contains every centimeter of me.

Each step along the way to what I thought was Cygnus's rescue, Lazarus was there: worming his way into Yinha's confidence, luring me into his tent, forging Cygnus's letter—no wonder it didn't sound like my brother wrote it. And all that energy I spent figuring out Cygnus's babbling? Squandered. The code was probably scripted. I think back to Lazarus's long, lingering keystrokes before the document opened; any password would have worked if his fingerprints authorized it. Lazarus may even have baited Micah River, sending his supposed friend to his death because it solidified the Sanctuarists' need for his aid and magnified the stakes of Cygnus's rescue.

From the moment Wes told his father about the broken engagement, I was doomed. Questioning Lazarus in Shelter, hesitating to fix his shattered reputation, rejecting his "advances"—all that only made him more determined to see me gone. He couldn't let me endanger the perfect life he wanted to build here on the Moon—a life that must include many, many Lunar women, just as Murray claimed.

"I have shed my past self, the self that Saint Oda refuses to accept." Lazarus's eyes never leave mine. "You will not besmirch the name of Tarazed Pi, *little Sage*, because the dead give no testimony—and you will join their ranks shortly. I am the victor. The truth belongs to me: I am a new man."

How can you call yourself a man at all? I try to scream through my gag.

"Thank you, Tarazed." Wolf rubs his hands together as if liquefying an insect between his palms. "Now, we must proceed with Miss Phaet's penance."

Andromeda's hand clenches on the table. "But . . . Wolf, we haven't voted on the matter. I was not made aware of this . . . this operation to entrap and murder Phaet."

"Murder, you say? It is but keeping the peace." Hydrus smiles sadly. His dimples look like puncture wounds. "Because of her, thousands have been displaced to the Shelter Department, including some of our best researchers. With chaos on the bases, progress has screeched to a halt. It is a national *emergency*, Andromeda, which was why we simply could not tell you ahead of time. You would have decreased our efficiency with questions and objections, as you did when we prevented Phaet's parents from harming the bases any further."

My heart lurches. *Parents.* Both of them?

"You are all too cruel," Andromeda whispers, looking from me to my brother. Cygnus shakes as he draws short, shallow breaths.

Cassini ignores Andromeda. "Phaet must comprehend the sacrifices we make for the public good, painful as they are."

"I agree," Hydrus says. "Journalists, it's time for a break."

The Journalists click off their recording devices, shutting off the live stream to air senseless segments about Committee-backed improvements to base life—advertisements, really. I catch looks of bewilderment on the citizens' faces before the ceiling screens black out.

"Phaet. We're *here.*" As soon as I turn to face Hydrus's voice, he *winks* at me, as if he'll share some juicy secret. I shudder, knowing that whatever gladdens him will only hurt me—all the more so if he can't share it with the bases. "Phaet Theta, you never knew your father as we did. He was as disruptive as your mother, if not more so."

I shake my head. Dad was a Geologist, a cheerful man who

loved his children too much to jeopardize our safety.

"But we never punish anybody unjustly."

What did you do to him? I demand them to tell me by knocking my shoulder into the cell. But I can guess at the answer.

"For your family's sake, we told you he died in an accident, in a leaky vehicle out on the Far Side. But with the Geology Department's resources, we would have given him a newer model if we wanted him to come back," Hydrus says.

A scream lodges in my chest. I won't let out unintelligible cries of anger, not in front of these murderers.

"We saved you from a turbulent upbringing," Nebulus says, shrugging. "Your father was a radical, and would have inundated your young mind with lies. He needed to be isolated."

"No," Wolf says. "He needed to be eliminated."

* * *

Dad. They took him from my siblings and me, leaving us half-orphaned at ages six, four, and two and a half. As much as I thought I was numbed to the Committee's evil, I'm unwilling to believe them. But if this is true, so many things make sense. The Committee told me, after they killed Mom, "You're as delusional as your parents." I wondered then why they mentioned both of them.

They sent Dad on that Geology mission in a faulty vehicle, knowing a moonquake was coming. Did Mom suspect? Did she *know?* And is that why, when we were grown, she started a revolution to protect her children from the Committee forever?

Umbriel pats my shoulder, tries to mumble something into my ear. I shrug him off, numb but for the simmering fury in my chest, and manage to catch Cygnus's eye. He's silently crying;

the tears have washed some of the makeup off his cheeks, revealing maroon bruises and burst blood vessels.

For ten years, we thought Dad's death was an accident. We even wondered if it happened because he wasn't being careful enough out in the vacuum of space.

The Committee grants Cygnus and me precious moments of peace, though not intentionally. They've all turned on Andromeda.

Cassini sneers at her. "We know about how you tried to finagle your way into stopping Atlas Theta's removal—his wife's, too. You are obviously trying the same thing now—do you think us fools? But we do admire your guile. Even if you've had your Dovetail sympathies from the beginning, your treachery hasn't prevented us from removing your . . . shall we call them *friends*?"

My last hopes vanish into the recycled air of the jail cell. Not even Andromeda can help Umbriel and me now. But she doesn't seem to have given up; she nods to the Journalists, indicating that they should start recording again. Only a few send their recording pods back into flight, with much hesitation. Nebulus flicks his pointer finger upward, backing Andromeda. The Committee can't cut off contact with the population for too long without arousing suspicion.

Footage of the anxious Lunar citizens lights up the ceiling, comforting me somewhat. They give us every speck of their attention, as if needing to know what they missed.

Andromeda's trying to appear calm, but I can hear the quiver in her breath. "It seems you five are expelling me from the Standing Committee. But that doesn't matter, not in light of the fact that Base IV voters expelled me earlier today, replacing me with Asterion Epsilon of the Reform and Equity Coalition."

Swathes of Base IV residents nod in agreement. Several

cheer. But the Base I crowd erupts in indignant shouts, unwilling to believe that an incumbent could have lost.

"Silence!" roars Wolf. The other Committee members fidget; they probably didn't anticipate a reaction from the viewers—or an outburst from Wolf, who seems to have lost control of himself. But they can't turn off the feed again, or residents of the less secure bases will demand to know what they're trying to hide. "Base IV dissidents, you are nothing," Wolf says. "You are bacteria on an agar plate, flies in a cage—"

"Wolf, allow me." Nebulus claps a hand over Wolf's mouth. "Do not follow Phaet Theta's path of lawlessness and discord. Let her . . . her removal serve as an example to you all." He turns to a Beetle standing by our glass cell. "Fill it with water. Slowly."

The Beetle pulls a lever. A stream as wide as my pointer finger trickles down from the ceiling, hitting the floor of our cell with a steady patter.

As if sleepwalking, I extend my hands to touch it. Cool, clear liquid runs through my fingers, inviting enough to drink. In a matter of minutes, it will fill the tank. And my lungs. The prospect is so disturbing that it feels fake, like an empty threat. But I know it's not.

Maybe it's good that I can't swim or float. I won't suffer as long.

Andromeda rests her head on the table. She appears to have given up, but . . . has she? Her right forefinger is moving across the back of her left hand.

"Wait. Her *friend* could prove useful to us," Lazarus says. Does he want to take even Umbriel away from me before I die?

"Perhaps," says Hydrus. "Let us ask. Ungag them. Let the bases hear their words of repentance—if they have any."

A metal arm next to the electric chair in our cell extends

until the end reaches Umbriel's face. The knife at its tip cuts through his gag, drawing blood from his cheek in the process. He winces but tries his best to ignore the pain.

Hydrus says to Umbriel, "If you agree to cooperate, you may live to see tomorrow."

Umbriel rests his cuffed hands on my left shoulder. "If you think I'd rather live without Phaet than die with her, you don't understand anything about friendship."

With a lump in my throat, I reach my hands up and squeeze his. He knows it means *thank you.*

Lazarus looks taken aback, but only for a second.

The knife comes toward my face. I hold still. Whoever's operating the thing slashes the tip of my nose before cutting off my gag—for fun, perhaps. I feel blood trickle from the wound, but it doesn't hurt. Much.

"*Friendship,*" Cassini says with a small laugh. "It cannot erase your crimes or destroy your enemies. And it cannot free you from that tank."

38

THE WATER HAS REACHED KNEE HEIGHT.
The chill in my lower legs brings me odd clarity of mind; I begin to assess the situation. The liquid's dripping from what must be the cooling unit's condenser; because hot air can hold more water than cold, the drop in temperature forms puddles of water pulled out of the air. *It's purer than regular water—it left behind most of the dissolved ions when it evaporated.* Not too different from the distilled water we used in lab.

I have a dagger and a diamond-bit drill in my boot, but neither can cut through the reinforced glass of the cell before the soldiers shoot us. There's Cygnus's metal torture chair bolted to the floor on one end of the room, and a number of metal rings attached to the walls—probably to chain up prisoners. The top of the tank looks like steel.

"Phaet Theta!" Wolf's voice booms. "Look at your so-called *supporters.* Look at their faces. They are afraid—they see what your crimes have cost you, and they are your friends no longer."

I close my eyes, trying to convince myself that his taunts mean nothing. When I open them, the bases' citizens stare back at me from the wall screens, some with malice, others with dwindling hope.

Flashes of movement draw my eyes to the screens on the large conference room's ceiling. The murmuring on the bases has escalated into shouting and stamping.

Is it because the Committee's killing us, or because—

The pie charts looming on the rectangular wall screen, which formerly showed large wedges of black, are now a rainbow of other colors. Half of Base IV's gleams gold, the color representing Asterion's Reform and Equity Coalition. The screen is labeled, RESULTS INCLUDING DOCTORED BALLOTS— CONFIDENTIAL. FOR INVESTIGATIVE PURPOSES ONLY. These must be the election results that take into account the makeshift write-in votes for Asterion and the other suppressed candidates. Did one of Sol's Journalist friends sneak them onto the screens while everyone else was distracted by the execution?

Hydrus follows my gaze, yet somehow the arrogance on his face remains. "Ah. Andromeda, I see you've asked your cronies to change the decorations."

"The Lunar people deserve the truth." There's a fever in Andromeda's eyes, burning away the exhaustion I noticed earlier. I've seen the same expression on Mom's face, on Sol Eta's—even on my own, as I stared down the camera that taped Mom's trial. "They deserve to know that the real tallies—including *all* the candidates—look very, very different."

Her words cause my home base to virtually explode. Disorder isn't confined to Shelter, the Atrium, and the hallways; it has spread to those departments most controlled by the Committee. In Biology and Medical, workers stand with palms facing outward, fingers pointed to the sides, and thumbs intertwined; their hands form a flock of birds whose feathers span the spectrum of human skin color. In InfoTech, workers seem to be highlighting and deleting gigabytes of data mined over the years from base residents; entire HeRP screens go red. In the middle of their dome, Journalism workers have knocked over shelves containing blue memory chips, which hold records of years and years of news. Then they ignite the towering pile. As the fire spreads, sparks jump between flames.

"Andromeda, all of *that*"—Nebulus points upward—"only proves that you're as much of a threat as Phaet Theta, if not more." He turns to the soldiers lining the walls. "Deposit her in the tank with the other traitors."

Callisto and seven or eight soldiers from the various bases—other bodyguards, I'm assuming—move forward. But Yinha, Nash, Eri, and two other members of the Base IV entourage rush to stop them. Four more soldiers remain where they are, conflicting emotions on their faces. One, from Base VI, toggles the power switch on his Lazy with a trembling hand—on, off, on, off—and sends a violet laser streaking toward the top of the tank. The glass begins to glow red, but before it can melt, a loyalist soldier takes down our would-be helper.

The water reaches the top of my thighs, and desperation sets in. Even if I have no idea how to get out, the Committee and their guards are distracted enough for me to try. I reach into my left boot with both hands and take out the diamond-bit drill. Bent down, with my eyes just above the waterline, I see the flash of an Electrostun. I study my handcuffs—specifically the bulge between my wrists, which contains the strong electromagnet.

That's it! Distilled water, electricity, and a long conducting wire. We have everything required to get out of here. My next steps materialize in my mind like mountains appearing through a thinning fog.

I press the drill into Umbriel's hands.

He frowns. "Phaet, the glass is four centimeters thick! We can't cut a hole through it in time—"

"Drill through the center of my handcuffs. Right there."

Without further protest, he gets to work. The drill tunnels through a thin layer of carbon fiber, exposing insulated copper wire coiled around an iron solenoid core.

"Free up one end of the wire. . . . Great. Hand it to me."

With my teeth, I slough the plastic insulating cover off the wire, and plunge under the water, which almost reaches my chest. Though my handcuffs cause me to fumble, I manage to tie the wire around a metal hook on the floor. I stand at the bottom, take a gulp of air, and bend down toward the metal chair, uncoiling the electromagnet. I slough off more plastic and tie the wire around one of the legs. Under the water pressure, my lungs seem to be sinking lower and lower in my chest, and a lump of pain is assembling in the back of my skull.

My legs flail as I try to gain traction on the tank floor, but my feet slip once, twice.

Big, bony hands grab my waist and boost me up.

I suck in air to the tune of "What the fuse are you doing? Wiring the tank?"

Nodding and gasping from me.

"Did your brain get squashed down there?" Umbriel continues. "If an electrical current hits any of this thing's metal parts, it's going to pass through the water and zap us to death! Look, Wolf thinks we're hilarious!"

The Committee member's face is all but pressed up against the glass. His prickly eyebrows vibrate with every chuckle; his mouth is open in an eerie expression of amusement. He'd rather watch us struggle than participate in the brawl happening behind him; he's that confident in the Committee's power.

When one soldier cocks an Electrostun in Andromeda's

direction, a Base IV soldier I don't know wallops him in the gut and wrenches the weapon from his hand. Eri and Nash stand back-to-back, picking off their adversaries. Yinha darts in circles around Lazarus, a knife in one hand and a truncheon in the other. "You're *sick*! You lying, murdering . . ." He evades her every move with ease, but doesn't try to hit back. What if someone other than Lazarus attacks her? She's not paying attention. I have to help—

Worry about yourself first. "Give me a boost, Umbriel."

He bends down so I can sit on his shoulders, but says, "You're still trying to wire the tank."

The water is now a meter and a half deep, but he straightens without much effort.

"This water is just runoff from the air-cooling unit. It evaporated and condensed, which should've gotten rid of ions and made it a poor conductor of electricity." I loop the wire through the rings attached to the steel ceiling. "In normal water, the current passes through dissolved ions, which this water mostly lacks."

"So what if this leftover water's a crummy conductor?" Umbriel says. "It's still a conductor!"

"Everything is, to some degree. If this works, we *will* be electrocuted. But not so badly that we'll die."

"I'll trust you on this." He still sounds skeptical. "But only because I'd rather not drown."

I jump off Umbriel's shoulders, into the water. It's up to my neck. Time to complete the circuit. There's just enough wire left in my handcuffs' electromagnet to tie around the first metal loop on the floor. Umbriel pulls a dagger from my boot and saws through the wire attached to the electromagnet in my handcuffs.

When I surface and stand on the tank's floor, the water

reaches my eyes. *All we need is an electrical current.* I jump up, try-ing to tread water the way Wes showed me, but I stay afloat for only three seconds. On my way back down, I take in a mouthful of water—and swallow it before it goes down my windpipe.

"Up you go, Captain." Umbriel squats down and boosts me to his shoulders again. He's twenty centimeters taller than me, so he'll last longer as the water continues to rise.

I take deep, gasping breaths and survey the scene from my perch. Several bodies lie on the floor. Callisto cowers under-neath the Committee table; she looks paralyzed, frozen the way she was on Earth, unable to decide on her next move. Although Lazarus has Yinha in a headlock, she pummels him with her elbows and the soles of her feet, trying to shake him off. An-dromeda's bodyguards are picking at the bonds around Cyg-nus's ankles; they've already freed his arms. As Nash and Eri maneuver Andromeda toward the doors, which loyalist soldiers have barricaded, Eri fires currents from her Electrostun at the enemy. Did she lose her Lazy? How? The jagged electricity use-lessly tickles their ballistic shields and armor.

"Eri!" I scream, forcing as much precious air through my voice box as I can. I make a gun shape with my right hand, pointing upward with my left at the tank's metal lid.

A horrified look crosses her face. Still, she nods.

I jump back into the water and give her the thumbs-up. Before anyone can knock the Electrostun out of her hand, she takes aim and fires a pellet, crackling with electricity, at the top of the tank.

Just before it hits, Umbriel and I jump.

39

ELECTROCUTION FEELS LIKE A MOONQUAKE on fast-forward—and then some. Every muscle contracts, causing my body to shake like a leaf in a storm. The water's too hot, as is the pain, but there's no escape. Time itself stretches, expanding with the fluid, so I'm able to make infinite wishes for agony to release me before—

The tank explodes. The superheated air below the lid has expanded, blowing it off and cracking the glass walls. Shards fly outward; water gushes into the Committee's conference room, taking Umbriel and me with it.

I land, belly down. Glass knives slice into my legs. Nothing hurts too badly—yet. My nerves are still recovering their ability to send and receive action potentials.

Decibel by decibel, my hearing returns. Nearby, Umbriel cradles his crooked left arm and howls in pain. It takes me a minute to register that screams are also coming from the Committee members.

"It's Wolf!" croaks Janus. "I'm not feeling a pulse. Call a Medic!"

"Not worth our time," says Hydrus. "He's dead."

"Wolf? Dead? *No!*"

Wolf's body looks even more angular and twisted in its stillness. Shrapnel from the explosion has mangled the top half of his face but has left his smiling mouth intact. He must have stood by the tank, wearing that grin, until the moment it blew.

Someone pulls me up and drags me toward the exit. My head lolls back; I watch the ceiling screens, the riots and explosions on Bases IV and VI—VI has revolted too?—with an odd feeling of detachment. My legs dangle, limp and useless, unable to support my weight.

"Phaet," a woman's voice says in my ear. "It's Yinha. Now's our chance to move."

"Ya . . . ha." It's all my numb tongue can manage.

Bodies in various states of consciousness litter the floor. Eri leans against a wall, still gawking at the smoking Electrostun in her hand. Nash is hunkered down in front of her; she picks off the Committee loyalists rushing at them. Wincing, Umbriel tests his left leg to see if it can support his weight—I'm amazed that he's standing at all. Near me, Cygnus has crawled under the Committee's table, and Yinha stands vigil over both of us. None of the blurry outlines in my field of vision resembles Lazarus's lithe form—has he fled the bloodbath?

A few meters to my right, Andromeda is clutching her left leg with one hand. Blood leaks copiously from a recent wound. Still, she hasn't given up fighting; she drives her other fist downward, into the skull of the soldier who must've cut her.

But even as she fends him off, Nebulus's left hand reaches for her head. His right clutches a Lazy.

"Mom!" Callisto shouts. "*Mom!*"

As Nebulus's fingers close around Andromeda's neck, Callisto emerges from underneath the table and smashes her truncheon against Nebulus's rib cage. There's a sickening crunch, and Nebulus collapses; the Lazy slips from his gnarled fingers and clatters to the floor.

Callisto takes advantage of her former comrades' shock by sprinting to the doors, firing Lazy shots into the face of the soldier standing guard. She holds the doors open and shouts, "Come on! All of you, get over here!"

Nash and Eri shield Andromeda; they lift her off the cluttered ground and half carry, half push her through the exit. Yinha follows, all but carrying me. Andromeda's two loyal bodyguards, whom I've never met, follow us, holding up Umbriel and Cygnus. Callisto fires more shots into the Committee's boardroom, and then punches the controls to shut the doors.

A shadow about Lazarus's size and shape has made it to the end of the hallway. *Of course he escaped before the real fight started.* My legs itch to chase him down; my hands long to throttle him. But before I can get a clearer view, he turns a corner and disappears. I stumble, cursing under my breath.

Alarms are blaring throughout Governance; I hear Militia boots clacking behind us. *Where next?* Defense's hangar is across Base I, and the hallways are a congealed mess of people. Our party of ten will never make it.

"Emergency shuttle. Elevator . . . Take two rights and a left." Andromeda chokes out the words. Nash and Eri tug her forward. A trail of blood from the gash on Andromeda's shin follows them. So do we.

But after the second right turn, we collide head-on with a five-man Militia squad.

"Injured and non-Militia in the middle!" Yinha shouts. In one motion, she pushes me to safety and back-kicks a private in the belly. Through her visor, I see her grimacing.

I'm an awful soldier, she once said to me. *Too soft to kill people.*

Our small group clusters around Andromeda, Cygnus, and

Umbriel, forming a circle with our backs to the middle. Beside me, Andromeda's bodyguard stows the Lazy he's been firing at the oncoming soldiers and feints left to slip behind a soldier's ballistic shield. He clubs her head with the back of his fist and grabs the shield.

Now that I'm able to move my fingers, I wrap them around my dagger. I make a minor contribution by sticking the blade into the unarmored space between a corporal's neck and shoulder—just hard enough to bring him to his knees.

"Move out!" Yinha hollers.

Eri moves in beside me, supporting my body weight. She's even smaller than I am, so our progress is excruciatingly slow. Still, our group manages to advance, abandoning one of Andromeda's bodyguards. When I look back, he's a crumpled heap on the ground.

Andromeda presses her fingertip to a sensor, and two pieces of marble wall slide apart to reveal an elevator, obviously intended for the Committee's emergency use. The footsteps behind us get louder. Yinha, Nash, Callisto, and Andromeda's remaining bodyguard help Andromeda, Umbriel, and Cygnus into the elevator. They're packed so close, I doubt both Eri and I will fit. I push Eri in front of me, intending to board last, but she shoves me inside the cylinder ahead of her.

"Dovetail can't lose you, Phaet!" She squeezes in. We've packed the elevator well past its weight limit. "Hurry! Shut the doors!"

The lift begins to close, but the doors pop open again when they meet the resistance of Eri's left shoulder.

"Fuse!" Nash pushes the button with her fingertips and then punches it with her fist. "Why doesn't this thing . . ."

The soldiers behind us have caught up. One launches himself at Eri; he jams his dagger between her shoulder and chest armor and drags the blade downward, through skin and ribs and lungs.

Nash screams, her voice the incarnation of anguish. With explosive momentum, she swings her truncheon at the attacker's helmet. His comrades catch his limp body, pulling him back. His head hangs at the wrong angle from his neck.

We squeeze more tightly to make room for Eri. The doors finally seal shut. I want to look away from Eri before someone confirms what I know—and refuse to believe—but I can't disrespect my comrade, my *friend*, in that way.

Nash flips up Eri's visor. Her tears fall on Eri's cheeks.

"Nash . . . I couldn't have asked for a better friend. I love you so much," Eri whispers. "Tell my parents that . . . that I'm sorry."

Her eyes find mine; I hold her hand, squeezing it as if I can anchor her to life by willing her to stay.

"Phaet, you were great up there. Save the whole . . . fizzing . . . Moon for me. Okay? And don't forget . . . Wes—"

She leaves us. All we see are two empty eyes and a smile that's dying on her mouth.

40

THE ELEVATOR DESCENDS, FILLED WITH screams and sobs. I watch Eri's blood pool around my boots. How could someone who was so *alive* be so dead? And all because a stupid elevator was too small.

Why did Eri even come to Base I? Yinha and Nash and I were more than adequate to defend Andromeda. . . .

Eri came for Dovetail, for a cause she believed in, despite the comfortable life she led under Committee rule. She loved Wes—and she died for what he believed in too: justice, and defending the defenseless.

When we reach the tiny emergency Governance hangar, we leave Eri's body behind.

It's a sacrilege. But we are burdened enough without her dead weight.

The eight of us board the Destroyer, which has a seating capacity of five. Callisto and Nash, who don't even glance at each other, man the wing weaponry. Yinha helps Cygnus into the rear of the cabin, and then she takes the pilot position, her hands trembling. Andromeda pulls a first-aid kit off the wall. Blood loss has blanched her skin. With sluggish hands, she disinfects and binds her leg wound, and then uses tweezers to pull glass shards out of my right calf and thigh, while her remaining bodyguard sees to Umbriel's broken arm and Cygnus's old wounds.

The first gate to the air lock begins to close. Other ships sputter to life around us.

We're not alone.

"C'mon," Yinha says, her teeth clenched.

She pushes us toward the exit. The Destroyer clips the ground twice; our right wing collides with another ship's, and we lose a small cannon. But we make it into the air lock. The second gate is about to shut when the left wing tip operator—Callisto—looses two large grenades. One flies forward in an arc, landing just under the gate's edge. The other flies backward. As the pilot of our first pursuant ship swerves to avoid it, the ship behind it rams into the right wing.

The grenade explodes. When the gate closes on Callisto's first grenade, it blows as well. Shrapnel, fire, and smoke fill the air lock. We fly straight through. As the Destroyer is knocked about, Yinha releases the controls, shielding her eyes with her hands.

Several seconds later, the ship hurtles into space and the sun's vicious radiation. The light seems to prick the back of my eye sockets.

Five two-person Pygmette speeders follow us, their interior compartments sheathed for spaceflight.

"Fuse," says Yinha. "We're being swarmed."

Mouth set grimly, she pushes the Destroyer to its top speed, making narrow turns to shake off our pursuers. But their Pygmettes are a quarter of our size and several times more agile. As we zigzag across the highlands surrounding the Peary Crater, she narrowly avoids clipping the Destroyer's wings on mountains and rills.

Andromeda's finger jerks as she applies disinfecting cream to my wounds. "I'm so sorry you found out about your father that way, Phaet. I swear to whatever gods there might be in this universe, I did everything I could to save him—Mira too. But you . . ."

The ship's belly scrapes the ground, accompanied by the sound of shearing metal.

"Watch it, Yinha!" Nash yells.

"Someone take copilot," Yinha says. I've seen her skillfully steer a Pygmette on a joyride through a clear sky—but this is different. "Or pilot. It's a grit-storm out here."

"I can," I say.

"Ten minutes ago, you zapped yourself," Umbriel says. "And me." His voice still sounds halting, disjointed.

"So there's no chance of me falling asleep at the controls," I quip.

Yinha swerves to avoid the Pygmettes' missiles, swearing on several unstable chemical elements that if someone doesn't help her, we'll crash. Andromeda applies the last piece of medical tape to my leg. "Phaet, will you be all right?"

"Yes, as long as the ship is." I inch toward the cockpit, wincing with every step; the ship's jerking nearly throws me off balance twice. "I've piloted under pressure before."

Yinha quickly scoots into the copilot's chair, allowing me to take the controls.

From their seats behind me, Nash and Callisto loose artillery at our enemies. Whenever either fires a weapon with substantial mass, it pushes our ship in the opposite direction.

"One down," Nash says as her wing tip grenade catches a Pygmette.

But it's only one of five. . . .

Pilot now. Feel later.

Behind me, Andromeda has moved closer to her daughter. "Thank you, Callisto. Thank you for doing what was right."

When Callisto responds, her voice is cold as winter wind.

"Save it, Mo—" She stops herself before she can call Andromeda her mother. "What does *right* even mean? Clobbering your old friends, and mine? How about going against every idea I've been force-fed since my fetus-hood?"

"You saved your poor old mother's life," Andromeda points out.

"Yeah, there's that. Even though you put me in such an awful position. . . ." Her voice trails off as she aims and fires, aims and fires. "I picked you over them. You over Jupiter, over everything I ever worked for. Didn't you at least *consider* what your Committee could've done to me, to our family, as payback for you being so two-faced? No? Of course not. You were too busy double-dealing."

I shake my head, pitying my archenemy. In her pathetic attempt at sarcasm, her voice carries more grief than anger or indifference.

Andromeda says, "Callisto, dear, I'd never let them hurt you—"

"Stop acting like you still have power—any power. You planned to jump ship regardless of what happened to me. Grit move, Mom."

At least your mother told you which side she was on.

Tears blur my vision, and when I reach up to scrub them away, the ship jerks. One of the Pygmettes' grenades has scraped us. I regain control of myself and fix my eyes on the horizon. We've almost passed the Plato Crater, which means we're just north of Mare Imbrium, a dark basalt "sea" of low elevation formed by lava flows. We have to reach Base IV.

Mare Imbrium . . . The name strikes me as dangerous, but I don't know why. I sift through my memories for a clue, but I can't recall all the geology I learned in Primary. All I see is my father's obscure face; time has scratched away the lens of memory through which I'm viewing him. If he were here, he'd remember why pilots avoid this place.

Our ship weaves between the mountains surrounding the mare, and it's all I can do to keep the Pygmettes from gaining on us. I head straight for the dark basalt sea: the most direct route home. *What is it that's so dangerous about flying here?*

"Don't fly into the basin," breathes Andromeda. She sounds exhausted. "My pilots—they usually go around."

I push the ship to go faster—the usual can't apply now. *We need to reach the base, get real medical care for everyone. . . .*

We reach the edge of the mare too quickly to change course. The light-gray regolith drops away, and I follow the sheer cliff downward for thousands of meters. My guts seem to push upward on my lungs. When we reach the bottom, I fly us parallel to the seafloor. For a moment, my lungs push down on my guts. Somewhere behind me, Cygnus wails, his fingers in his ears. *Poor boy can't take all those g's.*

The basalt looks black in the sunlight, sprawling layers of rock twisting over one another. There are no friendly gray peaks to hide behind. Despite my best efforts, our enemies inch closer.

I'm failing as a pilot. My friends shouldn't have had such faith in me.

But at least the Pygmettes aren't firing. The enemy probably wants some of us alive—Andromeda, and maybe me—for an on-base execution, so that they can hold on to the evidence. They'll try to surround us, then latch their ships onto ours and capture us.

I push the throttle as far as it'll go. The ship accelerates—but it's turning slightly to the left, toward the center of the mare.

What the fuse?

Behind me, Nash grunts in frustration. "The wing weapons

are all wonky," she says. "The grenades won't fly straight."

"They keep curving to our left!" Yinha shouts. She's switched seats with Callisto and has taken over left wing controls.

Mascon. Mass concentration. Dad's department, Geology, along with Physics, studied it extensively before he died—I mean, before the Committee killed him. The asteroid impact event that scooped out Mare Imbrium compressed the basalt sea's center, making it denser than the rest of the lunar crust. Now, the center of Mare Imbrium has a strong gravitational pull that can affect satellites, space debris . . . and, potentially, small spaceships.

"Use lasers to burn the ships," I tell Nash and Yinha. *Lasers don't have mass, so gravity won't affect their trajectory.* "It'll take longer, but at least you won't miss."

"Fine. We'll give 'em a light show," Yinha says.

I increase the altitude of the ship, trying to prevent us from crashing onto the mare's floor should gravity suddenly change. Then I fly us to the right, closer to the towering cliff that rings the mare.

"What do you think you're doing, Stripes?" shouts Nash.

Just as I'd hoped, two of the Pygmettes zip below us. Two fly above. All four are positioned to our left, trying to trap us against the wall of Mare Imbrium.

As the enemy approaches, Yinha and Nash manage to burn through most of the hull of one of the Pygmettes above. Before they can finish, the ship turns tail and flies back toward Base I. Smart—they'd rather give up than lose all their air to the near vacuum. Yinha and Nash shoot at the other ship above us, which is flying high, and it increases its altitude to evade the laser barrage.

Deterred by the lasers, all three of the remaining ships zip away, toward the center of Mare Imbrium. I inch our Destroyer away from the wall, firing the bottom thrusters.

Our ship should hold steady, I tell myself. It's bigger, so the mascon will have a proportionally smaller effect on it.

Yinha and Nash burn through most of another ship's hull. It too flees the scene.

Two left. I fly lower, pushing the enemy Pygmettes closer to the basin floor. They lose altitude—intentionally at first. But then they both dip at random moments. One ship's pilot loses control; likely surprised by the mascon's effects, he steers his ship right, up, and then left before crashing into the regolith. The other ship rises sharply to avoid colliding with the basin floor. The Pygmette crosses our field of vision—a perfect target.

"Grenade it!" I shout to Yinha and Nash. "Aim farther up and to the right!"

Two grenades leave our wing tips. One—Nash's—curves too far to the left. Yinha's flies to the right of our target until the mascon pulls it left.

In a pitifully small explosion, the last Pygmette falls to pieces.

I turn our ship away from the slaughter. We gradually climb the hundreds of meters out of the dark basalt sea. Nothing but mountainous gray terrain lies between us and home.

41

BASE IV DEFENSE WELCOMES US WITH OPEN gates; on every side, ships of all sizes hobble into space, where they meet with immediate resistance from Dovetail-aligned craft. The Committee holdouts are attempting to flee. Most of them don't bother to fire at us; I doubt they have competent pilots or wingmen on board.

"Loyalists," Yinha snarls. "They're finally getting some heat."

We easily blend into the melee, and with help from Yinha as copilot, we dodge the other ships and pull into the hangar.

"Let them leave," Andromeda says. "Better for them to be with their kind than wreaking havoc inside Dovetail's new sanctuary."

"Should we take their leaders prisoner?" Yinha asks. "That'll get us leverage in future talks with the Committee— or whatever's left of it, now that Wolf's gone."

"Good point," Andromeda says. I strain to hear her weak voice. "It might prevent them from using scorched-moon tactics on Base IV too. My former colleagues won't want to accidentally harm their assets. So, yes, take prisoners."

Yinha's face is grim. "Bonus points for the General and Jupiter."

*   *   *

We sneak into the unlit rear of the hangar on foot and split into two groups. Nash will take Cygnus, Umbriel, and Andromeda to the Medical quarters, Militia's on-site hospital, so that they can receive care—if the Medics are still working. Andromeda tries to resist, claiming that Dovetail needs her, but a burst of pain causes her to clutch her still-bleeding leg, and she reluctantly agrees.

"See you soon, Cygnus," I say to my brother, and it sounds more like a wish than a promise.

His only response is to knit his brow—in what? Confusion? Doubt?

Before I can work it out, Yinha, Callisto, and a bodyguard corporal named Pictor pull me into the packed hallways. We dodge Lazy fire, Electrostun pellets, and careening bodies. As we pass the entrances to the research departments, we see loyalist scientists fleeing, their arms full of expensive equipment, former comrades hot on their tails. I shake my head, appalled. So much progress, and it's all going to waste. Is this a necessary side effect of rebellion?

Ahead of us, a black-haired man with a broad forehead argues with three Militia soldiers. He has smart, side-parted hair that covers the tips of his large ears. His eyes are sleepless and scared. With his body, he blocks the door to the Nanoengineering Department. "No, no—not the lab. Not eight years of our work. The Committee has no right."

"If you don't move, Rho, we'll hack off your other leg too!" shouts a private.

Covering his face with his hands, the man limps away from the door. He looks to be in his thirties—too young to be walking like that. I catch a glimpse of a carbon-fiber prosthetic between his right shoe and pant seam. Clearly, he has enough money to buy a replacement leg, but not enough to have the flesh regrown via expensive progenitor cells.

"I'm coming, Bai!" Yinha bats the private who threatened him with her truncheon, then tosses the weapon to the Nano-engineer. "Go on without me," she calls to us.

That's her brother. The one Yinha told me about in the midst of a long-ago moonquake. *Bai was a special private, lost his leg on a recon mission,* she said. *Right around the time I got promoted.* She became a training instructor, in part, so that she could stay on the Moon and help him with routine tasks.

"I don't want to leave you here!" I protest, ducking to avoid an Electrostun pellet.

"I need my brother!" Yinha pulls out her own Electrostun and clubs a soldier in the head with the butt. "And Dovetail needs his contraptions. Ask Asterion, if you see him." She kicks the last soldier in the groin before his truncheon can strike Bai. *"Go!"*

Bai scans in his thumbprint, his retina, even his tongue before the Nanoengineering doors slide open.

"Stop standing around and get Phaet to some place without guns!" Yinha yells to Callisto and Pictor. She puts her arm around Bai's shoulders and guides him into Nanoengineering. *"Move!"* The door hisses shut behind them.

How could she leave us? I'm confused and angry—until I realize that I'd do the same in her position. I already did. Yinha and I have both given up everything for our brothers. In a way, that makes us sisters.

Exchanging tense glances, Callisto, Pictor, and I jog away. Near the entrance to the Defense Department, which opens into a grand, arched hallway, we find the General and Jupiter, surrounded by a cluster of loyal Militia, many of whom have officer insignia. Screaming civilians hug the walls to avoid the cross fire; others run, hoping that the lasers and dozens of full-speed Pygmettes and Destroyers will miss them. The smoking, acrid remains of two Pygmettes caught in a collision smolder on my right.

Amidst the fracas, I recognize the plump figure and green robes of Caeli Phi, Umbriel's mother, who's sitting in the passenger seat of one vehicle. With wild eyes, she scans the crowd; I wonder if she's dreading the reappearance of the family she betrayed. She looks more frightened than devastated by the fact that one of her sons sustained potentially life-threatening injuries on national television. Umbriel, Ariel, and Atlas aren't here to see it, but I am. I glare at her, even though she's too paranoid to focus her eyes on any one person in the melee.

On another Pygmette, my former boss, Major Skat Yotta, sits behind Jupiter, who's steering. Skat's strip of dark hair, which runs down the center of his scalp, isn't ruffled by the twisting and swerving of their Pygmette. Neither is his facial expression—he looks serene, if not bored.

On the Militia cluster's outskirts, angry Base IV residents—including a handful of deserters—press closer, waving makeshift weapons and shouting threats. The loyalists spray some kind of aerosol at them; instantly, the affected demonstrators' eyes tear up. People vomit and collapse. The Militia has broken out the tear gas. I expected nothing less.

Jupiter swerves in front of our party. When he notices Callisto, he pulls his Pygmette to a stop. *"You."*

In Primary, I watched couples address each other with that same word, but in more affectionate tones. Venom saturates Jupiter's voice. There's no room for love of any kind.

Pictor aims his Lazy at him, trying to shove Callisto to safety. She shrugs him off.

"Oh, Jupe, forgive me. I would've died if I hadn't—"

"Turned traitor?" Now Jupiter points his Electrostun at Callisto. His eyes never leave her face, even as Skat taps his shoulder, urging him to go. "It's bad enough that your mom did it. But you went along."

With a cry, Callisto falls to her knees. "They were going to kill me! How could I love you if I were dead?"

"Don't talk to me." Jupiter's deep voice wavers.

"Fine! Shoot me. I—"

Even as Jupiter lowers his weapon, jagged white electricity rattles Callisto's body, picks her up, and throws her down again on the floor. Shockingly, Callisto, the daughter of Base IV's former leader, has lost her right to personal safety. I hear a Pygmette zipping away and twist to track the shooter.

His hulking figure dwarfs the speeder. "My son's words," the General bellows backward at us, "are *commands.*"

"Dad? Where you going?" Cursing, Jupiter follows his father's speeder toward the entrance of Defense.

"Get them!" Pictor yells.

Everyone present turns our way. Militia loyalists and deserters, civilians, Dovetail members—their eyes find me, and for a moment, everything goes silent.

"The Girl Sage lives," a woman murmurs, her eyes wide.

Yes, I did the unthinkable. I escaped from Base I, the Committee stronghold. But I only survived because a girl sacrificed her life for me—a girl who'd saved me twice before, in the Atrium and on Earth. She protected me like a sister would. Did I even deserve it?

A Pygmette turns tail and follows Jupiter and the General. As it skids around corners, its riders shoot at the fleeing officers.

Our appearance seems to have shifted the course of the base-wide scuffle, bringing more people over to Dovetail's side.

They just want to be on the winning team, I think, a shadow of foreboding falling over me. *Ideals mean nothing when people are guarding their lives.*

A newly Dovetail-aligned Pygmette speeds toward me, shooting at Militia soldiers in its path. I run to build up momentum for a jump.

"Sage!" someone calls from the crowd. "Are you *thinking?*"

I leap and land with my feet on the backseat. Although I bang my hip on the backrest, I manage to hold on and shift into a sitting position.

"Hey, Stripes!" yells the pilot. "Nice show you put on back at Base I!"

Orion? Last August, when I asked him to help abort our hoax of an Earth recon mission because my mother's life was at stake, he seemed to value his career—all our careers—more than one human's fate. "Why are you helping us?" I cry.

"Want the truth?" Orion swerves around a clump of civilians, dodging Skat's scattered Lazy fire. He puts on speed; the General has nearly reached the Defense entrance, and Jupiter and Skat's Pygmette is close behind. "My parents taught me to do whatever keeps me alive."

I appreciate his honesty. But it also tells me that Dovetail can't trust Orion. If the Committee can better guarantee his safety, he'll switch sides again.

Concentrate, I tell myself. How can we stop the General and Jupiter? Pygmettes have light weapons, but I can't reach them: they're in front of Orion. If he multitasks, adding shooting to steering, we might crash.

We're nearing Jupiter's Pygmette. I aim my Lazy at its black exhaust tube, which protrudes from the vehicle's rear. Because a reflective silver layer coats most of the Pygmette, the laser will backfire or hit innocents if I miss.

I don't aim at Jupiter or Skat—Andromeda said to take prisoners, not to kill. Before I pull the trigger, I remember the soldiers on the Odan beach. My victims. The images fill me with self-loathing. *Killing again would kill me too, but slower.*

Holding my arm steady, I fire a series of quick laser bursts at the tube. If I can melt it, seal it off, then the Pygmette will stop running before the engine pressure gets too high—one of its many safety features.

The General passes through the open doors to Defense. The doors begin to close; at the rate everyone's moving, Jupiter and Skat will pass through, but not Orion and I. I fire more frequently. The polymer composing our targets' exhaust tube glows red and sags. Skat's head twitches backward; for perhaps the first time in his life, he looks troubled. His hand fumbles at his utility belt, trying to find a Lazy, an Electrostun, anything.

The space between the doors narrows—Jupiter's Pygmette barely squeezes through. I clamp my forefinger on the trigger, firing a continuous stream of violet. Through the crack between the doors, I see the Pygmette's blinking lights turn off. The vehicle slows down, gravity pulling it toward the floor. It bounces, flips over, bounces again, and wobbles on its belly as Defense's doors slam shut.

42

THE GENERAL ESCAPES THROUGH THE hangar. With him goes the loyalists' belligerence. In minutes, they fall apart, a scattered mess that Dovetail easily puts down.

Leading our prisoners, Jupiter and Skat, by a chain attached to their ship, Orion and I cruise toward the Atrium, where our new leaders have called for a general assembly. People around us stare upward in bewilderment and admiration. Some cheer, which makes me squirm. Don't they know that this victory marks the beginning of a long struggle?

Callisto has partially recovered; I see her crying into her sleeve, and all I can do is pity her. After her electrocution wounds heal, accepting her mother's choices and Jupiter's rejection will take long, painful months.

Jupiter. In handcuffs, the General's son rambles to anyone who will listen—namely, Orion and me—about his father. "He'll come back for me, blast it. They all will!"

His voice has an undercurrent of doubt; he's unsure whether he's been abandoned. The Committee is not always loyal to its own.

Even as I derive a guilty sort of amusement from watching this Militia bully in his weakest state, I catch sight of three people in the crowd. The stream of affection I feel washes away all else.

"Orion, do the honors," I say, pointing my chin at Jupiter and Skat. Orion grins and turns the vehicle toward Penitentiary, dragging our prisoners' Pygmette along. He'll put our prisoners in solitary confinement. I jump from our ship and run through the path made for me by the base residents. I nod at every smile or *thank you* directed my way, but there's no time for more. Soon I'm there, and I gather Ariel, his father Atlas, and Anka in my arms.

"Aieee!" Anka ends up in the center; she cranes her neck, searching for a place where she can breathe. Atlas cries tears of joy, or sadness, or both. Gray has invaded his dark, curly hair, probably a result of cracking tough cases in Law while contending with Caeli's desertion and Umbriel's absence. It's strange to see him without his wife. Did she make it out? Or has she been taken prisoner?

I decide not to ask.

"Phaet, you couldn't be a *little* louder when you got back?" Ariel says sarcastically. He's lost weight, like everyone else on Base IV, and his long eyelashes have thinned, but otherwise he's the same boy I grew up with. "If you wanted me or Dad to find you, you didn't have to plow over half a hallway."

Anka laughs from her stomach and bares her teeth in a grin. It's a relief to watch her girlishness resurface.

Umbriel and Cygnus appear in my peripheral vision. Joy seems to be the only thing keeping my brother awake and vertically oriented. I'm sure he'll fall into a deep sleep after this is over. I'm so full of love that my body feels like an inadequate vessel with which to contain it. For this brief, beautiful moment, our exodus is over.

*   *   *

Asterion, Andromeda, and a newly freed Sol Eta address us from the Atrium's third-level balcony. Because the Committee always broadcast their public addresses while sitting at their conference table, the balcony hasn't been used for its original purpose in decades.

The solemn expressions of all three quell the base's sense of celebration. Andromeda leans on a crutch, her left leg bandaged to the knee. Her skin is green under the lights. Asterion's round face was made for smiling, but today, scratches crisscross his skin; stress and gravity pull downward at his mouth and eyes. Sol holds her bald head high, twitching every few seconds as if tossing back the chin-length mane she once had. My right hand twitches too, longing to slap her.

She let my mother write her "Grievances" and die for them. A confrontation between us is long overdue.

"Thank you for voting on my behalf today." Asterion's voice, though comforting, drills straight into my brain. "Thank you for voting at all. Participating in the democratic process isn't only your right as citizens; it's your responsibility."

Andromeda's eyes fall on Callisto. She looks alarmed to see her daughter in tears, wearing clothes burned black, but she gathers herself and speaks to the base in ringing tones. "You, Base IV, have chosen your leader by majority rule. But before I cede executive authority to Asterion Epsilon, I declare Base IV to be governed by democratic principles—as a free and independent state."

I add a weak whoop to the raucous cheering. I've just watched the impossible happen. The bases were meant to coexist indefinitely. A hundred years ago, our founders considered themselves humanity's last hope. Through scientific advancement, order, and frugality, we would endure even if the Earth became a puddle of pollutants, and we would do it together.

Now Base IV is free, but alone, after a century of discontent.

"Asterion will serve as your interim president while a Constitution is drafted."

"Thank you, Andromeda." Asterion turns to the audience and gives us a warm smile. "With regards to the Constitution, we will arrange a nomination process so that you, the people, can choose who will draft this crucial document."

Hope buds within me, tender and green as a springtime shoot. If he's as earnest as my interactions with him suggested, and as persistent as his scientific work has hinted, Asterion will keep promises in a way the Committee never did.

Sol steps forward. She looks fifteen years older, and so sorrowful.

"In the aftermath of Mira Theta's death last August, I inherited her duties as leader of Operation Dovetail." Her once-powerful voice has been reduced to a weak chafing. "I will continue to lead the struggle to change the situation of our brothers and sisters on the other five bases." She pauses to cough. "Currently, we are alone. The Committee will order the Militia to invade us. They will remove us from the Moon's energy grid and cut off our communication channels. They will make our existence as difficult as they can."

Nods from the audience. We've dived too far into revolt to surface now.

"But I'm not without a strategy," Sol says. "We have innovative defensive instruments"—could she mean *weapons*?—"in development, thanks to a collaboration between the Chemistry and Nanoengineering Departments."

Interesting. My gut tells me that Asterion and Yinha's brother, Bai, are involved in this, and I tremble to think of what contraptions they could be building.

"Within months," Sol says, "we should be able to bring Base VI over to our side. Their researchers have been angry ever since the Committee cut their funding, and Wolf's death means the inauguration of a sure-to-be-unpopular interim Committee representative. Rebellion will soon brew there in earnest. This alliance will provide us with bright minds, another supply of solar energy, and a hold over the equatorial region. From there, we will set our sights on Base II, whose citizens are tired of producing goods and energy for Base I functions and working long hours for little pay. Once we've liberated them, we will use Base II as a launchpad to attack Base I with all our strength."

Put like that, taking over the Moon sounds deceptively simple. Easy, even. But I know that allying ourselves with the other bases will require backbreaking work from Dovetail—and from me, the Girl Sage.

Sol clears her throat, the pain evident on her face. "I understand that not all of you will support using our few resources to expand Dovetail's base and fighting power. Please know that I will not abuse Asterion's power or Andromeda's knowledge for that purpose."

My anger dissipates as she begins coughing again. I won't challenge her—for now.

Andromeda pats Sol on the back and turns to address the audience once more. "Regarding our future, I feel obligated to share vital information with you, the people. These revelations may not be welcome, but they are true."

Umbriel gives me a glance heavy with worry. Can he and I take any more surprises? Can the new legion of Dovetail members?

"Pacifia and the bases instigated aggression with Battery Bay, not vice versa, as the Committee has long led you to believe,"

Andromeda says. *No surprises there.* "They have deployed nuclear weapons in orbit around Earth. With Pacifia, the Committee has been planning coordinated attacks on the city of Battery Bay, where the known fugitive and Dovetail-aligned agent Wesley Carlyle is stationed with his family."

My breath catches at the sound of his name. Wes, Murray, the whole family—in danger of being captured or shot or nuked. I can't fight the familiar feeling in my gut, the tiny voice telling me I have to do something. But Battery Bay . . . what can be done? What can I do?

Andromeda sighs. "All these actions point toward my former colleagues' final goal. They have worked toward this end for decades."

I shake my head, tempted to put my fingers in my ears, as I did when I was little, whenever I needed to shut out voices, words, ideas I didn't want to hear. Andromeda's next words won't surprise me, but they'll still hurt.

"The Standing Committee is planning to recolonize the Earth," Andromeda says. "And achieve world hegemony."

It's a shame the Moon wasn't enough for them.

43

GASPS AND WHISPERS BREAK OUT ACROSS
the audience, filling the Atrium with a threatening hum. But
people should've known this was coming. The Committee's
collaboration with Pacifia, Earth Recon's scrounging materials
from Earthbound cities . . . Their love of power, a lack of lunar
natural resources, and perhaps even claustrophobia would natu-
rally drive them to thirst after humanity's home planet.

"Lady A has got to be making this up," Anka says. "The
Committee must be idiots to think they can take over the
whole *planet*."

"The Committee are anything but idiots," I say. "They're
addicted to power."

Around us, other incredulous and angry people are also debating with one another. "Earthbound," someone next to me scoffs
to his neighbor, a young woman with a Medic badge. "We have
enough problems without worrying about their power plays."

"They're so useless," the medic says. "True, some of them are
enemies of *our* enemy, but they'll never be our friends. They'll
only bring their sewage up here and feed it to us for breakfast."

I wish I could chastise them. Battery Bay and Base IV share
a common adversary: the Committee. The Batterers don't have
the resources to withstand the combined might of Pacifian numbers and Lunar technology, and neither do we. But Andromeda
can't propose an alliance without inciting disgust among Base

IV's citizens, whose prejudices—stoked by more than a century of propaganda—are still lodged firmly in place. I hold back a frustrated growl, realizing I'll need to help Andromeda change their perceptions.

"The Committee is confident that after thirty years of undisputed rule on the Moon, they can govern the Earth, even restore it to its former glory," Andromeda says. The crowd falls silent again, filling the hall with a haunting hush. "Though they deny this fact, the Committee—Wolf Omega most of all—are . . . *were* orders of magnitude more arrogant than my dear friend Mira Theta or her daughter Phaet, whom they so often mocked."

From the balcony, Andromeda's eyes seek me out. People are looking my way, cheering, but the claps and calls don't bring me joy. I'm *drained*, burdened by today's events. All I want is to rest.

"Girl Sage!" the voices cry.

Base IV's people need me now. But my legs can hardly bear my own weight—how will I stand for them?

"Phaet," Asterion says, "you showed us your intelligence and skill when you ranked first in your trainee class. You demonstrated your moral strength on the day of Mira's trial. And today, you proved that each and every one of us can rise from the brink of death—and win. In honor of your mother, and in service of the cause to which you have devoted yourself, will you join us?"

His request astounds me, makes me shake my head. *Why would they elevate a sixteen-year-old girl, place her beside the new leadership?* I can't do it—can't draw attention to myself, forget my roots, act prideful. The greatest honor anyone could grant me would be a peaceful few days with my reunited family.

But would I enjoy that peace? Someone's still missing.

Wes. Eri begged me not to forget him; she died with his name on her lips. His city is gone; his people are refugees. But I swear to myself that I'll find them on Battery Bay and fight until their archipelago is safe again. If I'm still alive at the end of it, I'll dig my hands into the soil and help rebuild the home they've lost.

From the balcony, Asterion, Andromeda, and Sol stare at me expectantly. So do my family, and the crowd that surrounds us. It's like I've sprouted hundreds of surrogate family members. Is there room in my heart for all of them?

As Yinha steers a Pygmette in my direction, I remember the old myth she told me. The peasant girl's ribbons of white hair, blowing in a lightning storm. The cruel landlord's death, her provincial village liberated. Between the Lunar citizens here, and the Odans in Battery Bay, I have a planetary village to worry about.

I climb into the passenger seat. The craft rises higher, higher, and the assembly below blurs into a dazzling wash of color. My family's faces shrink, and then fade.

It's no longer appropriate to stare downward. I must lift my head.

I near the balcony, cheered on from below, but I don't feel as if I'm flying. I'm suspended on a chill gust of wind, a dove wandering into war.